WAYFARER

NEW FICTION BY KOREAN WOMEN

＊＊＊

Kim Hye-Ja

edited and translated by
Bruce and Ju-Chan Fulton

J'Accuse

WOMEN IN TRANSLATION
· Seattle ·

Publication of this book was made possible in part with financial support
from the National Endowment for the Arts and the Korean Culture and Arts
Foundation.

Cover painting: *Autumn* (detail) by Shin Pong-ja
Cover design by Clare Conrad
Text design by Stacy M. Lewis and Rebecca Engrav

Library of Congress Cataloging-in-Publication Data
Wayfarer: new fiction by Korean women / edited and translated by Bruce and
    Ju-Chan Fulton.
        p.   sm.
    ISBN 1-879679-09-4 (alk. Paper)
    1. Korean fiction—20th century—Translations into English. 2. Women
Authors, Korean—20th century. I. Fulton, Bruce. II. Fulton, Ju-Chan.
PL984.EW39   1997
895. 7'340899287—DC21   96-39431
                                                                      CIP

First edition, March, 1997
Printed in the United States

Women in Translation
523 North 84th Street
Seattle WA 98103

CONTENTS

———— ✦✦✦ ————

INTRODUCTION

For much of Korean history, literate and literary Korean women have been wayfarers in search of acceptance and recognition of their artistic aspirations. Although Korean literature in its written record dates back well over a thousand years, it was not until the promulgation of *hangŭl,* the Korean script, in the mid-1400s that Korean women had ready access to a medium of literary expression. Until then, and indeed until the dawn of modernization in Korea at the turn of the present century, most Korean literature was composed in Chinese. For a parallel in the English-speaking world, consider what American literature would be like if it had been written mostly in Latin until this century. The learning of Chinese writing, requiring the memorization of thousands of ideographs, is a formidable proposition in the best of circumstances. For Korean women in traditional times, the task was all but impossible, for Korean women were not encouraged to read and write in the first place. The rare women who did manage to learn were discouraged from displaying their learning—and whatever writing they may have done—outside the home. In public life, the operating principle of gender roles was *namjon yŏbi* ("men respected, women demeaned"). A woman's role was very specifically a domestic one, and the attachment of a woman's name to a work of literature circulated outside the home would have flouted traditional role expectations.

Korean literature written in Chinese was thus the domain of men, especially wellborn men, who had the means and leisure to master a difficult foreign writing system. Korean men also had the incentive to pass the government civil service examinations (closed to women), which required mastery of Chinese writing and accomplishment in literary knowledge and expression.

The negligible amount of Korean women's writing in Chinese that has survived—some 1800 works, according to one estimate—suggests that the venerable Korean premodern literary tradition would have been all the richer for a greater presence of women's voices. In particular, the poems in Chinese written by women entertainers known as *kisaeng,* are passionate and lyrical, ironic and witty. The best-known *kisaeng* poet, Hwang Chin-i, has herself been celebrated in literature and film, and has long since become an inspiration for legions of artistic Korean women.

Hangŭl, the Korean alphabet, is one of most precisely phonetic scripts in the world; its rudiments can be grasped in a matter of hours. While learned Korean men for the most part disdained *hangŭl* as something befitting only women and the lowborn (the script was also called *amgŭl,* or "female writing"), preferring their monopoly of the esoteric Chinese writing system, literate Korean women finally had an accessible medium of literary expression. Dissuaded from circulating their writing in public, they tended to concentrate on *naebang kasa,* long, open-ended instructive poems that passed from mother to daughter and remained within the home (the *naebang,* "inner quarters," was the domain of women in the traditional Korean home). Although the surviving examples of this unpublished poetry, thousands of them, date from the early 1700s, most have come to light only since the mid-1900s. Of all the *hangŭl* works *published* during the Chosŏn period (1392-1910), however, no more than two to three percent are thought to have been written by women. (The remainder, published by men, consist mainly of *shijo,* a native poetic form, and prose works intended for the broad audience that could be reached only through the simplicity of *hangŭl.*) In other words, while most Chosŏn women's writing went unpublished, enough men's writing in *hangŭl* was circulated to give the impression until recent decades that men dominated the production of literature in the native script as well as in Chinese. Such was the anonymity of women writers and their literature in traditional Korea.

Two connected developments at the turn of the 20th century drove much of early modern Korean history: the modernization movement that swept East Asia, and the Japanese colonization of the Korean peninsula from 1910 to 1945. One of the salient effects of these watershed events was the widespread adoption by Koreans, men and women, of *hangŭl* as their written language. *Hangŭl* thus became the medium of literary expression for most Koreans and, perhaps even more important, a means for Koreans to hold fast to a language and culture that the Japanese, in the later years of the colonial period, expressly wished to obliterate as part of their plan to hegemonize East Asia.

If the legitimacy of Korean women's literature ever needed justification, it no longer did in modern times, for it was Korean women by and large who had for centuries accepted and utilized the national script while most male writers preferred Chinese.

And yet even in early modern times, when women shared in the creation of a modern Korean literature—journeying to Japan for their higher education and gaining exposure to foreign literatures in Japanese translation; returning to Korea to help establish Korean literary magazines and their associated circles; enduring jail terms for their activism in keeping the Korean language and script alive; editing, writing, and publishing—they were not fully accepted. They were branded *yŏryu chakka,* "female writers," and were merely tolerated by the preponderantly male Korean literary establishment as long as they confined themselves to tales of love triangles, of frustrated, silently suffering women, or of the harsh realities of Koreans during the colonial period. Those women writers who departed from the traditional cycle of subservience to father and then husband and then son, who attempted to chart their own life course, and who wrote of women who did the same, found themselves adrift, no longer welcomed by Korean society. Consider the fate of three of the pioneering women writers of the 1920s and 1930s: Na Hye-sŏk turned to art, Kim Wŏn-ju became a nun, and Kim Myŏng-sun died insane in Japan. Other promising women writers—Paek Shin-ae, Kang Kyŏng-ae, and Yi Sŏn-hŭi—died young. Successful, long-lived women writers such as Pak Hwa-sŏng and Ch'oe Chŏng-hŭi learned early how to write for two audiences: their predominantly female readership on the one hand, and the patriarchal Korean literary establishment on the other.

In the 1970s Korean women fiction writers began to come into their own. Korea's rapid economic development in recent decades has meant that more women are being educated, joining the work force, and, at least until motherhood, enjoying the leisure for pursuits such as reading (one survey indicates that the great majority of Korean book buyers are women). Women have come to play a greater role in many spheres of Korean public life, literature included. Among the eight women represented in this collection, all attended college; two studied creative writing, three studied Korean literature, and three studied English literature. All have made a profession of writing. This interest in literature as a career has produced a flowering of Korean women's literature in the 1990s. Now more than ever before, Korean women are winning literary prizes, appearing on bestseller lists, serializing their novels in newspapers, and finding their way into translation. They are, in other words, receiving unprecedented critical and commercial success. But even this long overdue recognition has not come without cost. The Korean literary establishment, still overwhelmingly male, has publicly speculated about the "feminization" of contemporary Korean literature.

Korean women writers' ongoing struggle for visibility is reflected in the stories in this collection. As we have seen, the anonymity of women writers in premodern Korea reflected traditional Korean gender roles, which militated against the public expression of women's learning. Public anonymity for women, vestiges of which survive in Korean society today, is revealed in the works in this collection. For example, in the minds of the male characters who have known the central figure in Ch'oe Yun's "The Last of Hanak'o," she survives only by her nickname, Hanak'o. And as we see in the person of "Ch'ŏri's mom" in Pak Wan-sŏ's "Identical Apartments," the common Korean way to address a married woman with children is still to refer to her as the mother of one of her children. The extent to which a Korean woman's identity continues to be defined by her domestic role is seen in the situation of the protagonists in this anthology who are not married. Among these five women, one is recently divorced, one is widowed, and one is a mistress; all face uncertain futures economically. Of the main characters in the remaining three stories, all of them married, only one works, and she is clearly subservient to her husband in the workplace. Korean women still reign at home, but the stark despair that awaits them if they are suddenly deprived of the domestic sphere is all too clear in the title story.

A common thread among the women characters in these stories is the richness of their interior lives, a richness seldom apparent to those around them, and especially to men. Consider the protagonist of Kim Chi-wŏn's "Almaden," whose emotional depth is brought to the surface by a customer at her New York liquor store. The brilliance of "The Last of Hanak'o" lies in Ch'oe Yun's superbly ironic depiction of a group of young men's complete ignorance of the personally and professionally enriching life that a young woman friend is forging. These men see in Hanak'o a caricature of female friendship, a kind of pen pal, a nonthreatening date who knows how to make them comfortable, collectively or individually. The significance of Hanak'o's relationship with her female companion eludes them. Mun-ja in Sŏ Yŏng-ŭn's "Dear Distant Love" has an even more formidable inner strength. This is a depressing story upon first reading, and Mun-ja's situation is degrading. But clearly she is utterly confident that her trials will eventually serve her well, as they have the desert nomads she so vividly describes as a parallel to her own life.

Korean women writers display a much broader range of themes and voices today than in the past. There is an easy flow to Kim Chi-wŏn's works, for example, many of which deal with the emotional adjustments of Koreans, and especially women, to life in an alien land. The evanescence of love is a recurring concern in her stories, as in "Almaden" (Almaden, 1979).

Ch'oe Yun is perhaps the best example of the literary career to which South Korean women now aspire. In addition to writing award-winning fiction and essays, she teaches French literature at a Seoul university and, with her husband, Patrick Maurus, has set new standards in the translation of Korean literature into French. Ch'oe has read widely in Korean and other literatures, and there is a variety and sophistication to her work, evident in "The Last of Hanak'o" (Hanak'o nŭn ŏpta, 1994). In her fiction she prefers nonsentimental, polyphonic narratives and likes to experiment with language, as she does in her debut work, *There a Petal Silently Falls* (Chŏgi sori ŏpshi hanjŏm kkonnip i chigo, 1988), which includes lyrical passages depicting the horrors of the 1980 massacre by Korean troops of citizens of the southern city of Kwangju. The movie version of this story, *A Petal* (Kkonnip), is one of the masterpieces of Korean cinema.

Kong Chi-yŏng is an impassioned, provocative writer. "I find a problem and then write about it," she has said. Many of her works concern student and labor activists or young career women trying to establish professional as well as personal identities. Kong's stories are reminiscent of South Korean fiction of the 1970s, which was notable for grappling with the social problems that attended the burst of industrialization under President Park Chung Hee. Kong's sense of group solidarity is evident in "Human Decency" (Ingan e taehan yeŭi, 1993) in her use of the Korean terms *sŏnbae* and *hubae,* which refer most commonly to graduates of the same school (the former having graduated before oneself, the latter after), and which involve a structured set of social relationships, *sŏnbae* mentoring *hubae* and *hubae* deferring to *sŏnbae*. Kong is also interested in domestic problems. The movie version of her 1993 novel *Go Alone Like the Horn of a Rhinoceros* (Muso ŭi ppul ch'ŏrŏm honja sŏ kara—a reference to devout Buddhists who set out alone on the road to enlightenment), for which she wrote the screenplay, was immensely popular among women but elicited mixed feelings from men, presumably for its portrayals of the inadequacies, sexual and emotional, of the three husbands portrayed therein. In Kong's works, as in Ch'oe's, we find a progression toward non-gender-specific voices that perhaps mirrors the slow but inexorable trend toward equality for women in Korean society.

In sharp contrast to the raw energy of Kong's "Human Decency" is the clean precision of Kim Min-suk's "Scarlet Fingernails" (Pongsunga kkonmul, 1987). Each, however, deals with the problems of individuals who ran afoul of the anti-communism laws enacted along with South Korea's notorious Yushin Constitution of the 1970s, and the effects of their transgressions on their families. This story is a compelling example of what might be called the "sins of the fathers" theme in contemporary Korean fiction, which has also been taken up by Pak Wan-sŏ, one of the other writers in this collection. This theme is in turn part of a wider body of literature often called *pundan munhak*—the literature of the territorial division of Korea and the separation of millions of family members following the civil war of 1950–53. The term *pundak munhak* takes on a special significance when we realize that North Korean literature, which in recent decades seems to consist mostly of formulaic pieces that laud the accomplishments of Kim Il Sung, is virtually unknown to the outside world. Properly speaking, then, references here to "Korean literature" in the post–World War II period designate South Korean literature alone.

Independence and perseverance are hallmarks of Sŏ Yŏng-ŭn's protagonists as well as of the career of the author herself. Sŏ's fictional world is populated with lonely, marginal souls striving to escape a mundane existence. Many of these characters are uncompromising individuals struggling to hold their own in an equally uncompromising society. In Sŏ's stories individualism is presented as an option for those who have difficulty fitting into Korea's highly structured society. But individualism offers no salvation unless it is accompanied by the kind of self-awareness revealed by Mun-ja in Sŏ's story "Dear Distant Love" (Mŏn kŭdae, 1983).

Pak Wan-sŏ began publishing rather late in life, after raising five children. Her debut work appeared in 1970, when she was almost forty, but Pak has since become one of Korea's most respected writers, enjoying immense popularity and a solid critical reputation. Her great success is due in large part to her superb storytelling. Drawing on her own experiences in Korea's turbulent modern history, she has imbued her fiction with an empathic quality that gives her readers a feeling of intimacy. It is as if they are listening to a neighborhood elder who has witnessed everything—hence Pak's nickname *yŏp chip ajuma*, "the auntie next door." Pak is a productive writer who has covered a wide range of thematic ground. Her "Identical Apartments" (Talmŭn pang tŭl, 1974) is a witty description of the sterility of apartment living in modern Seoul.

Kong Sŏn-ok is one of the new wave of Korean women writers, along with Kong Chi-yŏng, Kim Hyŏng-gyŏng, and others. Her rough-hewn devil-may-care approach in "The Flowering of Our Lives" (Uri saengae ŭi kkot, 1993) is striking. The narrator of that story is perhaps the most complex character in this anthology. In turns indignant, despairing, sad, brazen, and sympathetic, she has begun to come to terms with her contradictory impulses. Here is a vivid example of the sensibility of Korean women writers of the 1990s. More than any of the other stories in this volume, this one is for and about women.

Contemporary writing by South Korean women, it may be

argued, begins with O Chŏng-hŭi, author of the title story in this collection. Since her literary debut in 1968, while she was still a college student, O has produced a body of short fiction that is by turns elegant, elusive, deceptive, and unsettling. O has always been intensely interested in family life, but breaks new ground in depicting not only the surface routines of family members' interactions but also the bleak horizons of solitude, insanity, death, divorce, and desertion that may lurk just beneath. To control this volatile thematic mix O employed in her first volume of fiction a series of nameless first-person narrators that tend simultaneously to engage and distance the reader. The stories in her subsequent collections tend to be more approachable. "Wayfarer" (Sullyeja ŭi norae, 1983) is a bit more wistful and sad than many of her other works, but is characterized by the same careful construction and terse but suggestive dialog. O has always excelled at psychological portraits, and the tableau of Hye-ja in "Wayfarer" is no exception. Without ignoring the upheavals that have attended the rapid modernization of Korean society, this and other of O's stories transcend cultural boundaries to address universal themes of emotional rootlessness and a yearning for permanence, both in the immediate context of the family and in the larger society. In doing so they speak to the quest of Korean women writers for acceptance both at home and abroad and to their anticipation of the day when they will no longer be distinguished by their gender but will be known simply as *writers*.

WAYFARER

ALMADEN

Kim Chi-wŏn

The young man usually dropped by the woman's West Side wine and spirit shop around five p.m. for a bottle of Almaden chablis. He arrived with a throng of rush-hour customers after a slow day, and the woman hadn't yet recognized him as one of the regulars. A newcomer to the business, she was still learning such basics as the shelf location and prices of the wines, and although the man brought the same item to the counter every day, she invariably checked the price and looked up the tax. Some customers who stuck to one brand would tell her the price, but not this man.

His face and body were a solid match for each other. The curly, rust-colored hair, the firm, glistening forehead, the stubbornly protruding nose, the forceful line of the lips, the broad chest, and his moderate height combined to make him look trim and fresh.

One day she noticed him standing in front of the wine display.

"Are you all out of Almaden?"

3

The voice was calm and impersonal.

"We moved it—it's over there now."

The man's gaze settled on the bottles she indicated. His movements were precise, with no wasted motion. When he thumped the wine down on the counter, the woman saw the thin gold chains, three of them, circling his wrist; another was draped over the lush chest hair showing through his black satin jacket and the shirt unbuttoned to the navel. There were several theaters in the neighborhood, and she wondered if he was an actor.

That day, while the woman checked the price as usual and added the tax, he stood stock-still looking at her, eyes intent. She felt extremely uncomfortable. After he paid and marched off, the woman unconsciously heaved a sigh. Sometime later she realized she had memorized the price of the man's bottle of Almaden— two dollars and thirty-two cents, tax included.

In the beginning the woman had thought there wasn't much to tending a wine and spirit shop: you stand behind the counter, you bag the customers' purchases, you take their money. But a closer look revealed much more—ordering the right amount of the various brands, making sure you get what you order, paying the bills and the taxes, renewing your liquor license . . . and at the least little mistake you find yourself reported to the New York State Liquor Authority, or so she'd been told. When the woman lay in bed at night, all of these complexities would grow in her mind, blossoming from concern into borderline terror.

"Oh-oh, look at this," she said to her husband one day. "We already paid it—there's the check number in the account book— but they're billing us again."

Her husband drew near and looked over her shoulder.

"No, it's not the same one. The invoice number's different, see?"

He sounded strangely exuberant, as if he relished the prospect of paying another bill.

"Well, that's odd," said the woman, but when she realized her husband was right she fell silent.

As she filed the invoice, she wondered why she and her husband were never in sync when they talked. Even when she mentioned something she thought interesting, he would cut her short: "Go on home and get the stew going, will you?" She felt as if he had the soul of a beggar; he was a hungry man who could never be satisfied. Or was this simply an illusion? Now and then she would listen closely to how her husband sounded with others. Did he speak to them the way he spoke to her, in a scratchy tone of voice, in half-sentences? The layers of irritation that clouded his brow, the discontent that framed his lips—did he reveal them only to her? When she caught herself examining him like this, as if she were observing a stranger, she felt disgusted almost to the point of nausea.

Once in a while the woman daydreamed that she was walking in the woods with an affectionate man while the leaves danced in wild abandon. The forest path appearing in these reveries was like a beautiful detail in a photograph. But this imaginary path had no beginning, nor could she visualize what lay at the end. She thought only of being there with this man. Even my fantasies are drying up, she often reflected. As cut flowers yearn to root themselves again, she longed to nurture and expand her fantasies; instead she ended up empty and spent.

Summer arrived, and school was out at the university nearby. Many of the woman's regular customers went on vacation. One day she realized the neighborhood streets were nearly empty, but seemingly the next day the cafes and streets were full of tourists from other parts of the country and abroad. It was the off-season for her, but not for the restaurants and souvenir shops. Fewer people came periodically for a jug.

Instead, more couples came to buy a bottle of wine for dinner at a restaurant. The women's faces had a rapturous glow; some held roses presented by their men. Sometimes a couple kissed as the woman made change. Money in hand, she waited for their lips to part; she looked in embarrassment at the flowers, now starting to droop, in the other woman's hand. They seemed beautiful, these people, and she envied them their enjoyment, their night out, their bottle of wine. She felt these were the chosen people, people whose eyes didn't have to be dark, whose hair didn't have to be black, people who weren't afraid to express their affection.

In Korea, where the woman had been wooed and married, lovers didn't embrace in parks, subways, or other public places. She had sometimes wondered if the people here felt they had to show off their love. But now she considered their behavior a carefree, honest expression of their feelings.

The days grew hot and the man who bought the Almaden appeared without his satin jacket or the shirt unbuttoned to the navel. His muscular chest was covered with the same curly, rust-colored hair as his head. His chest looked almost as fleshy as hers. And when she saw his protruding nipples, she felt a warm prickle in her bosom. In the past, the woman had disdained this type of man, who seemed to use physical beauty as his main weapon. She had never felt any sexual attraction to the body itself—chest hair, nipples, and the rest. The fleeting attraction the opposite sex had held for her came from such things as a sincere voice, a wrist with a large watch, a neatly tailored coat collar, a graceful hand holding a pen, a gentle smile, a sense of humor. Now, the impact of this man's bare torso seen close up made her realize she was no different from men who looked at a woman with large breasts and buttocks as if she were a pinup girl. She lowered her eyes in shame.

The price of Almaden rose from $2.32 to $2.54, and the unspoken tension between the man who bought it and the woman who sold it also rose. After the man had left, the woman sometimes felt peculiar about the tension of their encounters. As with the narrow woodland path of her imagination, the path whose beginning and end she didn't know, she never thought of the man when he wasn't at the store. When evening approached, she didn't stop to think that this was the time he would soon appear. But then his yellow convertible with the black top would pull up and he would stride inside, take his Almaden from the shelf, and plop it down on the counter. Once again she would feel at a loss.

One day a little girl in the shop called out "Mommy!" The woman saw the man, as he was picking out his bottle of Almaden, quickly turn toward the girl and then toward her, as if wondering whether it was her daughter. When a sharp-featured Latina answered, she thought he seemed relieved.

The next day, when the man brought his Almaden to the counter the woman was busy with another customer, and so her husband waited on him.

"We have some in the cooler, you know." Her husband didn't seem aware that the man was a regular customer.

"I use it for cooking, so it doesn't have to be expensive and I don't need it chilled," the other readily replied.

"And what do you cook with it?"

"Tonight it's chicken. I'll add some of the wine and drink what's left." And then, with a glance at the woman, who was just then dropping some change in the till, "Nice sister you got there."

Hearing this, the woman felt warm blood gather in her face.

She couldn't move. The woman felt sorry for herself. If only she *were* her husband's sister, as Almaden had said.

The woman put in tiring days but often went sleepless at night. When she couldn't fall asleep she drank a glass of wine, went back to bed, and imagined herself sitting across a candlelit table from Almaden sharing a meal he had prepared. When her husband was hungry, he complained, "What the hell is a wife for, anyway?" Almaden, though, would probably say, "I'd better fix myself something." As in her daydreams of the forest path, the woman had no idea how she had come to be sitting across from Almaden at his table lit with a red candle. Judging from the relatively cheap brand of wine he bought, he probably wasn't very rich, probably lived alone. He said he cooked for himself, and she knew he did his own grocery shopping and picked up his own laundry. Beautiful women likely frequented his apartment. She imagined Almaden's large-knuckled fingers stroking her skin. In between these fantasies the woman was bothered by money concerns, shoplifters, her husband's disdain. As if she were wrestling with a goblin, her head flipped back and forth on the pillow while she let her mind wander, and finally her sleepless night would yield to a gray dawn. She would rise in the morning tired and angry with herself.

Before the woman knew it, autumn had arrived. The days grew shorter and by six o'clock it was dark. One day the woman left for the laundromat with a sack of laundry. The streetlights shone in the dusk. Her sweater pocket drooped under the weight of her key ring and change for the washer and dryer. The woman stopped at a corner, waiting for the light to turn. Just then Almaden drove up. Discovering the woman, he stopped and leaned out the window to look at her. The crosswalk light changed to a flickering walk signal. While the woman crossed the street, Almaden remained motionless at the wheel of his car. Is he wondering whether to offer me a ride? the woman thought in delight. Later, amid the noise of twenty whirling washers, she tried to think what to say if Almaden were to ask her out. She felt giddy, as if standing at the edge of a swirling rapid.

As the holiday season approached, the woman and her husband stocked their shop with the brands recommended in the newspaper wine columns. They arranged gift wrap, ribbons, greeting cards. Colored lights twinkled in the display windows. The storefront looked inviting with the artificial snow sprayed on the windows and the bottles nestled within. When it snowed, the woman's heart thrilled and she would turn up the music on the radio.

The woman began to take an occasional peek toward the street around the time of Almaden's arrival. One evening, in the midst of a snowstorm, he pulled up in his car and marched inside, speckled with white. Encouraged by the sight of the fluffy snow, she smiled at him for the first time. Nature, it seemed, brought humans closer to each other.

He selected his Almaden and plunked it down in front of her. His lush chest hair, displayed so proudly on warmer days, was hidden deep inside a gray turtleneck sweater.

"Can you trust me?"

His voice shook. It sounded distinctly higher than usual.

The woman looked at him, jolted by his words, wondering what he meant. The snow on his hair was melting. She noticed the color of his eyes—green bordering on ash-gray.

"Do you think you can trust me?"

She didn't know what to say.

"I'm out of money, but I'll pay you tomorrow—all right?"

The woman barely managed to say yes. She didn't know the

man's name or address, so after he left she simply wrote "Almaden—$2.54" in her account book.

That winter the snow piled up a foot or two at a time. The woman and her husband bought rock salt to sprinkle on the sidewalk. Then there would be a warm spell, soon followed by more snow and a cold snap.

Finally the breezes turned warm and spring arrived. Ever since that snowy day, the man hadn't returned. The woman didn't want to believe it had all been planned, just for the sake of a few dollars. A bottle of Almaden now cost $2.69.

Whenever she took up her account book and her eye came to rest on "Almaden—$2.54," she realized she had no way of seeing this man again if he didn't return—no matter how vivid her image of him and his car. She was left trying to reassure herself: The world was an endless expanse, its people an infinite multitude.

THE LAST OF HANAK'O

Ch'oe Yun

It is forbidden to venture near the canal railing on stormy days. Take precautions in the fog, particularly the winter fog. . . . Then enter the labyrinth. And bear in mind, the more frightened you are, the more lost you will be.

He had finished his business in Rome, caught the train, and arrived in Venice after dark. Dreaming an exhausting dream, wandering among fantasies he had yet to confront, through a dawn window frosted with desultory breath he had seen this spectral sign, the words assembled by his unconscious from the travel guides he'd read since arriving in Italy.

He had awakened to find the train crossing the steel bridge that connects Venice with the mainland. Outside was darkness, a darkness not quite ripe. It was barely eight o'clock. And then a real sign rose out of the gloom, "Venezia, Santa Lucia," and the train rolled to a stop. He followed the stream of people detraining and emerged from the station.

Before him lay the most peculiar city he had visited in his

11

thirty-two years. A floating city full of buildings crowned with weighty ornaments, it swayed on the canals like a gigantic cruise ship on the verge of sinking.

But there was no railing and no fog.

As he boarded the small boat that would take him to his lodgings, he awoke from the peculiar state of hypnosis that had gradually overtaken him since the start of his journey. The other passengers were silent as ghosts. "So this is Venice," he muttered to himself. "What now?"

At his request a room had been reserved for him by one of the suppliers in Rome at a *pensione* near the Rialto, not far from the center of the old city, this city of water and fog. A small room that looked down on winding canals and a street lined with worn buildings that time had permeated with moisture, fading their ancient wall paintings. A man at the supplier's said he had stayed at this *pensione,* and if it sounded acceptable, he would go ahead and book a room.

Well, why not?

It seemed so unreal, being in Venice. What was he doing there? Mustering the courage that had been shrinking since his arrival in Italy? Or escaping that which was fanning his courage?

It was all so sudden, so coincidental. It had been four days at best since he had left his daily routine, but the surreal sense of time one experiences while traveling had made the previous day feel like several years ago.

One day—his perception of time was skewed now and he couldn't precisely date it—there had been a call from K. It could easily have been five or six months earlier. K had returned from a distant business trip, he had said. K, a friend from high school. A partner in crime during college, and then a partner in business. The two of them and a few others from high school and college had fallen into a routine of gathering at least a couple of times a month. It wasn't that they had anything special to say, or were anxious to see one another, and most of them were engaged in different lines of work; it was simply that they were friends. Occasionally these friends got together, and if it happened to be the weekend they all brought a kid or two along with the wife. They were like the model families you see in health food ads. If K had returned from a business trip, he couldn't very well get back to work without calling him first. Of course they had talked about hats—their line of business—and exchanged virtually all the business-related information worth passing on. And a few dirty jokes too.

Chemistry and sociology—their majors in college—had nothing to do with hats, but through sheer coincidence he and K, after stints at one or two other companies, had both settled on the hat business. This was the reason for the special connection between the two, among those others who met regularly. They were serious when they talked about hats. They didn't have much else to talk about now, and so they talked for quite some time about business. But it wasn't he alone who sensed that their conversation was forced and overdrawn. They knew each other better than that. And now K changed the subject. As if something had just occurred to him.

"Do you remember . . . Hanak'o?"

Silence.

"Someone said she's in Italy."

"Really? And?"

"I'm just telling you. I thought you might have been wondering about her."

"Why me?"

"Well, don't you think everyone wonders about her—a little bit, anyway?"

Just like I didn't ask K for particulars—who had seen Hanak'o, when, where, what she was doing—I'm sure K avoided asking detailed questions of whoever had passed on the news, he told himself. Gracefully reserved, these two, they were well versed in the practice of etiquette. There was a brief, awkward silence between them, but he salvaged the conversation with a spicy joke. And a few days later when they were drinking, K mentioned not a word of the phone call to the others or, of course, to him. He too acted as if the call had slipped his mind. Looking back, he felt he actually had forgotten it. And in truth he had.

As always when the discussion turned serious at their drinking parties, they grew animated bringing up examples of the world going to ruin, as if they had decided to change the world just like that. This was a sign that the party was winding down. They were no longer young; their monolithic society had grown slowly more daunting, and they had no proven methods for taking pleasure from life. . . . And so they met frequently.

They had their own code word. A code word for a woman. Hanak'o.

There was a woman. This woman had a name, to be sure, a name that did not exactly charm their metropolitan sensibility. But this was not the reason for their code word. And not once had they used that nickname to her face. One evening, after a tedious, pointless day, the usual group were drinking, and the nickname—a spur-of-the-moment joke—became their code word. They were passing through one of life's darker stages, in which they enjoyed creating code words. Most of them were in their early twenties, and all were approaching graduation from college.

One day one of the group had introduced a college woman who appeared to be of similar age. A woman of unusually small stature, whose soft voice blended well with theirs in conversation, who would tilt her head to the left and, with utter gravity and an earnest expression, throw questions at them when bravado got the best of their logic.

"Why do you think that way?" she would ask. Or she would say, her eyes slightly melancholy, something like, "It's because we're all young—I mean, we don't know what to do with our youth." And so on, embarrassing them all. That was Hanak'o.

So much of it is murky now, he told himself. When was it exactly, which of our gatherings had provided the occasion, and who had introduced her—was it P, or Y, was it K, or me, was it someone else we knew at the time, someone who's since grown distant?

Yes, she had the prettiest nose. Her features in general conveyed no particular atmosphere; they didn't make you sit up and take notice. But that nose of hers: now *that* was pretty. Seen from head on or in profile, it was a thing of beauty. And thus her nickname, Hanak'o—The Nose. But this code word had yet to be formalized during that period of their gatherings. And before she was permanently stuck with this nickname, the first thing that came to mind when you thought of her was not necessarily her nose. That she was now called Hanak'o was the result of a mistake they all wanted to hide. A small mistake that hid many truths, that had arisen in drunkenness, that no one wanted to admit or even retrace thoroughly. We all have a secret person we can't deal with comfortably without a nickname, and for them that person was Hanak'o.

Most of them had been classmates since high school, and in their last year of college, with employment tests and job interviews awaiting them, they met almost daily to prepare. And during their company apprenticeship they manufactured any excuse to gather. Once or twice a month one of them would call Hanak'o and she, alone or accompanied by a friend—always the same friend, it seemed she had no other—would join them. He had no memories of this friend, not even her name. His only recollection was that she had never remained to the end of the evening. Just when the gathering seemed to be developing momentum she would excuse herself, saying she lived far away, then whisper a few words into Hanak'o's ear and rush out, Cinderella-like, as if afraid the subway was about to turn into a pumpkin. None of them made even a pretense of detaining her. For the one who drew their attention was not this silent woman but Hanak'o, she of the occasional witty joke, she whose remarks, even the remarks that brought exclamations, were invariably delivered in a gentle voice.

When a change of atmosphere became necessary for their gatherings, when they tired of the psychological warfare with their fussy girlfriends, or when they grew weary of the same old faces but met nonetheless to tilt a glass of beer—these were the times they called Hanak'o. She willingly accepted their invitations, and to the best of his memory she had never turned them down for a reason that was less than plausible; she had menstrual cramps, she would explain, or a friend from back home was visiting. True or not, it didn't matter, for her tone was always sincere. They considered her sincerity curiously interesting, worthy of appreciation, and contrary to their expectations they found her persuasive. They saw her more frequently after they began their company apprenticeships.

They knew little about her. She was a fine arts major, but whether she painted, sculpted, or both, they weren't sure. No one in their circle was well versed in the arts, and so the occasional particulars she revealed to them sounded quite vague. They knew the word *matière,* but not until after college did they feel compelled to know why it was important to distinguish among stone, earth, and wood. Her family life was a blank; all they knew was her telephone number and the address jotted on the occasional letter that reached them. During the few years they knew her, either her address had changed on various occasions or she was using several addresses simultaneously. Once it was a dormitory, often it was in care of so-and-so, once it was a certain studio, and so forth.

For some reason her lifestyle, which could have seemed a bit strange, never stimulated their curiosity. Or might they instead have felt awkward attempting to express to her their curiosity when that lifestyle seemed completely natural to her?

Hanak'o was not the first woman to join their gatherings, but there were few women who lasted as long as she did without upsetting the balance of the meetings. He wondered why that was. Was it the unobtrusive way that she remained beside them, like the air or a comfortable temperature, before disappearing? Until that incident, after which she disappeared once and for all? Yes, until then she was an unobtrusive presence, and none of them expected for a moment that one day she would vanish to some unknown place where she would fail to answer their call.

With the map he had bought near the station he located the inn that the man in Rome had recommended. "Take the *vaporetto,* get out at the Rialto but don't cross the bridge, and then take two lefts. . . ." He'd spent the entire day on the train and was thoroughly exhausted. There'd been no rest since his arrival in Italy, and the melancholy he'd almost been savoring when he left Seoul had pursued him all along. He stood beside a youth with a handsome profile who skillfully brought in the line and secured it whenever a boat arrived at the dock. As he gazed at the buildings floating on the water, the warm orange glow of the lights inside them deepened the gloom he felt in this chill, moist air of early winter.

What the hell am I supposed to do for two days here? Don't know a damn thing about the city or the country. Maybe I should go on a tour.

"Listen—no matter how busy you are, you've got to see Venice." That's what K had said after going to Italy and making contact with the suppliers.

Yes, he thought. Everyone wants to come at least once to Venice. A city preferred by newlyweds and lovers. A desolate smile briefly played about his lips. All he could imagine in Venice, this city that made him feel as if everything were slowly sinking into the sea, were dark, dark things. But it wasn't just K's suggestion that had spurred him to come here. His objective wasn't Venice. It was an address in another city very close by.

"Don't cross the bridge, but instead take a left, then another left. . . ." Pensione Albergo Guerrato, where he was booked for two nights, was an old, four-story building he was sure he would grow tired of seeing over the next two days. A woman with a limp who owned a frighteningly large dog worked there. She had a good command of Italian, English, and French.

The room to which she guided him was number 7 on the third floor. According to the man in Rome, the room looked down on a cozy street that was worth viewing for its colorful daytime array of fruits and vegetables. Somewhat farther off were the Canalazzo and the partly hidden, lamplit Rialto. In the still of the night the street was empty. Infrequently the sound of young people laughing rang in the distance and then vanished without an echo. And very near, the peaceful sound of boats slicing through water aroused in him an odd loneliness. If only there were a face, a person who could caress the tense scales of life as gently as that. . . . Why, wherever he went, did he hear the sound of something crumbling? He was past thirty, and this sudden visitation of sentiment baffled him.

They knew little about Hanak'o's background. Strangely enough, apart from learning that she had taught children at an art institute with some college classmates before graduation, they had never openly questioned her about herself—what she did for a living, what her blood type was, if she had brothers and sisters. And if something remotely similar to such topics came up in conversation, she would be sure to nonchalantly steer the discussion elsewhere. She seemed to do this on purpose, as if she felt time spent talking about herself would be wasted for the others.

But now that he thought about it, he seemed to recall her saying that she had majored in sculpture. And he remembered her face when she added, smiling, that her sculpting experience actually consisted of working as an assistant for a famous sculptor, wrestling with blocks of stone three or four times taller than she. Hanak'o really was no bigger than a child, and none of them, even in their imagination, could visualize this rare disclosure from her. They had known her for a little over three years, but during their gatherings she had never drawn attention to anything related to herself. Always the same expression. The face lifted up slightly askew at a forty-five-degree angle so that her Natalie Wood nose was prominent. And that was all.

The room was quite small. It had a high ceiling with projecting molded corners, the kind of ceiling he'd seen several times since arriving in Italy. He lingered briefly in front of the telephone, then lifted the receiver, listened momentarily to the dial tone, and replaced it. Was it daytime on the other side of the globe? That's how far away his life with his wife was. In four years' time the widening of that distance had accelerated shamefully. In the beginning there had been rather sincere conversation. But their seesaw debates couched in such lofty expressions as *existence, value system,* and *joint property* quickly became outright arguments. The purchase of the most trivial item or his habit of squeezing the toothpaste tube from the middle or allowing a trace of smoke to continue from a cigarette he had crushed out—these trifling matters produced quarrels that provoked them to deny each other's very being and shook them to their roots.

The final disagreement, caused by the firm silence, the fault-finding vigilance they kept toward each other, as if their vocabularies had evaporated, was violent and long-standing, like a howl followed by complete silence. If not that cause, any other would have sufficed. There were the inevitable periodic disputes they held in order to reject each other. And all along, their play-acting toward the world continued. Together as husband and wife they visited relatives, attended social functions, and when the play was over they returned to their cold war.

Would he have taken this business trip to Italy in such a hurry if there hadn't been that discord, those petty, tiresome disagreements that left their inadequacies exposed in the most degrading manner? Would he have left without telling anyone, as if escaping, dressed as when he went to work, carrying a clumsily packed travel bag? He shook his head without conviction. If there had been no disagreements, would he have recalled what K had said about Hanak'o? Would he have approached with utmost secrecy those of her relatives he knew, and through these and other people, and over the course of several days, obtained her address in Italy?

He thought with a hint of pleasure, like one who possessed a top-secret file, of the hours he had devoted to tracing Hanak'o's address. And he tried to imagine the expression on his wife's face if she were to learn the true intent behind this trip to Italy. But it didn't offer that strong a feeling of compensation. Their malicious insensitivity toward each other was too deep for him to divert his mood through such fancies. Their quarrels were a shabby excuse for the fact that neither of them could deal skillfully with the frequent anxieties and disagreements that had twisted their relationship. If it had been otherwise, regret would have followed their quarrels.

"What in the hell am I doing here? And what am I supposed to do the next two days?" Muttering, he produced a guidebook from his bag and lay down on the bed. The ceiling receded higher toward nothingness. The other side of the globe felt more distant. He gradually fell asleep, thinking he wouldn't be troubled for at least ten hours.

He awoke the next morning to a noisy fog outside the window. Just as the guidebook had said. And just as the man at the supplier's in Rome had said, both sides of the street directly below were packed with the displays of the morning produce market. He left the window open and went down to the dining room. It was early and only a few people were having breakfast. They were young and looked American, and they spoke in undertones, perhaps about the weather, for the woman who operated the *pensione* could be heard reassuring them in her husky voice that the skies would clear later in the day. Two cups of coffee and a slice of toast: a simple order, and once he was done he returned to his room, oddly tired. Eight a.m. In the Seoul of his imagination it was the previous night.

He gazed vacantly at the names in large type in the guidebook that lay open before him—Piazza San Marco, Torcello,

Salute. . . . He decided that he hated traveling by himself. In all of his business trips this was the first time he had a two-day void to fill. It was almost as if he had planned it that way. But hell, this was, after all, the first time he had traveled alone. Before, it was always business, or else he was part of a tour group. A succession of faces surfaced rapidly in his mind—his wife, friends, colleagues at work—but in terms of a hoped-for traveling companion, none lingered in his brain for more than a second. And then the silhouette of Hanak'o walking away on a riverbank at twilight flashed through his mind like a distant shadow. "The hours at tourist attractions are quite unpredictable in Venice during the off-season. If you want to squeeze more into your schedule, you have to get an early start. After three o'clock everything closes down." The voice of K, a passionate consumer of information, echoed faintly in his ear.

He picked up the telephone, then opened his address book to a phone number that had been jotted down almost as an afterthought. Not a number in Seoul, but Hanak'o's number.

I'll just tell her I'm here on business and her name came up, he told himself. Maybe she's forgotten that little unpleasantness back then.

For the first time he was faintly curious about what Hanak'o was doing here on the far side of the globe. If memory served him correctly, he had never heard it mentioned that she had family or friends in Italy or that she had studied Italian. But then those weren't the reasons he had come here, either. Obtaining her address and phone number had involved contacting at least four people. True, he could have gone about it more efficiently. But he didn't wish to identify himself during his search, and the unfriendly tone of the man who had finally given him the desired information, who had said he was her classmate, had discouraged direct inquiries about her present situation.

The area code was that of a small city about an hour by train from Venice. It was supposed to be a tiny city; what could she be doing there? At that moment—and he had no idea why—the thought of a nunnery or a similarly still place came to mind. Maybe it's all the churches, he thought. Seems like there's one down every alley. Maybe she's not exactly a nun, but something like that. But when her face actually took its place in this mental picture, it didn't sit quite right with him. He'd had the same feeling several times before, and had never been able to pinpoint it. Something vaguely unfamiliar that irritated him and soured his mood.

He obtained an outside line . . . then punched in the numbers all at once. A ring . . . continued ringing. . . . He concentrated on the regular, repetitive rhythm as if it offered some sort of message he must decipher. No answer. Was it too early? By his watch it was past eight-thirty. With the light heart of someone putting off homework he gently replaced the receiver.

He considered: From the Rialto I ought to be able to walk to San Marco without asking directions. No, I shouldn't ask directions even if I get lost in that mazelike tangle of alleys. He left, taking a business card with the *pensione*'s address and phone number. He vaguely looked for someone who resembled Hanak'o—looked among the people standing inside the large glass windows of cafes drinking cappucino, the people cleaning the display windows of the high-fashion clothing and leather shops, people scurrying down the narrow shop-lined street, market baskets in hand.

It was strange the way memories of Hanak'o forced themselves upon him like this. Forced? "Perhaps I should say 'stubbornly persist,'" he muttered. Were those memories connected to being in a place not far from where she lived? Or to the foggy labyrinth of alleys and the water that was unfailingly revealed at the end of every one of them he followed? Yes, that was it. Strangely enough, Hanak'o had been associated with water. And maybe that's why it seemed natural that everyone had thought of the riverside for what turned out to be their last trip.

They had all vaguely realized that from time to time Hanak'o saw one of them apart from the group. He himself was one of those she met separately. But no one ever mentioned this. That is, until their contact with her was cut off. He didn't know how it was with the others, but his meetings with her followed a ritual-istic sequence. First of all, she would select a cafe rather than the tearoom where the group met.

"It's got the most comfortable sofas, makes you feel glad you're there—want to try it?" This was how she put it.

Yes. Places that made you feel good. There was probably no one better than Hanak'o at picking places in Seoul that were com-fortable and suited one's mood. Whether she chose a tearoom or a place to drink, it would be an utterly commonplace location on a street they had often used, prompting them to wonder why they had never discovered it before. A place, though, with one special characteristic that was sure to leave an impression. Some-thing memorable—comfortable seatbacks, distinctive decorations, unique teacups . . . she never forgot to point them out, and even a person like him, who tended to be obtuse in this respect, found himself responding to such features before long. And so a seem-ingly ordinary place was transformed into something that left a mark in his recollections. Like someone who kept a list of Seoul's hidden landmarks, she would guide him to a place "that made you feel good," wherever it might be, as if secretly inviting him to her own home.

After talking for a short time at this place they would walk the streets. Then have a simple meal. The strange thing was, they all demonstrated an incomprehensible stinginess, which they themselves recognized, when it came to Hanak'o, and not just during their college days, when it would have been quite natural, but after they had found jobs as well. This stinginess remained unchanged even after they had become rather well-to-do. Unlike his dates with other women, he generally selected the most shabby, inexpensive restaurants and he didn't necessarily pay. After the meal, a game or two of table tennis or bowling. Then back they would walk to the original place.

And then . . . drawn by a mysterious power to engage in a rite of confession, he had told Hanak'o everything indecent, unspeakable, and private about himself. About everything except the girl he was dating. The age at which he'd begun to masturbate, his shameful hidden habits, even secret dissatisfactions with close friends that Hanak'o knew. She listened to these accounts, head cocked inquisitively, always hearing him out until the end without interruption. The smile that played about her mouth never changed, no matter how shocking the account, and so he sometimes exaggerated these confessions of his hidden vices. He knew of no other woman who would give undivided attention to these trivial accounts. Sometimes he imagined her reenacting the same scene with a friend of his. This did not make him the least bit jealous.

"I appreciate your opening yourself up to me—it must be hard for you to talk about this."

On rare occasions she expressed her tiredness in this fashion. It was her way of telling him she wanted to go home.

Instead of waiting with her at the dark bus stop, he would leave for the subway. Again, she never objected, and when he looked back, her expression somehow made it seem that she was elsewhere already. Why had they extended Hanak'o only the bare minimum of patience and consideration?

Suddenly thirsty, he entered a cafe with unusually transparent windows. Like the other patrons he drank cappucino, the soft fresh cream clinging to the roof of his mouth. He stood like the others, and tried to make himself look as animated. He suppressed his desire to ask directions to San Marco. Back outside, instead of following the signs, he chose crowded streets and wandered numerous alleys and small plazas. With the self-assurance of someone who refused to be fascinated by the city's attractions, he pulled up his collar and buttoned it, then followed a foggy canal and crossed a small bridge. He was surprised at how fast he was walking.

He wondered if J had been the first of them to try something with her. J, the first of their group to marry. Once, he had received a midnight call from J. He had carefully set the receiver down beside the bed and taken the call in another room. And then, afraid his wife might overhear, he had remembered to replace the bedside phone in its cradle. Because J was drunk, and had brought up Hanak'o. They had been out of touch with her for more than a year by then. To his wife, who had looked up at him wonderingly, he had responded as if the call was unimportant: "It's just J. Sounds like he's drunk out of his mind."

J's drunken ramblings had stimulated his curiosity until sleep was banished from his mind. "This might come as a surprise to you, but there was a time in my life when I really didn't know what to do. I was so stupid. If I'd just pushed a little harder, who knows what would have happened? It's all right, don't worry, the wife's off visiting her family. Hold on, I'll get the letter. Hanak'o wrote back to me. Let's see—I hid it way down there somewhere.

Okay, got it. Now listen. I'll just give you the important stuff."
And in a tone exaggerated by his drunkenness he began reading:

"J, you always were a clown when it came to talking about something important. And don't think I'm rejecting you out of hand. I understand you're going through a difficult period, and you simply had to write a letter like this. But think about it, J. Am I really the right person for this letter? You ought to go away for a week or so. After that, if you've found the answer . . . then we can talk some more."

As he listened to J's drunken drawl, which made the contents of the letter sound ridiculous, he imagined himself in Hanak'o's situation with J before him, and felt irritated enough to punch him. But because his curiosity was greater, the irritation was short-lived.

"You remember how Hanak'o writes, don't you? If you knew the kind of letter I sent her, you'd probably faint. You see, I proposed to her—a very passionate proposal. It was something I had to do. None of you knew a thing. Recently I started thinking about it again. Of course, a week after I proposed, I set the wedding date for the wife. How am I going to get rid of this letter? Oh, Hanak'o is on my mind!"

J really did indulge in tongue-twisted romantic reminiscing, and he had given J's confession a proper hearing. J's case was somewhat unique, but all of them, himself included, had saved up a letter or two from her. Like trophies. After she had disappeared from their gatherings, it was briefly fashionable for them to read aloud to one another the letters they'd occasionally received from her, primarily during the early period of their meetings, when they were in college. It was then, when they gathered over drinks, that they had coined the nickname Hanak'o. She who never failed to answer their letters. She wrote letters that for some unknown reason touched their hearts, making them wonder if she was born to answer all the letters in the world. That there was a woman whose correspondence with them was somehow so profound, so philosophical and elegant, made them arrogant. Hanak'o was the first woman to arouse in him a desire to write letters. During his courtship he had never been taken with an urge to write to his future wife. Once he had embellished a letter to Hanak'o with a line lifted from a poem, and in her reply she had jokingly written, "You're trying to make me guess the title of that poem, aren't you?" There had been nothing about his relationship with Hanak'o to injure his pride; he had no fear that she would take something the wrong way. And now, despite that incident back then, he was using this business trip as an excuse to look her up. Why was that?

"After all, we're friends."

Once he had blundered, and this was how she had smoothed it over. Of course he didn't remember exactly what it was he had said. But the uncomfortable ripples it had caused remained fresh in his mind.

Hanak'o had never been notified about any of their weddings. He couldn't speak for his friends, but in his own case it had been simple carelessness. Needless to say, when he had been preparing the invitations, he had thought of inviting her. But his busy schedule had made him forget. It was the kind of forgetfulness that is unconsciously planned. Those of his friends who had married later couldn't invite Hanak'o because they were out of contact with her, but at least in the case of P and J, who married while they were still seeing her, they had clearly not invited her. After J's wedding he had apologized to her on J's behalf.

"You don't really consider weddings that important, do you?" she had responded.

In the distance appeared the steeples of San Marco that he had seen in photos. The wave of humanity that had already surged ashore told him he was approaching the plaza. If only it had been the two gilt lions in the plaza staring resolutely out to sea, he might have been moved. Ordinarily he tended to enjoy throngs of people. But there were simply too many people here, too many vendors, too many flocks of unusually fat pigeons, and no room to move about. He purchased an admission ticket for the basilica, but as he was about to enter he realized he had left his camera and binoculars at the *pensione*. And the guidebook he had made a point of purchasing, which described the mosaics inside the basilica. He was crestfallen. But that didn't mean he had any intention of going all the way back to the *pensione*.

Pushed inside by the line, he was surprised at the scale of the gorgeously colored mosaics on their golden backgrounds that covered the dome, the walls, even the pillars, with no space left untouched, a sight that drew exclamations from all the sightseers. Otherwise, he felt only the profound boredom of someone ill prepared for his trip. People throughout the world marveled when they set foot inside this basilica, but the sleepy mixture of thoughts in his head wandered in another time and place.

He sat down at the end of a pew and, recalling what he knew about the Bible, identified a few of the mosaic scenes. And there he remained, slothful and bored, waiting for time to pass. Hearing a Korean voice among the many languages flitting past his ear, he focused on it. It was the bright voice of a young woman explaining to an elderly man the mosaic on the ceiling directly above where he himself sat, a scene from the Book of Exodus. An affectionate father and daughter, he thought.

Again he asked himself what he was doing there. He thought of his daughter at home. She was almost two. Suppressing a sudden surge of frustration, he rose. The young woman offered her father the vacated seat. The exit was more crowded than the entrance.

He walked to the harbor and deeply inhaled the air. Time and again his gaze was drawn to the telephone booths scattered along the waterfront. In Seoul it was probably a gloomy early-winter evening. The fog had lifted from the water. Just then there was a loud cry. A crowd of people flocked the short distance to its source. Instantly a circle formed, and before he knew it, he found himself at its inner edge. There, three men were exchanging punches with the skill of professional boxers, while cursing in Italian. He saw that it was two against one, but everyone looked on wide-eyed with no thought of stopping them. Too, the single man was putting up a good fight.

The circle gradually widened, and the faces of more onlookers appeared on the balconies of the luxury hotel that stood beside the water. Back and forth they went at each other, three healthy-looking young men in leather jackets, tight-lipped except for an occasional outcry and their rough breathing. Finally the two partners cornered the other, who had fallen, and began kicking him with studied intent. While it seemed that silence ruled the fight itself, the crowd, on the contrary, became more vocal. He did not know the language of this country, and to him the people looked like they were cheering an innocent wrestling match. The spectacle became more violent, and he felt himself making tight fists. No one dared break up the fight. He felt a thrill watching the kicks and punches of the two partners. "Go on, one more. Finish him off, and get it over with. . . ." Just then the police waded through the crowd, and in no time they had separated the three men and were leading them off.

The crowd broke up and the pay telephones reappeared, beckoning him. Without hesitation he extracted a telephone number.

A number whose location was not on the opposite side of the globe but rather in a small city nearby. After three or four "hellos" in Italian he heard a gay, high-pitched woman's voice speaking rapidly and at length, saying something he didn't understand. In hurried English he asked for Hanak'o, using her real name, of course. He was put on hold, and then came the gay, raucous blend of several voices speaking in Italian. . . . And then a bright voice that he knew. Hanak'o's voice. Speaking not Italian but the Korean that he had hoped to hear. At that very moment the *vaporetto* deposited a group of passengers. Arms around each other's waists, smiling young couples stepped onto a small landing and walked past him. Only then was he released from the caution that had seized him. Suddenly he felt exhilarated.

He gave his name, then produced an awkward, exaggerated laugh. Without waiting for a reply, he launched into a wordy explanation: He was on a business trip. While the contract was being drawn up he had come to Venice. He would have to return to Rome. But first he wanted to see her. He'd gone to a lot of trouble to find out where she lived and to obtain her telephone number. On and on he chattered, frequently repeating the loud, incongruous laugh, giving her no opportunity to speak, as if he were trying to avoid something. And then there was an abrupt silence like that of a radio quieted by a power failure. Finally she was able to respond.

"It's good to hear from you. Why don't you come over?" she said in a loud, bright, laughing voice.

And then her voice slowly became the composed, low-pitched tone he remembered so well. Amiably and deliberately she told him the name of the train station, her work address, the name and appearance of the interior decoration firm where she'd been hired as a designer, and other particulars. But there wasn't as much to see in her city as in Venice, she added apologetically.

Although everything about her seemed the same, something had changed. Not her voice. Nor was her tone any less friendly. . . . Hadn't she sounded genuinely delighted to hear from him? Suddenly his resolve weakened. To see her he would have to catch a train, wander around looking for the street she'd mentioned, enter her office, wait beside her desk until she'd finished her work, be invited to her living space, eat a home-cooked meal, as the people in this country liked to do, and have a pleasant chat—was he really in the mood for all of this? And if she was married, he would have to observe proprieties and make conversation with her husband. . . . He asked her a question, cunningly, he thought.

"How many children do you have?"

She laughed.

He detected something in her voice. "I hope I won't be disrupting your work," he said.

After a brief silence she countered with a question of her own: "Don't you know me any better than that?" Then, at the sound of the tone signaling the end of the allotted time, she added, "You're not going to be like J, are you, calling but not visiting? Or P, leaving before he even finished his coffee? Come on over. I'm glad to hear from you—really."

As soon as she had finished, the line went dead. With the click of the telephone something connected in his mind. P had called her? And J?

He recalled the last drinking party they'd had before this trip. He had wanted to keep the trip a secret. The party mellowed him, though, and his plans had popped out of his mouth almost before he realized it. And then someone who hadn't attended the group gatherings for the longest time had unexpectedly brought up Hanak'o's name. "Who came up with that name, anyway? Makes her sound Japanese. Wouldn't 'K'ohana' sound more Korean? Some nickname! She'd be pissed if she knew." And then someone else had said, "She'll never find out." He recalled that J and P had each chimed in during that conversation. And he recalled very clearly K's phone call several months earlier informing him about Hanak'o. But none of them had said he had actually seen or talked with her; rather they had supposedly heard through a third party that she was living in Italy.

After declaring to Hanak'o that he would leave on the spot, he instead left the harbor and walked down an alley that followed a small canal. There he saw houses with a thick layer of moss that looked damper than usual now that it was winter, houses whose wall seemed about to collapse into the water. He saw a small bridge at the end of a wall, and narrow house fronts that seemed to suggest that life was like a game of house here. Occasionally he heard music from the houses, or the everyday bustling noises that come from inside a home, as if these sounds were meant to expose in starker contrast the mossy, sad-looking exteriors that had lost their paint and made the city seem to tilt even farther toward the water.

He allowed his pace to be dictated by the endless variation of the canals, alleys, and bridges. A street sign that captured his gaze became a vague guidepost telling him that the Rialto was growing ever more distant. With a gloomy smile he gave himself up to the freedom of the disheartened soul who walks an unfamiliar city without map or destination, to the repose of the person who wanders a maze in silence in a land whose language he neither speaks nor understands. Several times, like an overtone of this city, there sounded lightly in his ears the voice of Hanak'o; no, the voice of Chang Chin-ja—her real name—an interior designer who worked for a firm called Scobeni: "Don't you know me any better than that?" No better than that? Like a riddle with many pitfalls, the question drew him deeper and deeper into this city of mazes.

Through the window a train departed for the cities to the north. In the lights of the dusky station he saw once again the white sign reading "Venezia, Santa Lucia." His train, the night train for Rome, would leave at any moment. It was too early for sleeping, and only the seats on the upper level had been made into beds. Two passengers were at a window talking with well-wishers. Early though it was, he climbed up to the berth he'd reserved and lay down. The train slowly left the station and began to cross the steel bridge to the mainland. It was about the same hour as when he had arrived. Looking more distant from where he lay, the orange lamps appearing at intervals above the water formed a long curve like a procession of monks. The lamps, which marked the channel for nighttime boat traffic, were each suspended by a black band from a pointed piling, as if between a pair of clasped hands. The train accelerated and soon the water had disappeared from his field of vision, leaving him feeling yet again as if something in the far distance was collapsing.

There it went, the city of his momentary stay. Now the train was passing through a dark landscape of fewer and fewer lights and no visible human presence. The passengers below busily reclined their seatbacks to make beds, and then suddenly there was silence. The voices in the corridor became murmurs and the train raced toward thick darkness. Three of the berths in the upper level remained unoccupied. Later that night, when everyone was asleep, people boarding at some station or other would climb up looking for those berths. Maybe Bologna, Florence. . . .

How could that incident have come about? Could you even call it an incident?

He had no idea how they'd discovered that drinking place in the boggy, marshlike area near the reed grass. It had all started when two of them happened to buy used cars around the same time. A group of seven had left Seoul during a three-day holiday and driven as far as the Naktong River. Their original goal had been to find a beach that they liked. But they ended up at the river. The group included himself, plus Hanak'o and her woman friend. They had divided up into the two cars, whose owners then took advantage of the journey to practice their driving skills. At the Naktong, a sign advertising sashimi and spicy fish soup had caught their eye, and they had followed a narrow dirt road until the restaurant appeared. Although it was extremely isolated, they decided to make it their destination for the night. To enter the restaurant they first had to cross a muddy yard that threatened to swallow up their feet. And he seemed to recall a weedlike grass at the side of the yard that gave off a nauseating odor. Was it late autumn? he wondered. Or early winter, like now?

While the meal was being prepared, they walked along the riverbank. No light appeared in any direction, making them feel as if they were at the end of the world. Back at the restaurant they ate and drank leisurely, and as the night wore on, the excitement of the trip gave way to a melancholy unease. The restaurant seemed to be part of a home, and as soon as they entered the room where they would spend the night, the strange mood, which didn't seem to have originated in any one of them, spread through them all. It was as if this house was cut off from the world and would sink into the marsh at any moment. It was clear that W, one of the drivers, regretted having come such a long way to this place. One of the others kept saying he had to call Seoul, and another complained that he had forgotten an important business meeting the following day and didn't know how to notify the other party. At the time, P was the secret envy of the others because of his upcoming marriage with the daughter of a wealthy family, and although he had insisted on short notice that they take this trip, he had reacted the most irritably when someone raised the delicate question of where they would all sleep. He himself had felt inexplicably hostile toward Hanak'o and her friend, whose expressions hardened as they observed the change in the others.

Perhaps during this trip they had let down their guard to reveal the despondency they all felt after two or three years of life in the real world. Or maybe the combination of the fatigue of daily life, the alcohol, and their long day of travel had triggered a strange chemical reaction that caused irreversible uneasiness.

One of them went outside, then returned with news that the lodging question was settled, and why not drink some more. This was a friend whose participation in their group had grown infrequent after he started working for a bank. He had given the owner a huge sum, he crowed, in return for a second room.

After that, everything went downhill. . . . Seven hours together in the cars had left them with nothing to talk about, and so they sang songs. Well, it was more like screaming than singing. Like the squealing of pigs. Everyone focused on the two women, who were quietly nursing their drinks and attempting to conceal their puzzlement at the deterioration in the group's mood, and tried to intimidate them into singing. Any pretense at fun and games was over. They all knew that Hanak'o detested being pressured to sing, and in point of fact her singing was terrible. Knowing this, they demanded, half jokingly, half threateningly, that she sing. Hanak'o's friend stood up instead, prepared to sing in her place.

But all of them shouted together for Hanak'o. With an awkward smile her friend sat down. But Hanak'o, for some reason, would not oblige them. And there seemed to be a slight change in her expression.

Then someone bolted up. "Who wants to bet me whether she'll sing?" he said, gritting his teeth as he approached her. At the same time, someone sitting across from Hanak'o took her by the arms and tried to lift her. Hanak'o's friend rose partway, trying to free her. He himself stood and tried to pull Hanak'o up from behind. Someone threw a bottle against the wall. Someone yelled, just for the sake of yelling. And then someone grabbed the three of them, Hanak'o and the two who were trying to make her stand up, and all three plopped back down to the floor.

He tried to remember how long they had harassed her. No one had tried to put a stop to it. Stop it? You could be sure everyone gladly connived in it. Whether Hanak'o sang or not wasn't the issue. Her friend's meaningless outcry did nothing to stop them. It wasn't much of a cry anyway, but rather a weak, ridiculous sound that probably didn't carry outside the room. The scene was one of odd frenzy—pushing and shoving, breaking glass, screaming and shouting—as if they were each in their own way observing a strict method to the collective harassment, each playing an assigned role to perfection, all of them now trying to outdo one another. It could be said, at that point, at least, that none of them was genuinely drunk. They were faking drunkenness, all of them. Perhaps Hanak'o too.

Hanak'o and her friend were standing now. Their faces were pale. Hanak'o's hair, which she wore pulled back, was disheveled and unseemly. Her blouse was twisted to the side. Someone pointed out her appearance and burst into laughter. The laugh was instantly infectious, and before long there was a whole-scale frenzy of laughter. It spread even to the two women, who had accepted their punishment, and they laughed in spite of themselves. But their faces were terribly contorted, and they might actually have been crying—it was impossible to tell. Laughing hysterically, they picked up their bags. And then their coats. And then, still laughing, they opened the door, admitting the chill night wind and the stink of the weeds, and walked out into a darkness that was several times thicker now. He had no memory of them laughing after that. The only thing visible beyond the yard was the long, faint line of the riverbank; only an old, dim light bulb illuminated the yard. By that time the dwindling outlines of the women had darkened and then dissolved in the gloom. Nothing was distinguishable save the blades of grass that were occasionally turned up by the wind so that they reflected the faint light from the bulb.

They gazed toward the dark expanse where the two women had vanished, but no one ran to call them back. They were all well aware that the women would have to walk for a dangerously long time through the darkness before they found another dwelling or came out on the main road. But they continued their frenzied laughing. They were like wind-up toys, unable to stop. Someone closed the door. They all sank into silence, and when they fully realized what had happened, they drank until dawn. The next day they returned to Seoul in leaden silence.

And this was how Hanak'o had disappeared from their gatherings. It was then, after her name, Chang Chin-ja, happened to come up in their conversation, that she formally became Hanak'o. This use of her nickname resulted from the subtle interplay of two contradictory desires: to speak of her on the one hand, and to refrain from doing so on the other. Although she would appear by that nickname in their idle talk over drinks, they kept a firm silence about the identity of the shadow that had vanished into the darkness that night when they were all adrift along the Naktong.

And now he was lost, as lost as he had been the night of that trip, which had seemed darker because it was unfamiliar. He turned away from the darkness and curled up toward the wall of his berth. Someone passed by quickly in the corridor, whistling a soft, peaceful tune. Loud snoring rose from the seats below. The three empty berths remained unoccupied.

You'll call home as soon as you get to Rome, he told himself. His feelings hadn't changed a bit. "I really feel your absence," you'll tell her. "We'll have to take a family trip to Venice sometime." You'll say that to her on the phone, even if you can't promise it and your voice lacks conviction. Everything will work out. Just like it has so far. But what if the wife says, "It won't work this time. Let's talk. Let's be honest with each other for once." His face wore a sharp scowl as he fell asleep.

Back in Seoul, he arranged a gathering over drinks. As usual, they ended up talking shop, discussing the world situation, and talking about business prospects. Like J, P, or whomever, he talked long and loud about the exotic beauty of Italy, the gondolas of Venice (but had that famous attraction ever actually entered his mind?). And then they all got drunk, and as they always did before scattering for the following day's work, they concluded by summarizing the various matters they'd been rambling on about: the world would keep turning; their children were growing up so well; they'd get along fine as long as they avoided basic sources of friction with the wives; and maybe the next day they'd be a little bit richer and not quite so tired.

◆◆◆

"Don't you know me any better than that?" From time to time Hanak'o's question echoed in his ear, as if spoken by a ghostly voice. But for a vast number of reasons his life was too busy for him to respond to such a question. His business with the Italian firms that provided raw materials for hats flourished, but he never again volunteered for a trip to Rome. He was never able to satisfy all his desires, but because he received promotions in keeping with his age, it was unnecessary for him to go there on business himself. He had more important matters to decide, matters that kept him busy. So busy that there was no possibility of taking his wife and daughter, who was soon to enter grade school, on a family trip to Venice.

For as long as his business had prospered, his company had regularly received a monthly English-language newsletter in the form of a publicity pamphlet for foreign buyers, issued by the Italian ministry of commerce. Several years had passed since his trip to Venice when one day the monthly copy of the journal arrived with a feature on two Asian women: "Korean Duo Design Chairs With Asian Charm; Interviewed As They Depart For Home." Accompanying the interview was a large photo showing Hanak'o's face and the broadly smiling face of the woman who seemed to be her only friend, a woman he could remember nothing about, not even her name. The interview revealed how the pair had become a unique and highly promising design team, beginning with their chance participation in an international interior design contest sponsored by Italy. There was a brief account of Hanak'o's school days, all of which was new to him. She had been close to them at the time; how and when had she led a life such as this, unknown to them? The interview conveyed a tone of respect for the pair's single-minded devotion to chair design and to the unique charm of their designs, which aimed simultaneously at bodily comfort and sensuous beauty. The remainder of the feature was taken up with photos and a technical discussion of their designs, along with their plans, and steps they had already taken to open up offices in Korea as well as Italy. The article spoke of the two women alternately as business partners and companions.

Hanak'o's face was angled halfway toward the smiling face of her friend, making her prominent nose even more noticeable.

HUMAN DECENCY

Kong Chi-yŏng

Yi Min-ja certainly was an attractive woman. Attractive enough
to make me understand my editor's change of heart. When I arrived at the place in southern Kyŏnggi Province where she stays
when she's in Korea, she had just returned from her morning
walk. I found her in her yard, where wildflowers were blossoming. She was perhaps an inch or so over five feet tall, her straight
hair drawn together in a ponytail, and she wore unstarched off-
white cotton pants and a loose-fitting wool sweater the color of
eggplants. It was that time of spring when you never know what
to expect from the weather. A heat wave had arrived a few days
earlier, just like in early summer, and I had left my jacket back at
the office. When I climbed out of the car the chilly wind whipped
me and it just kept coming. The purple lilacs beside the hedge
looked like they were cringing. The bright blossoms of the weeping cherries next to the hedge, the dazzling white flowers of wild
magnolias, the plain pink flowers of double-blossom cherry trees,
even the hazy spring scenery in the valley close behind the house—

everything seemed to shiver painfully in the cold air. And yet Yi Min-ja, despite her small figure and short stature, shorter even than the shrubs behind us, looked willfully, refreshingly pure, like a lone wildflower blooming in the wind. The impression she gave me was—how shall I say it?—unique and somehow mysterious, as if she possessed a magic that protected her from the wind and the capricious spring chill and made her look younger than her age of forty-eight. Maybe that impression was due in turn to the log house into which she welcomed the photographer and me, a house that seemed completely original and fresh out of a children's book. Its broad wooden floor had the deep reddish-brown sheen that comes from years of treatment with perilla oil. Above the fireplace was one of her paintings; it showed a preschool-aged girl sitting cross-legged on a green globe. While I inspected the painting, the artist appeared barefoot with tea. The tea had an extraordinary fragrance, and its taste was slightly bitter, as if it had been prepared from wild grasses.

She had us sit on floor cushions covered with coarse, rough cotton. Then she sat down on the bare floor, saying, "Once when I was in India I drank nothing but this tea for a month. My meditation master, Magahota Meeruhonjee made it himself. It helps clarify the mind."

I finally remembered to take out my notebook. It had remained in my bag while I tried to deal with the overpowering impression presented by the house and the singular mood that Yi projected.

"I'm sorry, his name was—"

I stopped short, noticing she was staring at me. Her eyes seemed to be asking if I had fulfilled the writer's courtesy of reading her book before interviewing her.

"I read your book," I hastened to add, "but the master's name didn't stick. It's not a name I'm familiar with. . . . I'm sorry."

"Ma-ga-ho-ta Mee-ru-hon-jee," she repeated with a subtly inviting smile that reminded me of the stone Buddha in Sŏkkul Grotto.

As she pronounced the name I bent over my notebook to jot it down, thinking, "He's not my master—why should I bother memorizing such an odd name?" But what was the point of dwelling on that? When I looked up, she still wore that penetrating smile. It unsettled me.

"I guess I'm forcing a name on you without any context. I wonder if I can describe him in words," she said, unnerving me more. And yet her voice was warm, her expression gentle. Her expression, if I can call it that, had a trace of something I can only describe as plant life, something that would set plantain leaves trembling and bring rain down upon them. She had a look of complete fulfillment even when she was alone in her spacious yard. I now regretted disapproving of her for having lived abroad. There was nothing foreign about her small, narrow eyes, regular nose, and thin lips; she was Korean, the same as I. Now that she had returned to her homeland, why should it matter whether her master was Indian, American, or some other nationality? I quickly drank the piquant tea.

I looked up, prepared to ask my next question, and as my eyes met hers I ventured a smile. She carefully refilled my cup and politely offered it to me with both hands. As I watched her I suddenly imagined myself nestled in her spare bosom asking about the meaning of life. I imagined her stroking my hair, and myself saying, "Yes, I want to be alive."

It was clear she had a certain power. The power of, well, one who is fulfilled just by the fact of her existence. After my editor met her at her one-woman show, our office had become a veritable Indian meditation site. This was a man whose charismatic aura of experience could draw tears from anyone in the office except a hardened writer (though at drinking parties he gave the impression of an aging romantic with literary aspirations) and here he was talking rapturously about her paintings and about meditation. And we writers, worn out from research, deadlines, meager pay, and writing—as we smoked cigarettes, phoned contributors to dun them for their articles, or else crumpled up our own articles, we began surreptitiously to listen to what he was saying about Yi Min-ja's lifestyle.

"At age twenty-one she takes Grand Prize in the Republic of Korea National Exhibition; after graduation she moves to the U.S.; she's a huge success in New York; she moves to France and holds one successful show after another; she's the only Korean artist represented by Sotheby's. . . . And then one day she realizes that her successes and achievements have left her hollow. She goes to India, studies under the master Magahota Meeruhonjee, wanders for three years barefoot all over India, travels to Africa and sketches, and one day on safari while she's gazing at the snowy summit of Kilimanjaro, she has another awakening and comes back to Korea to settle down."

"The stuff of dreams," blurted a writer who had a smart mouth. Not that I didn't acknowledge his sarcastic intent. But I found myself wondering if perhaps the account really was true. For when I was on my way home after a tipsy post-deadline gathering with the other writers, when I was brought to an abrupt stop by the realization that there was nothing but darkness down every street, when I wondered what the hell kind of life I was living, I felt a yearning to be free and fearless; I felt certain things come to life inside me, and among them was a curiosity about freedom, wandering, transcendence, the achievement of a dream.

One of my responsibilities at work was selecting a book for

that month's topic, interviewing the author, and writing a six-page feature. When the editor did an about-face and asked me to postpone my story on Kwŏn O-gyu to the following month and do a feature on Yi Min-ja instead, I must confess I hesitated. I had already started the feature on Kwŏn, and there was the matter of my negative reaction to Yi because she had lived abroad. But I didn't put up a fight—which would have gained me nothing anyway—perhaps because the hope Yi had given my editor was now spreading to me. A hope that my long years of living alone, and more recently the years I had worked for this women's magazine, all those lonely hours that felt so long, would be infused with a different color. So I put away the negatives of Kwŏn that I'd received from the photographer, along with Kwŏn's book *Human Decency* and the notes I'd made on him, and after I marked the manila envelope "June" I left to interview Yi.

And now as I climbed into our car and gazed at her log house set against the outline of the distant, wind-swept hills with their pastel blossoms, at the very moment I caught myself wishing I could live in such a house, a sorrow long dormant deep inside me shot forth like a young radish poking out through dirt and trash. Why a sorrow like a radish shoot? That much I think I can answer. There's a kitchen garden behind the house I recently moved into. One Sunday when I had nothing else to do, I dug up the soil to see if I could plant something. More accurately, rather than breaking ground I dug into a dump site. There was plastic, there were cookie wrappers, and eventually lumps of cement, not to mention stones and rocks. The stones and plastic bags were no problem, but my spade proved useless with the cement, and I was tempted to give up. But the idea of losing a fight with a junkyard and taking my tool back inside didn't sit right with me. All right, I told myself, as long as I've started, I might as well see it through to the end. So I bought a shovel, one that came up to my waist. My first job was to dig up the cement, and then I fertilized the patch, but it was still so sandy and rocky that I wondered if seeds could possibly grow there. Just for fun I planted some radish seeds. But wouldn't you know it, the weather turned chilly as soon as Arbor Day passed. For several days I went out back and waited to see if a sprout might appear. I gazed at the soil, darkened by the fertilizer, but there was no sign of a radish shoot. I was prepared to blame myself for planting too early in the spring, when just a few days ago those seeds I had given up for dead shot through the rocks and plastic remaining in the junky soil, to reveal sprouts the size of mung beans.

Now, when I leave for work I simply have to go around back to see how much the sprouts have grown. And this is why I'm quick to use the metaphor of a radish shoot to describe that unexpected outpouring deep inside me.

But if anyone were to ask why sorrow shot forth in me, I would probably equivocate. I would shake my head, saying that maybe it was something other than sorrow.

My hour-long interview with Yi Min-ja having ended, I climbed into the car and waved goodbye, but as I watched her plantain-like face that still seemed so friendly, all I could think of was the rented room beside the gate of a shabby Korean-style house at the end of a winding alley in Samyang-dong where Kwŏn O-gyu had lived since his release from prison two years earlier. This was the man whose magazine feature had been postponed to the following month for the sake of Yi and her bestselling book. All I could think of was his room beside a tiny yard that was thinly layered with cement, where on one side rustic-looking rhododendrons and flowerless Kaffir lilies grew in blue plastic flowerpots, where there was a slender pipe and faucet and a brick-red washbasin of reconstituted rubber thrown beside it, a room that cast a slender curtain of shade like dark watercolors much thinned with water. But if anyone had asked why I associated such scenes with sorrow, I couldn't have offered a word in reply.

"Freedom Is My Clothing, Meditation My Food: The Universe Cannot Confine Me." This was the title that occurred to me on our way back to the office. It had a nice ring to it. And it was a good sign that it had come to me so readily. In contrast, I had been at a loss for a title as I emerged from that winding alley after interviewing Kwŏn O-gyu. How could I come up with a title when I couldn't even think of how to *begin* my article about his book containing the letters he'd written while serving the life sentence handed down to him when he was twenty-eight? The title, not to mention the introduction and main body of the feature, was a blank. And so I felt like congratulating myself for my willingness to interview Yi Min-ja. If not for her, then again this month I would have been tagged Tchongsuni—the last one in with her articles.

"What do you think?" the photographer now asked me. "Are we going to run your piece on Yi Min-ja this month?"

I nodded.

"Sounds like the editor sweet-talked her into not giving an interview to any other women's magazine this month. A story like hers is an exclusive these days. Who cares about some guy stuck in prison for life, now that we've got a civilian government? Right?"

"What's your point?" I asked. Misgivings were cropping up in my mind like radish shoots. (I felt that as long as I was calling for an explanation, I might as well think in terms of radish shoots again. But then misgivings aren't something we normally associate with the fresh green color of a radish shoot. Sorrow, perhaps, but not misgivings. So let's just stick to the facts.) For some reason his words had sounded sarcastic, and so I had questioned him. And now I observed him. He had buried himself in the seatback and stretched out his legs.

"Oh, it's just that I'm thinking maybe I should get out of here for a while myself," he said after a brief silence.

"Where to?"

"Well, I don't really know. India, maybe? Africa? New York? Paris? . . . I could do some meditation. Maybe I'll see the light, too. Damn. . . ."

"Nothing wrong with that. But why 'Damn'?"

"Seemed like the perfect thing to say. Damn. . . ."

"Why look at the world from such a crooked angle? There's more than one road to salvation, you know. Not like in the past."

He seemed ready to add something, but instead deposited his heavy camera bag in the back seat and closed his eyes. I said no more and turned my attention to the expressway. I could see myself growing flustered and evasive if he had questioned my abrupt mention of a "road to salvation," and so I was thankful for his silence. In that sense, we tended to be a perfect match for each other.

But unlike the photographer, I didn't want to record our encounter with Yi Min-ja in terms of *meditation* or any other single word. For when I had seen her in the yard, her smile as refreshing as a wildflower, I had felt a kind of courage well up inside me. A courage that would help me accept the prospect of being alone now and for a good part of the future. Because now when I returned home alone at night, instead of sipping the cheap wine in the refrigerator, instead of lingering at the telephone deep into the night, until the radio stations went off the air and I could no longer hear trucks outside my window, wondering if someone would awaken me for a conversation in low voices, instead of dialing 700 and listening inattentively to my horoscope, I could try to meditate as she had instructed me. Sit cross-legged, preferably in the nude, she had said, and let all the things that are stressing you dissolve. Then start the breathing technique. Remember to use the abdominal muscles. Take in through the nose, down the airways, and collect in the stomach all the energy of the universe, then with your abdomen expel through the airways and mouth the bad energy collected in the stomach. The important thing, she had said, is to feel yourself breathe, simply feel it. When I'm alone, I thought now, maybe I really can do that breathing in the nude, that breathing I had tried with a clumsy smile a short while ago as she looked on.

Back at the office, the photographer and I found ourselves alone; everyone had gone out for lunch. I offered to treat him to a meal and he accepted. As I set down my bag on a chair to look for my wallet, the manila envelope with my story on Kwŏn O-gyu fell to the floor. I thought of picking it up, but decided not to bother. Locating my wallet, I placed it in my armpit and we caught the elevator. After pushing the button for the first floor, he spoke up:

"In the car you were asking me what I was getting at. Actually I was thinking of those black-and-white photos in the picture frame at the house in Samyang-dong. Didn't he say one of those men was executed and the other one died in prison? I should have shot those photos. If the article was going out this month, I was hoping to go there, maybe today, and photograph them."

He spoke nonchalantly, but from that point on he looked preoccupied. I wondered if he had noticed that I hadn't picked up the Kwŏn envelope. If not, then why would he have mentioned those photos all of a sudden? No, that wasn't it. I asked myself why everyone sounded cynical to me these days. I stuffed my hands in my jacket pockets and watched the floor number change in the elevator.

About those photos. It had been so balmy that day. The photographer had posed me in front of some fluttering cherry blossoms hanging over a wall on a residential street in Samyang-dong. The street narrowed to an alley farther up, and cherries and similar trees could no longer be seen. The alley became a desolate heap of concrete in which only such things as a wilting crab-leg cactus in front of a realtor's office caught our eye. We climbed that winding alley, and as we entered the home of Kwŏn O-gyu we were sweating so much that I forgot all about spring. The photographer was constantly mopping his face with a handkerchief. The doorbell was answered by Kwŏn's younger brother, who had looked after him in jail for almost twenty years. He ushered us inside to the veranda. Memory is a strange thing. At the time, I hadn't paid attention to the rhododendrons and Kaffir lilies in the blue plastic pots in the cement yard. I noticed only the refreshing feel of that thin layer of dark shade. But why, when I was waving goodbye to the artist Yi from our car, had I thought not of the perspiring photographer, or of Kwŏn's brother with his receding hairline, or of his sister-in-law bringing coffee and apples from the kitchen, but instead only the wornout washbasin of reconstituted rubber and the slender faucet in the yard? Anyway, there we sat on the veranda's wooden floor, the brother explaining with a rueful expression that Kwŏn had gone to the clinic because of a cold and would soon be back. He then handed us a business card that read "Kwŏn O-wŏn, Representative Director, Korean Ceramic Trade Association."

"Korean Ceramic Trade Association?" I asked casually.

"Actually, it's a small pottery shop at South Gate Market. . . . My given name is 'Five Wŏn'; with a name like that you don't get to be president of a big business." He chuckled nervously, perhaps wondering if we really thought he was a company president.

We produced our own cards.

"Please don't bother," he said, his face flushed. He kept smoothing back his hair, but this couldn't conceal the discomfort in his tone. Perhaps he was embarrassed by the large scale suggested by "Ceramic Trade Association," or by the fact that it was only a small shop, or that his given name didn't mean "Five Hundred Million Wŏn" but only "Five Wŏn." In any event he seemed uncomfortable watching us inspect his card. It was too bad he felt that way, I found myself thinking as we quickly put our cards away. He shouldn't have to worry about what other people thought of him. I glanced away, and that's when I discovered the photos. Hanging from the wall was the kind of picture frame you always see in the veranda of old traditional houses, and my eye was drawn to two small, faded photos. They were half the size of a business card, and were squeezed in alongside a large photo of two figures seated side by side who appeared to be the parents of the Kwŏns.

"That gentleman is Yi Mun-su," said Kwŏn's brother, following my gaze. "He was sentenced the same time as my brother, and executed. And that one is Hwang Mun-ch'ŏl. He was tortured to death. My brother kept those photos, then asked me to put them up here in the house. Their families are scattered all over, so we decided to hold their memorial services here."

I looked up at the photos. Yi Mun-su wore a black suit. His square face had piercing eyes. Hwang appeared to be a few years older. He wore a dark traditional topcoat. His face was gentle, his eyes narrow. One of them executed, the other dying after an intestine burst under torture. If this hadn't been explained to me, I might have taken them for the brothers' uncles. As I listened to

Kwŏn O-wŏn's explanation I jotted down the two names in my notebook.

I guess this is irrelevant, I told myself, but I'm not used to looking at photos of people who are dead now. Maybe because my family doesn't use framed photographs in the memorial ceremonies we hold. But now I have friends who remain only in photos. Once in a while I'll open my photo album and find myself counting those friends, who by joining me in photos helped record a period of my life, but who no longer exist in this world: the friend I used to teach Sunday school with who rescued a drowning classmate during orientation our first year in college but who himself ended up drowning; the classmate who died a questionable death in the army; the *sŏnbae* who died of a heart attack late one night in the darkness of a movie theater; the friend who hanged herself in her rented room; the *hubae* who was killed by a tear gas canister. There was a friend who was taken away and tortured, who needed treatment in a mental hospital when released, and who finally jumped from the tenth floor of an apartment building; and a *sŏnbae* who was out drinking till dawn with his *hubae,* and on the way home was hit by a taxi. All these ways in which they died. And then . . . there was a student. He had wavy hair, and a dimple when he smiled. He had a voice that blasted, once we got him to sing, and it often got us kicked out of drinking places. . . .

What would they be doing if they were alive now?

Well, they'd probably be wearing neckties and meeting *hubae* in a tearoom in the basement of their company building, or showing up at the wheel of a new car at evening alumni gatherings. Maybe I would have dropped out of touch with them long ago, like I have with many other friends, without wondering much about them, and maybe I would make my way along in life and at unexpected moments their faces would come to mind. Because it kept occurring to me that we were all in our twenties in the 1980s, and although I had said then that I wished I were dead, I wasn't dead; whereas those others who had run with us along the road out of the 1980s had fallen, never to rise. And because I was seized by the thought that I was the only one to make it out of that long tunnel, that all the others were dead. Which meant that the mere sight of a dark place would make me fearful that I'd find their blue, lifeless bodies lying there.

"How is Mr. Kwŏn's health?" I asked.

"He was all right for a while, but he's having a hard time now. Even little colds. . . . You'd think his germs might have learned to behave themselves in prison."

It wasn't a particularly funny joke, but he laughed as if he found it hilarious. It was a clumsy attempt to make amends for keeping a pair of young journalists waiting so long, and we forced ourselves to laugh along with him. In fact, the situation was a bit awkward and tedious. A short time later, his wife appeared with sliced apples and coffee. On that spring day that was no longer balmy but downright hot, we sat on the veranda drinking luke-warm coffee.

"That's my brother's room over there," Kwŏn O-wŏn said with a mortified expression as we sat in silence, awaiting the subject of our interview and nibbling slices of apple. The room he indicated was beside the front gate. A room with traditional sliding doors and thin, light yellow rice-paper panels that were translucent in the sunlight.

"Originally it had a hinged door. We used to rent it out, but after Brother was released, we had the tenants vacate, then bought some furniture and moved Brother in. We had him turn in early that first night because he was tired, and then we shut the door and went to bed. The next morning we didn't hear him stirring, and figured he was still asleep. We assumed he was exhausted, and decided not to wake him. I left for the shop, and my wife had something to do, so she left his breakfast on the veranda and went out. We were having the shop remodeled, and didn't have much time for anything. My wife left a note saying breakfast was on the meal tray and for lunch he should order noodles with black-bean sauce from a Chinese restaurant, and she wrote down the number for him to call and directions to our house. But by four in the afternoon, I'd called home several times and there was no answer. That seemed odd, so I rushed home. The meal tray hadn't been touched, and there was no sign of Brother. You can't believe the things that went through my mind. And then I heard banging from inside his room. I opened the door . . . and there was my brother, drenched with sweat, staring at me. 'Brother, why are you pounding on the door? Why didn't you come out?' I said. And then I realized he was so embarrassed he couldn't say anything. . . . I found out later that this happens a lot with lifers. Think about it. He'd been locked up for twenty years, and forgot how to open a door from the inside by himself. And so he skipped breakfast and lunch and just kept pounding on the door. He probably heard us leaving and wondered what if, what if, and began pounding. . . . It's hard to believe."

He quickly lowered his reddening eyes and took out a cigarette. The photographer coughed nervously and fumbled with his camera lens.

"I guess these things really happen when you lock up a human being. Scary, isn't it? My brother used to play rugby, you know. And in prison he worked out, did breathing exercises. But he's so weak now. He's still not used to walking around town. In his cell he could only take seven or eight steps before he'd have to turn around, then he'd take another seven or eight steps. He's still in the habit of doing that; he kind of flinches and pulls up. The first time we saw him do it on the street, we thought he wasn't feeling well. He said he wanted to rest for a moment. We were downtown showing him around. . . . And now I realize it was a habit. He thought he was going to bump into that jail-cell wall that was facing him for twenty years. It's like that wall is still part of him, and it's going to take a while to get rid of it."

The photographer was gazing at the red reconstituted-rubber washbasin in the corner of the yard. I slowly nibbled at my piece of apple.

A little over an hour after we arrived, the elder Kwŏn appeared. His sister-in-law opened the front gate and he rushed across the short interval to the veranda.

"I'm so sorry, inviting you young people here and then. . . ." He stepped onto the veranda, produced a handkerchief, and mopped his brow. "I was on my way to the clinic and got to thinking about a gentleman named Yi Sang-u. He was a partisan during the war. He got out of prison not too long ago, and it occurred to me he might not have long to live. So I called him out of curiosity, and it was just like I thought. . . . I took him to the general hospital just now. I'm very sorry."

His sister-in-law broke in as she served him a cup of ginseng tea: "Brother-in-Law, you're not well yourself. If you keep this up and get to feeling worse, what's going to happen? If someone needs tending, why not let the young folks do it? And what about your cold? Did you go to the clinic?"

"I'm fine. I'll get something at the drugstore. A cold's not the sort of thing to worry about. The point is that Mr. Yi doesn't have any family here in the South. And as a matter of fact, some young people who belong to a support group for prisoners with life sentences were at his house."

He smiled meekly, as if to apologize for having made us sit longer while he spoke with his sister-in-law. The smile produced a mass of crow's-feet around his eyes. It was strange. People say you get those wrinkles from laughing. Was it possible for a person spending twenty years in jail to have laughed enough to leave such deep furrows? I shifted my gaze from his eyes and looked at both brothers. The younger brother's face looked older, but he was losing his hair and was on the pudgy side, while the face of the elder brother was oval and narrow. People seeing them separately wouldn't have noticed a likeness, but together they somehow resembled each other. How can I say—they had a similar childlike expression you wouldn't notice when they were sitting quietly, but it jumped out at you when they laughed. You might see that expression if you stopped your car at a crosswalk and watched grade school children flocking across the street after dismissal. . . . There it was, my peculiar imagination acting up again. In the expressions of those two brothers who were well into their fifties, I perceived two children running along, school shoe pouches dangling, a second grader, the elder, clutching the hand of his little brother, a first grader. . .

I quickly awoke from my reveries, remembered I was on assignment, and offered Kwŏn O-gyu my card. He extracted a small magnifying glass from the pocket of his pale, sky blue dress shirt, peered at the card, and nodded. But as he looked at the card that identified me as a writer for the *Women's Monthly*, the strange feeling returned. What could the *Women's Monthly* possibly mean to a man who had spent twenty years in prison, a man who had forgotten how to open a door from the inside? Had he ever read it? Would he read such a magazine in the future? After talking with these two brothers who seemed too old for their age, I left with the photographer.

The only notes I took with me down the Samyang-dong alley were the names Yi Mun-su and Hwang Mun-ch'ŏl and next to them the words "executed" and "died in jail." Normally, when I return from interviewing an author, all sorts of phrases occur to me. But not this time—not even a title. All I could think of were things that would be difficult to make into a story: How was this man in his fifties supposed to find a wife? How was he to make a living when his book didn't sell very well? How could he spend the rest of his life caring for other life prisoners when he himself was not in good health?

The elevator arrived at the ground floor. Separately and silently the photographer and I walked to the door. While I was wondering what to eat, we emerged onto the street and were ambushed by the wind.

"What is it with this weather? No . . . we don't get typhoons in the spring, do we?"

We both looked up. The gray clouds covering the sky looked too massive and weighty, and for some peculiar reason the wind unsettled me.

"Looks like the sky's about to collapse, doesn't it." The photographer stuck his hands in his pockets. Without his heavy camera bag, he looked like he was swaggering. "Today's the second anniversary of Kang Kyŏng-dae's death." He spoke rapidly, crouching to avoid the wind.

"Today?"

"But doesn't it seem like it was twenty years ago?"

For lunch we had meat and a bottle of *soju*. We finished the liquor without saying much. Back outside, the photographer squinted his drink-reddened eyes and made a wry face.

"What if I told you I could hear sounds of sorrow and false accusation in the wind? Would you tell me I was crazy?"

Maybe some dust had blown into his mouth, because he spat. I managed to put my arm around his shoulders; it wasn't easy, him being six inches taller.

"No, I'd probably say you won't last long thinking like that."

"And I'd probably say you're right."

Two years ago today, April 1991, Kang Kyŏng-dae had been killed by a riot policeman's metal baton outside the gate to our school. And here we stood drink-sodden and bewildered on a windy street, smiling stupidly.

I picked up the envelope of materials on Kwŏn O-gyu that had dropped at my feet earlier. Inside, my eye came to rest on a sheaf of papers. It was a copy I'd made at the library of his indictment twenty-two years earlier. I'd underlined in red the passages I intended to quote in my story. According to the indictment, the Kwŏn O-gyu "ring," through Kwŏn's "Letter to Intellectuals, the Press, and the Clergy" and his essay "The Way of the Masses," had orchestrated student demonstrations; had given comfort to the North Korean Communists by using slogans with which the North typically defamed the South, such as "Comprador Nepotism" and "Capitalist Exploitation"; had charged that the Yushin administration was a military dictatorship; had plotted a violent revolution, designating the laborers and farmers as the major forces that would overthrow the Park Chung Hee government and launch a Communist revolution; and, in planning bloody demonstrations with Molotov cocktails and wooden clubs, was an incorrigible force supporting that revolution.

Such were the crimes that had earned him a life sentence. And as a full-time revolutionary who had graduated from college, who enjoyed a certain stature in society, and who had dedicated his life to the Communist revolution, he was differentiated from students, whose sentences could be commuted.

That era, compared with 1991, when Kang Kyŏng-dae had died, really felt like a different time to me. To think that printed matter and Molotov cocktails could be grounds for a life sentence. . . .

What to do? Are we really going to postpone Kwŏn until next month and run Yi as scheduled? With this thought I put away the materials. The wind was still gusting and kicking up dust outside the window. On the deadline board, those articles that had been completed were circled in red: "A Smart Wife Finds New Positions for Sex"; "Everything You Always Wanted to Know About Good Housekeeping"; "How to Cure a Womanizing Husband"; "One Woman's Struggle With Liver Cancer." Next to this month's book assignment was Yi Min-ja's name, and beside it a checkmark that demanded action. I was sure, before I hurried out that morning to interview her, that Kwŏn's name had appeared there. I hadn't formally consulted with the editor about carrying the Yi story this month. Although I'd earlier put the Kwŏn story back in its manila envelope and marked it for June, I still had mixed feelings. And now, even if I decided to argue with the editor, the words for the article were not coming to me, whether it should be Kwŏn or Yi, and so all I did was close up my notebook and chain-smoke two cigarettes. I had just crushed out the second one when the office girl told me I had a phone call.

To my surprise, the voice coming from the receiver was that of a *sŏnbae* named Kang. In a tone that sounded slightly uneasy he told me he was waiting in the basement tearoom.

I checked my watch. Barely two o'clock. Why was he here? I hadn't seen him in years, had only heard gossipy news of his divorce.

I waited for the elevator. The FULL light remained on as each of the floor numbers was displayed. While the elevator rose and fell, I looked down at the streets of Yŏuido, where the wind still swirled madly.

It's been five years, it suddenly occurred to me. Five years since I was hired as a temporary with some help from my uncle, who owned this magazine. At the time, I worked on household budget books. It was autumn, and the sun still blazed down crisply on every street. My job was to design and lay out a one-year budget book that had a recipe, a good-housekeeping hint, or information on buying a family car provided in the corner of each page. As I sat in the corner of the dark reference room looking at slides of recipes for foreign foods, I wondered how the people in those countries could have such bright faces, faces devoid of guilt and apology. How could they drink beer every day with salad and fruit slices? How could they go around so proudly in such expensive clothes? I would turn on the projector, each slide would click into place and light up—meat sauce for spaghetti, thousand islands dressing on a salad, sausage wrapped in iceberg lettuce and steamed—and I would carefully record the slide number on a slip of paper and stick it between the galleys of the budget book. And then I would ask myself: What the hell am I doing here looking at slides of exotic foreign food? My friends, the friends I had so passionately declared my love for, had they ever tried such food? Would they ever ride in a family car and practice good housekeeping by eating those foods? These thoughts created in my mind the illusion, as I jotted down slide numbers with my ball-point pen, that I was writing in the corners of the pages, "I want to die, I just want to die."

It was around that time that I had last seen Kang. He had waited for me in the basement tearoom. It had been almost three months since I'd sneaked away from the group. To disguise himself he had permed his hair and wore black-rimmed glasses. He had a weary expression, which brightened when he saw me. The perm was wearing off, and his hair stuck up every which way. But in contrast with this riotous spread of hair were the fine wrinkles, clearly visible in the dim light, on his gaunt face. Although I had seen those wrinkles every day, there in the tearoom they weighed on my mind, and to avoid looking at them as I sat down across from him, I quickly took a drink from his glass of water.

"Well, are you doing okay?" he asked ever so carefully.

I knew why he was being careful, and I lowered my gaze, but then wondered if that was the only reason. "No, to be honest, I wish I could die," I felt like saying. But that sounded trite, so all I did was nod, tight-lipped, eyes still downcast.

"I wanted to look you up right away, but I figured you had enough to deal with already. . . . Why didn't you tell us? You could have explained, put our minds at ease, and *then* left—"

At that point he stopped. For I was in tears. Even now I can't put my finger on the reason for those tears. But while I cried, head still bowed, I was thinking: My disappearance, my telling those of you in the group that I was going to the market for dinner things and then running away—it was because all of you were right. There was no excuse I could give you. I couldn't say, for example, that my father had taken ill, or that my family was short on money and I had to get a job, or that I suddenly felt sick and thought I was going to die. Every excuse I came up with was a dead end. . . . But I wasn't crying because the group members had been right. There was another reason: Every day with them had been nerve-wracking. I hated the tension of living day and night with fugitives, my nerves on end every time a siren went by outside our room. I was fed up with my heart hammering whenever I ventured out with mimeographed materials or books hidden in my bookbag and saw a riot policeman. I could no longer bear the hatred I felt, but I didn't think I could explain that hatred rationally, and so I ran away. It wasn't that I especially liked the place I had run to, this place where I now worked. In fact a different set of dislikes awaited me here: people who picked up a newspaper and looked only at the stock prices; people who sold their apartment when the price jumped, then bought themselves another apartment whose price would jump even higher; people who traded in their car; people forcing me to listen over beer to stories about their one-night stands. . . .

"Silly thing," he said with a smirk before giving me a gentle pat on the shoulders. My tears had almost stopped.

He said he had to run, and as he was leaving I offered him the pay envelope I'd just received for that month. He peered inside, extracted five 10,000-wŏn bills, and tucked them in his pocket.

"Does that make you feel better?" he asked. "You don't have to feel so guilty."

Clutching the pay envelope he'd returned to me with all the remaining 10,000-wŏn notes, I followed him down that building-lined street in Yŏŭido.

It was a dazzling autumn day.

"Go on back."

"All right." But I continued to follow him.

He turned toward me, solicitous, his hair sticking out in all directions on that windless day.

"Go on, now."

He walked a short distance farther, then turned back again. In exasperation he lit a cigarette.

"I might as well tell you. You would have found out sooner or later. Yun-sŏk's . . . in the hospital. He's in critical condition."

There was a student. He had wavy hair, and a dimple when he smiled. He had a voice that blasted, once we got him to sing, and it often got us kicked out of drinking places. . . .

Disregarding Kang's appointment, I caught up to him and, remembering he was a fugitive, led him off to the darkest place I could find: a place whose sign read "Western Liquor * Beer," and where all evening long young hostesses followed their male customers to partitioned rooms. But it was afternoon now, and the madam gave us a dubious look. We sat down side by side in one of the rooms, like lovers on a daytime date. Actually, we may have been the only ones who thought that; the madam probably knew better. A young couple going into a drinking place with partitioned rooms in the afternoon didn't have the expressions we wore, expressions that were in turn hardened, bewildered, then blank, as if we had been randomly assaulted while walking along the street.

We ordered two bottles of beer and a plate of dried snacks that were completely shriveled up, and when finally the madam had yawned and disappeared I asked him, "What do you mean?"

He finished two glasses of beer before answering.

"They were striking for a wage hike. The owner didn't want anything to do with them. As a last resort Yun-sŏk doused himself with paint thinner and went inside. But that owner is a notorious, pig-headed bastard, about as nasty a businessman as you can find. So Yun-sŏk, paint thinner and all, figured he'd try talking with him, and if the man was still acting obstinate he'd hold out a cigarette lighter and tell him, 'If you're not going to listen, I'll light myself up.' But he forgot how volatile the stuff is, and it was dripping all over the place. As soon as he lit the lighter, he was in flames. . . . The owner's in critical condition, too. It's in the evening edition."

Worried about Yun-sŏk, he left without finishing his beer. I gulped what was left, and on my way back to the office to look for more recipes for things like spaghetti sauce, salad with thousand islands dressing, and steamed sausage and lettuce, I bought a newspaper. The article, five lines of it, was on the very last page of the local-news section. The next morning I read that Yun-sŏk had died.

I had lived with Yun-sŏk for about five months. More precisely, I had let him and four other boys from the university stay at my apartment while they waited to be assigned to factories. Although these five, all of them my *hubae,* lived with me, I had little to do with them. In the prevailing political climate, we understood that we shouldn't ask about each other's affairs. Instead, we could only guess.

Once, shortly after they moved in, he threw a shot of *soju* at me. Before I could wipe the liquor from my face, he burst into tears. I knew his older brother had lost a hand working at a factory, and their mother worked in the factory cafeteria, and that he himself was desperately poor. In fact, I was amazed that he could afford to attend school.

"What do you know?" he sobbed. "You don't know anything . . . about . . . poverty."

I remember something else. It was the day he moved in. I was about to boil some water on the gas range for barley tea.

"Why boil water when you can get hot water out of the tap?" he asked.

Everyone laughed, but frankly, I was shaken. To think he'd never lived in a home with running hot water. . . . Boiled water, hot water—it was all the same to him. As he had said, apart from what I had read in books, I knew nothing except what the minimum wage was. If not for the jolt he gave me that first day, I would never have spoken to him again after the *soju* incident. But as I wiped the liquor dripping from my face, I felt like crying myself. Because of the apartment my parents had bought for me, because of the hot water that poured from the faucets. And my heart ached for the hand his brother had lost, and for the sixteen-hour days his mother worked in the cafeteria to earn his tuition. But apart from my heartache and regret, there was nothing I could do to help him. And so I thought the best thing was to wait until his anger had died down.

The next morning there was a knock on the door to my room. I opened the door, and there he was with an Indo apple, a green Japanese variety that comes out early in the summer. My gaze met his, and he promptly blushed and said, like a novice actor who had been practicing his lines, "Here, have an apple."

I poked my head out to look, and saw four other smiling faces watching us. It seemed the students had taken some time from their busy lives to enjoy those apples. I accepted the apple and managed in all sincerity to thank him. I was thankful that he'd apologized—I was older and should have approached him first—and grateful that he had gone to the trouble to offer me an apple he could have eaten himself. I knew he had better things to do and didn't get enough to eat.

We were reconciled by that apple, and through our reconciliation we became close. I frequently ate with them, and when I occasionally grilled meat for our meals I realized with concern how ravenous their appetites were. The day they left for the factories, we shared one last dinner. And once more Yun-sŏk sang in that blasting voice of his:

If the blue mountain calls me, say I have gone,
To death's dreamless season, there do I lie.
I have crossed that broad river,
I have gone, you must say.

The cry of souls in that fathomless place,
The bone-crushing pain of my people
*   in that more perilous place,*
To history I devote my small lone self,
I will fight and I will love.

This time there was no one to kick us out of a drinking place. Still, his voice blasted loud enough to make me wonder if I'd get kicked out of my apartment.

"Let's shake hands," he said, shyly extending his hand. It seemed for a moment that he might withdraw it, but then he took mine firmly in his and gazed at me. "How can I thank you? I used to feel like a poor, narrow-minded student trying to work his way through school. But I'm not like that anymore. You believe me, don't you?"

I nodded.

Smiling, he slowly released my hand. "Well, I definitely want to see you again. We, uh—"

I nodded again, but without conviction. "We live in a time where we can't make promises. You or I might be dragged away to jail," I almost said to him. But never, even in my dreams, had I thought that death in all its vastness would divide us. I had wished him good health and courage at his factory, had wanted him to look back on his youth and know he had nothing to be ashamed of.

Kang called me once more. We couldn't bring ourselves to openly mention the departed Yun-sŏk. Kang was still a fugitive, and I had my budget books to design, and so we hadn't attended the funeral. But in the interval between the beeps warning that his three minutes on the pay phone were almost up, and the moment when the line finally went dead, he blurted out, "Today, I went by myself . . . to his grave."

That was the last I had heard from Kang. I had then learned of his arrest, his divorce, his return to his father's house. . . . He still didn't know. He didn't know how much I had longed for him when he was a junior and I'd just entered the university. Just like Yun-sŏk, I suppose, at the time he left my apartment, had secretly longed for me.

Naive and shiny-eyed, Kang had gathered us together back then and said, "There's no magic formula. You just have to fight for anything you want to accomplish. Watch out for the little things, because the major problems actually look quite minor. We're going to begin fighting for those little things. Things around us, things inside us, things that seem trivial—those are the things we'll tackle first. All right?"

He had said this with a smile on his face and a glow in his good-natured eyes. And then he had fought those trivial things and gone to jail, the sight of him dragged into court, gagged, in white traditional prison garb bringing us to tears; he had mediated between Yun-sŏk and me after the *soju* incident and managed to calm us down; and he had worked in a factory and married a factory girl with only a middle school education.

And here I was, five years later, going to see him. A man now quoted as saying there was no use risking one's life for something trivial, a man who had inherited his father's bus company, who had fathered two daughters and then separated from the factory girl with the middle school education, after which she was committed to a mental hospital.

It wasn't just his life that had changed during those five years. The tearoom we used to meet in had turned into a cafe. The dim lights hanging from the ceiling had been replaced by small, bright lights, and the dusty-looking chairs between the dividers were gone in favor of plush sofas. It was odd: I often came here, but why was I noticing these changes only now when I was seeing Kang for the first time in five years? I went inside and looked for him. And looked some more. His favorite spot was unoccupied. He recognized me first. He was at a table out in the open, wearing a silk jacket the green color of mung beans. Instead of the black-rimmed glasses he wore a pair with sharp gold rims. The rough, unkempt, permed hair had been gently smoothed down, and he had gained weight.

"You've changed so much I didn't recognize you."

"Have I, now?" he said, smiling.

The fine wrinkles that had made his face look so haggard were no longer visible. Five years earlier, when he was a fugitive, he had always found a table tucked out of sight. Why had I thought he would still do so? When he had called my name just now as I peered into the corners, and I had turned to see him, I'd been struck by an illusion that he was sitting out in the open not in a cafe but in the world itself for all to see. A world that I had condemned, and that he had wanted to reform.

"Guess what? I'm getting married. I had some business nearby, and figured the least I could do was drop by and give you an invitation. . . ."

He smiled sheepishly, produced a gilded invitation from his pocket, and held it out to me.

"So, you still like to drink in the daytime? . . . You're old enough to know better, aren't you?" He smiled.

"'Still'?" I was surprised. "You mean there's something I still do?"

He lit a cigarette. We fell silent, and I recalled the beer we had drunk that afternoon five years earlier. I thought of the room salon with the sign "Western Liquor * Beer." I thought of how we had sat side by side like lovers, and how only after the madam had yawned and left had we spoken of Yun-sŏk. But Yun-sŏk was dead, Kang owned a bus company, and all we could talk about now was daytime drinking.

Kang coughed softly to break the silence and began talking about subjects that were too mundane considering he hadn't seen me in five years. He spoke in a lazy tone and I responded likewise. If he and I were now the individuals we had been five years before, then even though I had wished myself dead as I looked at slides of Western food with long, strange names, I might have spoken of Kwŏn O-gyu, prime mover of an affair that had shaken the nation in the early 1970s. I might have spoken of the life sentence he had received, the death sentence handed down to one of his comrades, the torture and the burst intestine suffered by the other, the one man executed and the other dying in jail, the twenty-odd years of Kwŏn's prime that he had spent in jail, the fact that he was now well into his fifties. I might have spoken of the idiosyncracies Kwŏn had developed during those years of confinement: forgetting how to open a door from the inside, depending on others to open it from the outside; stopping short while walking along the street, suffering under the illusion that the wall of his prison cell was coming at him. I could have described the heartache of his companions who had witnessed this.

And if I had done so, then Kang and I, smoking too many of our Milky Way cigarettes, sniffling to disguise the redness around our eyes, would perhaps have said in spite of this, "We'll win, because we're right. And people who know the truth won't deviate from it even with a knife at their throat."

But instead he spoke up out of apparent discomfort with my silence: "When I called, you said you'd been out on assignment. Have you been busy?"

"Mm-hmm, I have a deadline coming up."

I felt ill at ease looking at him as I drank my water. The delight of seeing each other after five years was eluding us, and the delight we used to take in each other's company was tucked out of sight. It wasn't as if death was about to separate us, but didn't this encounter actually represent a parting of the ways for us?

"It was a rush job. I had to go visit someone named Yi Min-ja. She has a book out—"

"Aha. Yi Min-ja."

Did he really know about her? My editor's praise for her best-selling book seemed more understandable now.

"My father recently bought one of her paintings. It seems she's a distant relative of ours."

"No. . . ."

We looked at each other and smiled at the coincidence.

"How did the interview go?"

"So-so."

"My fiancée bought her book on meditation techniques. She's so into meditation she gave me a copy and ordered me to read it. As if I had time for book reading." And then, since this talk of Yi Min-ja was smoothing over the awkwardness between us, he hastened to follow up: "What's she like in person?"

"Oh, unique, I guess you could say."

"Unique? How so?"

"Well, to give you an example, she's got a puppy. And all day long that puppy sits with its nose up against the rocks around the pond. I asked why it did that, and she said it was meditating. Well, that was interesting. So I asked what it was meditating about. And she said, 'Maybe it's thinking, "Hey, there's fish in that pond."'"

With a snort of laughter, Kang put down his lukewarm coffee. I laughed too. I felt thankful. If I had gone to Kwŏn O-gyu's house earlier that day, gone up the winding alley to that shabby Korean-style house with the shaded room beside the front gate, the tiny yard plastered over with cement, the blue plastic flower-pots with the rustic-looking rhododendrons, and the reconsti-tuted-rubber washbasin lying abandoned, I might not have been able to dispel the awkwardness between Kang and me. The two of us could no longer talk about Yun-sŏk, or about Kwŏn's im-prisonment, his torture, the years lost from his prime. I won-dered if I was overreacting. In any event, sitting out in the open in this cafe, facing this man in the gossamer-silk jacket the color of mung beans, I found myself not wanting to talk of such things.

He checked his watch, rose, and paid for the coffee. I stole a look at his wallet and saw several bank notes sticking out. Would he remember the autumn day I had offered him my pay, feeling that even if I gave it all to him I could never cleanse myself of the guilt I felt for running away from them? If not, did he occa-sionally think about the day he had visited Yun-sŏk's grave by himself and then sobbed to me over the phone? I considered this briefly, then produced a smile and offered my hand. He shook it tentatively.

I saw him off at the parking lot and then, while waiting for the elevator to take me back to the office on the seventh floor, I tried to imagine his wedding ceremony. There would be a revolving ice sculpture, a cake would be cut, and comrades from the old days would gather. Many people would attend. The *sŏnbae* who owned a computer company, the classmates who had full-time teaching positions, the girlfriends who had married and produced two babies apiece. . . . But there were others who would not attend. The *hubae* who was still a fugitive, the *sŏnbae* who was still in jail, and the friends who had died long, long ago. . . .

"Can we ever escape the 1980s?"

Once, when several of us were having drinks, someone had asked this.

"If we haven't, then it's too late now," another answered.

But then another friend, who because of his criminal record had given up hopes of hiring on at one of the big conglomerates and now worked for a small computer firm, spoke up: "Well, I haven't. Maybe all of you escaped, but not me. I couldn't."

All of us were very drunk, and we had broken up the party at that point. Would those friends of mine attend Kang's wedding as well?

I kept waiting for the elevator and finally I took the stairs. As I slowly climbed the dimly lighted steps I thought of Kwŏn O-gyu's book *Human Decency*, the negatives the photographer had given me, and the names of the man who had been executed and the man who had been tortured to death—the only notes I had taken at the interview. And I thought of people such as Yun-sŏk, who couldn't be interviewed, who had died such a senseless death.

◆◆◆

Why had I gone to see Yi Min-ja? Why had I accepted so readily an assignment I really didn't care for—accepted it and then thought it fine to write about Kwŏn's book for the following month? It was a minor thing. In the end, wouldn't the world keep turning whether it was Kwŏn or Yi I wanted to run this month? Hadn't I escaped the 1980s, that decade to which I had consigned my twenties? The dead were dead, and those who had been released from jail were free. The readers of our magazine didn't care for that sort of story anymore. It was a hit song whose time had passed. And what did this mean for me?

I had seen Kwŏn's name in a pamphlet mimeographed by some of my *sŏnbae*. While underlining and taking notes, we had criticized the blind spots and mistakes of their movement, as well as Kwŏn's anarchistic ideas. The 1970s innocence of the dozens in that secret society who thought they could bring down a dictatorship! He was an influence on me, but that was all. Even when many others were locked up and then died, all he did was sit in his cell. It was not because of him that the Park Chung Hee regime collapsed, or that Chun Doo Hwan was banished in disgrace to Paektam Monastery, or that an age of civilian government arrived. What, actually, was his influence on those of us who had used up our twenties during the 1980s?

Yun-sŏk hadn't been careful. He had set himself on fire for the sake of a 700-wŏn daily wage hike. Why had he forgotten how volatile paint thinner was? The company hadn't given the raise. The owner had survived and Yun-sŏk had died. His mother probably still works at the factory cafeteria. . . . And while I designed my budget books I would pause for a moment, stare into space, and mumble, "Idiot. Idiot." That's the only influence *he* had on me. . . .

But now in the 1990s, this decade of great ambition, it's

possible for Yi Min-ja to be different. At the very least, she can tell me about meditation techniques. She can speak proudly and serenely to all those who are lonely, who can't sleep, who feel alone and sad: "Just remember, the fact that we're alive in this universe makes us valuable." And so if along with her we drink that tea with the uncommon fragrance, we can find the courage to say, "Yes, I can get along well enough by myself." And wasn't it really to find that courage that I had visited her?

Is there nothing to grab onto when we feel so hollow? When we no longer sing songs of the movement, even if we're drinking together? When we no longer talk about the strikes at Inchon, Pup'yŏng, Ulsan? When we're no longer interested in who is a fugitive and who is still in jail, enduring the chill of a cold spring day? When someone says, "Movement? You're still talking about that?" and bursts into laughter? When we speak not of what is right and wrong but of what we like and dislike? When a married critic impregnates one of the women who works at his publishing company, when an author who has sent out wedding invitations brags that he's slept with twenty different bargirls? When a man declares in all sincerity that it's because the Eastern bloc collapsed that he inflicted emotional scars on a woman? For heaven's sake, please give me something to grab onto. . . . Was it these feelings I harbored when I visited Yi Min-ja? Tell me.

If someone had said to me, "Because you ran away from the group, you have nothing to say," then perhaps I would have said nothing. And if someone had called me a coward for running scared, I would honestly have been willing to apologize for my cowardice. Still, though, I was a child of the 1980s. How single-minded we children of the 1980s were to believe that right would triumph whatever the circumstances; how firmly we grew up believing that justice would win out in the end. We saw *sŏnbae* forced into military service for printing Lukacs in the school magazine, we saw friends taken into custody for reporting campus demonstrations in the school newspaper, and we held fast to the conviction that if one of us fought for a minor victory for justice, then those who came later could fight for a slightly greater victory, and we learned to believe that our sacrifices were never in vain. Now that the Eastern bloc is history, are sighs, resignation, and dissipation all that remain in our minds? Tell me.

I thought of Kwŏn O-gyu, sitting in jail for twenty years. I thought of Yi Min-ja, leaving with a shabby suitcase to study art in New York. Kwŏn, arrested when his secret society was forming. Yi, painting in New York. Kwŏn, sitting in jail. Yi, wandering barefoot in India. Kwŏn, taking seven paces in his cell, turning around, and taking seven more paces. Yi, on safari in Africa, snow-covered Mt. Kilimanjaro visible, suddenly asking herself, "What does it all mean?" Kwŏn, still sitting in jail, sitting for an insufferable twenty years, just sitting, enduring, waiting. Kang, running with a Molotov cocktail, me following along, blowing my nose in a tissue. Yun-sŏk, dying for the sake of a 700-wŏn pay hike. Me, hating it and running away. Kang, sitting out in the open in the cafe. Yun-sŏk, turned to dust. Me, drinking in the daytime; me, one big mess. . . . But today it's windy. The photographer said it's been two years since Kang Kyŏng-dae's death. And then this other Kang looks me up and offers me an invitation to his wedding—why today? The wind is up—why today? "Damn," I mutter to myself like the photographer had done on our way back to the office. "Who cares about the deadline?"

Once I saw a movie on "Weekend Masterpiece Theater." I can't remember the name or the actors. It is World War II, and a team of five special agents leave to blow up a Nazi dam. Young men carrying dynamite in one hand and holding a photo of their mother in the other. Going to their deaths. Blowing up their destiny along with the enemy dam. "If we think of duty," says their sergeant, "what's there to fear in death?" In fact, though, the young men don't want to die. Still, they go beneath the dam and detonate the dynamite. They all fall to the ground. Those poor men, I thought, imagining the magnificent scene that would follow—the dam collapsing, the water gushing out, the men swept away. But no, the movie didn't end like that. A few moments later the young men regained consciousness beneath the dam. They had only fainted. The sergeant saw them revive, and laughed.

"Stupid sons of bitches—do you know how many sticks of dynamite it takes to blow up a dam this big? Right now, water is seeping through the holes we made, and the dam is going to collapse from the force of that water. Come on, get up! Let's get out of here."

The *soju* from lunch finally hit me. My face was hot and the steps grew blurred. I paused at the landing and propped myself up on the railing like a worn-out old lady. Well, I guess I had better talk one last time about that radish shoot. What I said earlier about leaving Yi Min-ja's log house and feeling a sorrow like a young radish—it was a lie. Sorrow is sorrow, a radish shoot is a radish shoot, and there was never any comparison between them. I knew from the outset that I could never feel as much affection for Yi as I did for Kwŏn. It's true that she was more attractive and provided me with a more interesting time, and that Kwŏn's brother was tedious and Kwŏn himself talked only in hackneyed phrases about what I already knew. I'm sorry to say, I had to reflect on the lives the two brothers had led. I thought of them using up their twenties, as I had used up my twenties in the 1980s. Just as I think I can detect an odor from the period of my approaching thirties, I couldn't help associating the Kwŏns with our political history, which stank of filth at the time of their thirties and forties. And so now, one last time, I should talk about that radish shoot. This is the truth. This morning I gathered the leaves from my tea and sprinkled them around the radish, then covered them with more dirt. That earth is so sterile, I thought even the tea leaves might make a difference. I prayed. I hoped the weather would turn sultry, that the tea leaves would quickly turn to compost. And at the same time, I looked up to a spring sky that was still cold. If they don't decompose, then they won't do anything for the radish and there can be no fresh green shoot. It was only then that I found the words with which to begin my article on Kwŏn O-gyu:

"Here is a man who has held fast to his decency toward our times, our history, and our very humanity."

I slowly maneuvered my tipsy body up the steps until I saw the number seven. The distant outline of my yawning editor came into sight, and I set off toward him.

SCARLET FINGERNAILS

Kim Min-suk

"Mother, I'm off," my husband calls out toward my mother's room as he wedges his heel into his shoe.

"All right, see you later," Mother replies mechanically while she braids Ho-jŏng's hair.

After a glance in Ho-jŏng's direction, my husband opens the front door and goes out. I quickly follow. He pretends not to know I'm there, and starts down the stairs. I aim my voice at his back.

"I'm going to Uncle's in Hwagok-dong today."

"I know."

Since last year my husband has forsworn the elevator and walked the stairs to our eighth-floor apartment; he needs the exercise, he says. As he turns the corner at the landing, I look down on his balding head and slightly protruding stomach: the vertical image of my husband. A few more steps and it will disappear. But my expectation goes awry. That vertical image makes a 180-degree turn and comes back up, a little faster than when it went down.

He seems relieved to see I'm still outside the door. He stops a few steps from the top.

"I know you have to go, but don't take the kids. Understand?" he says in a low but firm voice.

Just before, he'd said, "I know," and now he asks if I understand. I have to wonder just what he knows and what I'm supposed to understand. Shafts of sunlight penetrate the window at the landing and impale his shoulder. Floating dust particles are captured in the light, as if in an aquarium. Without waiting for an answer, my husband goes back down the steps.

It's all right if I go, but not the children. He's right, of course. Where I'm concerned, he's always right. But it's not just the children who've never seen the man I'm going to visit today; I've never seen him either. The man who is my father. Mother doubtless feels the same as my husband. My husband says, "I know." Does that mean he's going too? Or is it his way of saying I'm allowed to go by myself without him? The only thing that's clear is that I'm not to take the children. Suddenly this certainty irritates me. I had no thought of taking them, and didn't need his reminder. Whether I see that man or not I'm his daughter, and whether the children go or not they're his grandchildren. That too is clear. I'll protect my children, just as Mother protected me. But protect from what? That's not so clear.

After my husband disappears I remain at the top of the steps, fascinated by the dust particles swimming in the pillars of light. I feel giddy. This morning it seems I think too often about what's clear and what's not clear. I don't seem to know the difference. Maybe it's because I slept poorly last night. I'm struck by an unintended, incongruous thought: My husband's a stranger to me. In this world there's just me and Mother, and she stays at home, left out. Today I'm about to betray her, my one and only ally.

A month ago Elder Uncle called me. "Next month on the twenty-first, your father turns sixty-one," he said in his thick Kyŏngsang accent. "Your grandma and I have petitioned for his release. The last time we were down there, the warden himself told me it would work out as long as your father keeps out of trouble. Your grandma has a wish: just once before she dies she wants to feed him a birthday meal at home. You should keep that in mind. This time make sure you and your husband come. You're still his daughter. I'm in no position to tell your mother what to do, but you should be a little more receptive than she is. You're old enough now, and you have children of your own; you ought to be able to understand how parents feel. Like it or not, children have duties to perform. Don't think I don't know how you feel; I do. But still, are you going to live the rest of your life without seeing your dad? There isn't that much time left. And it's not as if he can have visitors anytime he pleases. Your grandma's not well these days. You'd be setting her mind at ease by coming think of it that way. So make sure you come. All right?"

I didn't tell Mother any of this, though. Every day I put it off, hoping the petition would be rejected. But then three days ago Uncle called again, and Mother answered. Unfortunately, it's Uncle, and not Grandmother, that Mother has trouble dealing with. That's the way it is with a brother-in-law or sister-in-law, but there was something very particular in her attitude toward Uncle.

"It's her decision—what can I say to her now?" said Mother. "Here, you talk to her."

She put down the phone and disappeared into her room. Even from the rear she looked so stern that I almost couldn't deal with it. Wouldn't it be much simpler, I asked myself, if she just said no, like she does when Grandmother and Uncle invite us along, as they always do, on their trips to the prison in Taejŏn? Mother seemed angry with me. Because I hadn't told her about the previous call from Uncle? What is it that's bothering her? I wondered. Flustered, I said hello to Uncle. He told me the petition had been granted and asked me to come to his house on the evening of the fifteenth. The twenty-first on the lunar calendar would be the sixteenth on the solar, but Father would be released on the fifteenth. Uncle told me that since Mother hadn't objected, they would expect me there.

That evening in bed I told my husband about the phone call from Uncle, omitting, however, Uncle's wish that my husband and children join me. Before I could finish, my husband interrupted:

"He didn't say anything about me or the kids?"

I felt ashamed of myself, then flew off the handle.

"I haven't decided myself if I'm going. But you and the kids—"

"Why wouldn't you go? You've worried about your mother's feelings long enough. Don't you wonder what your father's like? If it was me, I'd go just out of curiosity."

With a dejected look he turned away and lit a cigarette.

"Curiosity? I don't have the peace of mind to be curious. Why would he want to see someone like me, or even think of me as his daughter? There's no reason to make a big production and involve you and the kids."

"The way you talk, it sounds like you've decided to go. I'm curious, but I don't feel comfortable at these big family gatherings. And I'd feel strange seeing your father. After all, it's been ten years since we were married and I've never met him. . . . I think I'll just forget about it."

"Yes, I know you're uncomfortable with *my* relatives. It's all you can do to show your face there once or twice a year. Well, they didn't ask you to come, so you don't need to worry."

Our conversation almost ended up in an argument. Until this morning he hadn't brought up the subject. And then he puts his foot down and says the children can't go. It bothers me when he acts like this without looking into the situation. Does he really think I want to take the children?

I hear Ho-jŏng whining from inside the front door: "Grandmother, can you do it for me again? It came off when I was sleeping. The color isn't pretty like yours."

I go inside and close the door. Maybe I've been watching the floating dust particles too long, because I feel dizzy. I collapse on the sofa and close my eyes.

"Not now," said Mother. "You'll have to pick some more balsam flowers. Not the ones that just bloomed, but the ones that are almost withering. They make a nicer color, remember? We'll dry them, and then after dinner we'll put the color on again."

Last night Mother and Ho-jŏng colored their fingernails. Mother's a champion at that. After drying the flowers for half a day she grinds the leaves in a mortar along with alum chips. After the mash is half dry she spreads it on the nails, then wraps them with balsam leaves, just like bandaging a cut, and winds thread around them nice and tight.

When I was little I used to go to bed early, and sometimes I'd be awakened by Mother applying balsam color on my little fingernails. Her face, flushed and perspiring, rapt with attention, was so lovely. I used to thrash around in my sleep, and the next morning some of the leaf wrappers were always missing, leaving the scarlet color of my nails uneven. I would compare my nails with Mother's and whine that mine weren't as beautiful. I colored all of my fingernails, but Mother colored only those on her ring and little fingers. At some point I lost interest in coloring my nails, but Mother never missed a year. When we moved to this apartment she continued to grow balsam in flowerpots. And now Ho-jŏng is her nail-coloring partner. A few years ago Mother heard somewhere that if you keep your nails colored until the winter's first snow, then your first love will appear, and she sighs every time she reluctantly clips her long, tinted nails. This year Mother is fifty-seven, an age when people usually don't care about things like their first love, and when I see her sigh I can't resist an urge to smile. But there are times when my smile is followed by a silent question: Who was Mother's first love? Did she really have what you could call a first love?

For several years I've been scolding my husband about leaving the newspaper lying around, but still he does it. I wish he were here so I could tell him. With this thought, I fold it up neatly and put it on the table. First I need to do the dishes. But I don't want to get up from the sofa. Ho-jŏng is out on the balcony picking balsam flowers.

"Hurry up, Ho-jŏng—you'll be late for kindergarten."

Ho-jŏng goes into Mother's room with a handful of scarlet flowers. Ho-jin has already left for school. He has afternoon classes today, so he'll get home too late to go with me. But Ho-jŏng comes home at lunchtime. Shall I take her with me? She still doesn't know any better, so perhaps she won't realize what's happening. This thought shocks me.

Mother began instructing me in earnest before I entered grade school:

"The teachers are going to ask you all sorts of questions. Be sure to speak clearly when you answer them. When they ask what your father does, tell them he was a middle school teacher and the Northerners kidnapped him during the war. Can you remember that?"

"What's 'kidnapped' mean?"

"It means they took him to the North."

"Did he die there?"

"Even your mom doesn't know that. Just say he was kidnapped."

When we received our homeroom assignments, a woman teacher asked me my name, address, and age, but that was all. And on the first day of school, no one asked me about my father. All my homeroom teacher did was take roll call.

I was disappointed as I walked up to my waiting mother in the hallway after school.

"Did your teacher ask you anything?"

"No, just called out our names."

"That's all?"

"Uh-huh. Just smiled and said I was cute."

In high spirits, Mother took my hand. From then on, at the beginning of every school year, she extracted the same pledge from me. Years later it became annoying. Why the pledge when no teacher ever asked about my father? I then realized that Mother showed up at school quite frequently—once a month or so—and she was still pretty enough to catch people's eye. As a result of these appearances, most of the teachers assumed that I had no father. But no one ever asked how I had lost my father. They seemed to think he was dead, or something almost as bad, and eventually I felt the same way myself. But until I entered high school Mother continued to insist he had been taken north during the war. This very insistence bred doubt in me: was it really true? But I rarely dwelled on this suspicion. Instead I took a ridiculous tack and created my own embellished image of Father.

We lived in Pusan throughout my grade school years. After the war broke out, a high school friend of Mother's had arrived as a refugee and established a kindergarten. Mother had taught there, though she lacked a teaching certificate.

My grade school, built during the Japanese occupation, had an unusually large auditorium where the pupils staged performances and occasionally saw movies. It had a wooden floor, where we sat, black canvas sneakers or rubber shoes in hand so we wouldn't lose them. Once—it must have been around the time of the holiday commemorating the March 1 Independence Movement—we were shown a movie about a freedom fighter during the occupation period. I've forgotten everything about it: the title, the name of the fighter, the actor who played him. What I do remember is Yang-ja.

In the movie, the freedom fighter was traced by the Japanese military police to his ancestral village, where he had returned under cover to see his wife and young son. The reunion was short-lived. Before his wife could feed him, the MPs were knocking at the door. He climbed over the back wall and went into the hills. Meanwhile, his wife took her time going to the door. The MPs said they had proof her husband was in the village. "Where is he hiding?!" they shouted. Then they ransacked the house looking for him. The police had fanned out along the road to the village and toward the shrine beyond the hills behind, and he had no place to run, they declared. His wife turned pale—she knew he had probably gone toward the shrine—and she signaled her son with her eyes. While the MPs were searching the loft, the boy stole over the wall and ran up into the hills to tell his father. When the MPs realized the boy was gone, they went after him.

The path was narrow and steep. It was autumn, and the boy's feet crunched loudly on the dead leaves. He heard the constant shrill whistling of the police, and he panted for breath. And then in midstep one of his black rubber shoes slipped off and bounced over the edge of a low outcrop. He looked down. The tip of the shoe was already torn, but still it was precious to the boy. Should he try to fetch it? If he did, the MPs would surely capture him. While the boy hesitated, from behind him the whistling grew louder.

At this point, a girl in the audience sprang up and screeched: "Hey! Put this one on, and move!"

She then heaved one of her sneakers toward the screen. The auditorium burst into wild applause. Several other children threw their shoes onto the stage as well. I can't remember if the boy in the movie found his shoe or left it behind, or whether he reached his father safely or was captured. All I remember is Shin Yang-ja, the girl who so quickly became the representative of our collective heart by jumping up and throwing her shoe. She was maybe three years older than I, but because she was a refugee from the North she had started school late and was in the same grade. I took a liking to her, and to win her favor, I gave her the double-strand fake pearl necklace I had bought with my New Year's money, the hair ribbon Mother had given me, and other offerings, and of course I spilled out to her the secret of my father. More than anything else, Yang-ja liked to hear secrets. She stuck out because of her height, and whenever short little me had something to tell her, she would tilt her tanned face toward me until her wavy hair almost touched my cheek.

"My father killed five Japanese. The MPs were chasing him and he hid in a tunnel in Grandmother's kitchen garden. So they arrested Elder Uncle instead, and my mom, even my cousin Chŏng-sun, and practically beat them to death. After they let them go, they found my father had sneaked away in the middle of the night. I guess he was afraid they'd be tortured until they confessed. He left a note saying he was going to Manchuria. And he changed out of his bloody pants. I think he was shot during one of his escapes. Mom told me she still keeps those pants in a trunk at home. One of these days I'll let you have a peek. But not now. Mom's got the trunk locked up."

This account was embellished with what I had seen at the time in movies and comic books, but a few particulars were based on the truth. After Chŏng-sun married she had continued to live with her family; her husband worked at their rice mill. When I went to Grandmother's in the countryside during school vacation, Chŏng-sun would show me the scars on her wrists and tell me that because of my father, the whole family had been taken into custody and given a terrible beating. But I had no interest in learning *why* it was because of Father. I merely went on imagining that he had been a freedom fighter, and that his family had suffered as a result. It was much more interesting that way, and I felt no need to ask questions. Of course, there weren't any freedom fighters after Liberation in 1945, and I was born in 1950 after the war broke out, but I couldn't have cared less about such discrepancies.

On this point Yang-ja was the same as me. She never questioned my accounts about Father being a freedom fighter during the Japanese occupation and then a right-winger who escaped the communists during the war, or who went to America and became a millionaire. It seemed the millionaire father had forgotten us for the time being, but the day would surely come when he would remember, and cross the ocean to take us back with him. Every time I finished one of these stories Yang-ja would look at me with dreamy eyes and smack her lips in anticipation. "Good for you," she would say. "Can he take me too?"

"Sure, why not?" I always put on a good face and sounded big-hearted then.

One of the stories I told Yang-ja was based on the truth. The traditional silk outfit Father used to wear was stored in our chest, neatly pressed and folded. And it was true that there was a dark stain on the trousers. But it was an inkstain, not a bloodstain. Every time Mother replaced the mothballs, the sight of that stain bothered her. "What a shame the ink got on it—it was such a nice outfit," she would sigh, as if hoping the stain would fade over time. And it really did seem to me that the color turned lighter. But instead it was probably just that I'd grown used to the sight of it.

Yang-ja's family lived in one of the back rooms in a two-story building across from the train station. At night they looked after the building, and during the day they tended a small wooden street stall. And then when Yang-ja was in sixth grade they moved away. I missed her at school, I missed her whenever I had cocoa at that streetside stall, and I missed her when I went to the quonset theater nearby and squeezed in among all the fatigue-clad soldiers on leave to watch a movie. After grade school my family moved to Seoul, and I haven't seen her since: Yang-ja, who used to avoid the fierce gaze of her mother (who would shout "Double Crown!" at her because of her twin hair whorls) so she could stick in my pocket a large candy with a peanut inside; Yang-ja, who kept the secrets about my father. I never told anyone else about him. Even today I think I would recognize Yang-ja and her wavy hair.

"Hey! Put this one on and move!" Perhaps Yang-ja at this very moment is giving someone her shoe.

◆◆◆

I finish the dishes and go into the laundry room to do the wash. There, soaking in the washbasin, are several quarts of soybeans.

"Mom, why are these soybeans here?"

"I'm making soybean soup."

"Why so much?"

"Well, you're going to Hwagok-dong today. You'll need to take *something.*"

I'm momentarily speechless. "I was going to take some meat and something to drink. . . ."

"He'll get sick if he drinks. Where he is, they don't even get to *smell* alcohol. That one always filled up on soybean soup in the summer anyway. You take it in the plastic bucket so there's enough for your uncle's family too."

It's hard to believe that with all her spite toward Father, and after just three years of living together, she still remembers his eating habits thirty-seven years later.

"Oh, stop it, Mom. Why don't we go together—"

"No! I never want to see his face again. I'm not making it for him. It's for *your* sake. As long as you're going to see your father, I don't want you giving anyone a bad impression."

"Well, maybe I shouldn't go either."

Mother's face immediately hardens. "Why not? Did your husband say something?"

"No. He said I should go. But if you don't want me to go, then I won't."

"I don't care either way. It's what your grandmother and uncle want, so do as you please. When have you ever listened to me, anyway?"

Until I married, or actually until I became a mother myself, I was a woman who hated her mother with all her heart. The woman I was couldn't forgive her mother for marrying such a man and giving birth to her. Perhaps this hatred and resentment should have been directed toward her father. But for that woman, her father never existed. And she couldn't very well have as an object of hatred and resentment a person she'd never seen.

"Should I cook the beans?" I ask.

"I'll do it. Why don't you go to the beauty parlor."

"Beauty parlor? It's not like I'm going to a wedding or something."

"So you're going to your uncle's looking like that? With your hair sticking out like a punk?"

"Nobody's going to think that." Still, I hurriedly prepare to leave. My mother has raised me herself, and she wants to take pride in showing my father, who has turned his back on her, that his daughter has grown into a beautiful woman.

Mother always enjoyed dressing me up. As far back as grade school my clothes and shoes were a bit overdone in view of our circumstances. At the time, ready-made clothing was awful. If you wanted something that fit, you had to have it tailored. And so all through the lower grades, Mother made all my clothes herself, even bathing suits. Mother's artistic sense was quite extraordinary, and I received a lot of praise for my dresses and blouses. In middle and high school she took me to high-class Western-style dress shops, picked out colors and designs, and had clothing made for me. These clothes were always fancier and more colorful than I would have preferred. Mother, on the other hand, never departed from gray, dark brown, or white. Her appearance was plain, her lifestyle frugal. From the time I went to college and began choosing my own clothes, I selected simple styles that were even darker than her clothes. My rebellion brought criticism: "These are your best years. What are you doing wearing old people's colors?" she always asked in disgust. "There are so many beautiful, pretty colors." I began to wonder if the scolding was meant to compensate for her own tendency to avoid such colors.

"These days even older people like to wear bright colors." Mother said this frequently, and I thought I detected a note of envy in her voice. "Well, why don't you try something more color-ful yourself, Mom?" I always replied. She would shake her head. "If a woman living alone dresses like that, people laugh." "Well, let them laugh. You're still a pretty woman, Mom." When I said this, Mother would produce a wan smile and look at me bash-fully out of the corner of her eye. At such times her face reminded me of the flowers of the trumpet vines that climbed the side wall of Grandmother's yard in the summer.

That yard was where I learned that Father—supposedly kid-napped to the North, and so in my mind as good as dead—was alive and had come south as a spy. The yard where trumpet vine flowers bloomed in a row just like a necklace with orange beads. Beneath the vines was a wooden platform in the shade created by a wisteria arbor, and during summer vacation I played there with my friend Mun-gŭm.

She was the same age as I. Her family ran the only inn in town, just across the road from Grandmother's rice mill. Mun-gŭm liked to play with makeup, and was forever applying then removing her mother's cosmetics on the sly, so that she always smelled of cheap face cream.

One day she asked, "Have you seen that movie about your father? I saw them filming it and everything. Chang Tong-hwi plays your father and Pok Hye-suk is your grandma who runs the rice mill. That movie's stirring up the whole town."

To Mun-gŭm's amazement, I had no idea what any of this meant. In confusion she rubbed her ears with fingertips red from the lipstick she'd just removed.

"They shot it last fall, and this spring there was a sneak preview at the Ch'ŏnil Theater. People who saw it say Chang Tonghwi doesn't look anything like your father. But Pok Hye-suk is the spitting image of your grandma. Everybody rushed over to see it, and the Ch'ŏnil had its biggest crowds ever. Probably everyone in town's seen it except your people. I guess that young guy Pak at the rice mill saw it too. You live in Seoul, and you haven't seen it? At the end of the preview they showed a slogan . . . yes, I remember: 'Surrender, and find the light,' with music and everything. The words get bigger and bigger—what a sight! People were whispering about the one who reported your father—the reward must have been a fortune. Do you have any idea who it was? After your father got caught, your grandma fainted, and she didn't come to for days. She tried to get him to turn himself in, begged him and begged him. But he was a rock-solid Red, and he wouldn't do it."

Suddenly it seemed like everything around me was freezing up. Those scarlet trumpet vine flowers, the green wisteria vines, Mun-gŭm's chattering mouth, my arms, my eyes, my eyelashes, my hair—in the blink of an eye everything was frozen in time. It was a scene that didn't make sense, like cold wind and snow blowing in on a summer stage setting. Blood began to trickle from my nose. I vomited my lunch. For four days straight I was racked with a high fever and was sick to my stomach, but I didn't tell a soul what I had heard from Mun-gŭm.

I'm back from the beauty parlor but still haven't made up my mind about going to Elder Uncle's. What's the purpose of seeing someone you've never met in thirty-seven years? To reestablish a father-daughter relationship with a sixty-one-year-old stranger?

There's no relationship to recover.

In the meantime Mother has made the soup and put it in the refrigerator in plastic containers.

"Why's it in the refrigerator if I'm going to take it to Uncle's? Extra work, isn't it?"

"I know, but it needs to cool. I also made some noodles. We can have them with the soup for lunch."

"Is it time for lunch?"

Then I realize it's already twelve-thirty. Ho-jŏng will be returning any moment.

"Ho-jŏng doesn't care for noodles, you know."

"Then stir-fry some rice and vegetables for her."

Mother is shredding cucumbers—a garnish for the soup. I feel I ought to be doing something, so I ask if I should peel some onions.

"I already did that."

I wish Ho-jŏng would arrive. But I also feel I should say something to Mother first, though I'm not sure what. And then in spite of myself the words jump out of my mouth: "Why didn't you remarry?"

Mother opens the refrigerator and locates carrots, onions, Vienna sausage.

"I would have, if he had died. But he's still alive. He could have kept to himself, but the damned old man crawls all the way back here—has to show everybody he's still alive. . . . He's worse than my worst enemy."

"But didn't you think he was dead? You were young then, Mom, and no one told you not to remarry, did they?"

This wasn't what I wanted to talk about while waiting for Ho-jŏng. I can't understand why I brought up this topic, which serves no useful purpose.

"You were a little girl then, and somehow I believed he was still alive. I don't know why, but I wanted to believe that. What an idiot I was."

Fortunately the doorbell rings. I jump up and go to the door. It's Ho-jŏng, and she's holding something made of clay.

"Look, it's Daddy! Teacher said I did a good job. Grandmother, will you color my nails!"

While I'm setting the clay figure on the living room table, Ho-jŏng goes to her grandmother and continues to pester her.

"I'll do it tonight when you're sleeping. Now wash your hands and get ready for lunch."

"But it keeps coming off at night. I want to do it in the daytime. Right now, please?"

"Then how about after you eat and have a bath? All right? Now go and wash up."

On the figure's still damp head sits a round lump of clay that makes me think of a bewigged English judge—Ho-jŏng's attempt at a head of hair. The arms are together in front of him, and between them is a long object that resembles a club. A rolled-up newspaper? Then I look carefully and see it's a necktie. Ho-jŏng favors her father over me. At her age, and in fact until I was much older, I never wondered what kind of man my father was. Was it merely a lack of interest? Or had I subconsciously felt that I should take no interest in him? It was for my own enjoyment that I made up stories about him for Yang-ja with such enthusiasm, and not because I longed for him. During those early years Mother missed no opportunity to pose her constant question: What would I do if Father were to return? I would smirk and say, "What do I need a father for? It's fun just the two of us. So I'll kick him out." This answer was my way of humoring her, but it also reflected my true feelings. It was a kind of game, that question, but after I was out of high school, Mother put a stop to it. At the time I wasn't aware that our game had ended. Mother, though, had no choice, for Father was in fact alive and had returned. Albeit not to us. But I was not aware of that fact until Mun-gǔm told me. And for years afterward I pretended to know nothing about it. Mother tried desperately to hide the truth from me, and I hated her for that, but the truth was too frightening for me to acknowledge. Perhaps the facts would simply disappear if I pretended to ignore them, and so I came to feel that they were irrelevant to me.

The spring after I learned the truth from Mun-gǔm, I let the fear inside me explode just once. Mother never learned the actual reason for that explosion.

It was a new school year, and as usual the homeroom teachers made the rounds of the students' homes. My teacher seemed to think it a bit odd that Mother and I lived by ourselves, and one day after school when I was helping him grade tests he casually questioned me.

"Sŭng-hye, does your father live apart from you?"

Later, when I considered the question, I wondered if he was asking if Father had a concubine, as men often did at the time. After all, on the student family questionnaire we had indicated that Father was alive. But at the time, like a thief with a guilty conscience, I immediately associated "apart from you" with jail and supposed that my teacher knew the whole story. I turned pale and couldn't answer. My teacher must have assumed I was ashamed, for he never mentioned the subject again.

On my way home from school that day I stopped at five different drugstores and bought twenty Seconal pills. As soon as I arrived home those twenty crimson capsules went down my throat. It didn't feel strange, because after Mun-gǔm's revelation the previous summer I had occasionally taken one or two of them. And so I sank into a deep sleep, with Mother's irritated voice sounding in my ear: "Eat your dinner and go to bed." It was the following evening when I woke up. Mother had realized something was wrong when I fell asleep so early, and somehow she saved me. I wonder if perhaps I was intent not so much on killing myself as on doing anything I could to relieve my unbearable fear. I never did reveal why I had tried to poison myself. I couldn't tell anyone how scared I was of becoming known as the daughter of a spy.

To this day I have never thought specifically about Father's suffering in jail. Instead, when I think about the injuries he's caused me, all I can do is grit my teeth and clench my fists. Can you call this a father-daughter relationship? Why should I play the role of an unwilling daughter? Why now?

"The noodles are getting soggy. Come and eat!"

I hear Mother's voice as if from a distance.

The telephone rings, awakening me from my nap. After lunch and the dishes I sank onto the sofa and ended up asleep. Probably a combination of a full stomach and not sleeping very well last night. Mother has answered the phone. I see it's almost four o'clock. The phone must have been ringing for some time; it seems I can still hear the sound of it inside my drowsy head.

"Brother-in-Law, when have I ever opposed you or Mother? I've always gone along with you, but this time I can't. And I don't think Ho-jŏng's dad would be comfortable either . . . Yes . . . She'll be leaving right away . . . No, I'm not stopping her . . . Yes . . . Take care . . . I'm very sorry."

Mother replaces the receiver. Her face is deathly pale. Whether it's that, or the grogginess from my nap, I don't know, but suddenly I'm irritated.

"What did they say?"

"He's already there. Your grandmother sounds disappointed—she seems to think I'm cold-hearted."

"Does she think turning sixty-one in jail is something to brag about? Is it a cause for celebration? Come on, Grandmother—"

But this is not what's on my mind, and I stop short. It's not that I don't understand the state of mind of Grandmother and Uncle. Rather, I notice that Mother's expression has hardened. And it's not the result of the badgering by Grandmother and Uncle just now. Instead, she's angry with *me*.

"How could you sleep at a time like this?" she finally blurts out. Perhaps my suspicion is correct. Is Mother upset with me for not visiting Father until now? Doesn't she know that my not visiting him, like my saying I'd kick him out in that game we used to play, is my way of humoring her, my sly, instinctive, protective coloring?

"A time like what? For heaven's sake—"

But before I can finish, Mother goes in her room and shuts the door. "For heaven's sake. . . ." What was I going to say next? "For heaven's sake, you mean it's time for me to see a father who ought to be dead?" "For heaven's sake, is this supposed to be some grand, happy occasion?" Feeling sad and victimized, as if Mother has somehow betrayed me, I massage my cheeks over and over.

In the spring of my sophomore year in college, with Mother's tacit approval, I was finally allowed to hear the story of Father. Mother sent me on an errand to Elder Uncle's in Hwagok-dong, probably after talking with him beforehand. Uncle sat down beside Grandmother and for the first time told me about my father.

"I wanted to tell you earlier, but Sister-in-Law—your mother—put her foot down, and besides, you were too young. That's why we haven't brought it up until today. In any event, you're old enough now to understand, and it's time you heard the story. I think you know your father used to be a middle school teacher in the town where we lived. It was all my fault. Things might have turned out all right if I hadn't called him back down to the countryside. But your grandma wanted him close by, so that's what I did. It seems he got mixed up with some bad elements when he was in college here, but we didn't know that at the time.

"Well, he comes back home, and he and the other young people are always going to some meeting or other, but what's so unusual about that? And then pretty soon the war breaks out and your father starts working for the Communist party. Sister-in-Law joins too. When the tables turn and the Reds are pushed north, your father tags along. But Sister-in-Law's expecting any day, so she stays behind. Later when our boys, the ROK soldiers, turn up, they take her away and she gets the scare of her life. But she didn't do nothing except teach other women some Commie songs, and here she is about to hatch, so it's our good luck we're able to get her out. But it cost us practically every grain of rice we had—and we grew about a thousand sacks' worth in a normal year.

"If we'd just kept him from going north . . . But it's no use thinking about that now; if we'd kept a tight leash on him, he probably would have been rounded up and killed. After you were born and Sister-in-Law was back on her feet, she left for Pusan. Told us she'd feel more comfortable in a place where no one knew her, and swore she'd get by with the help of a high school friend who ran a kindergarten there. Around the time you started middle school, they told her she couldn't work at the kindergarten anymore because she didn't have a certificate. So she decided she might as well move up to Seoul and go into business. That's when I sold your father's share of the land—about two and a half acres—and gave her the proceeds. She used that to open up a stationery shop near one of the schools, and that kept her going. She had peace and quiet for a few years, and then out of the blue your father shows up. The way he put it, he wanted to see his mom, so he volunteered to go south. He figured on staying one night, but Mom made him stay another night, and that's when they got him. Whether it was one of the hands at the rice mill who turned him in, or what, I don't know. *Aigo,* I get a chill whenever I think about it. He came down by boat through the West Sea, so they call him a spy, but he didn't do any spying. Just went straight to your grandmother's. It was the year you started high school. If he'd just renounced the Reds, things would have been better. But he said he wouldn't do it as long as he lived, and so they put him away for life. He's in the penitentiary at Taejŏn now. Your grandmother and I go there every month.

"I know you don't enjoy hearing this, but there's one more thing needs telling. It seems he started a new family up north. He must have thought he'd never be able to come back here again. He has two sons, and the woman teaches at a university. The boys' names are Sŭng-jae and Sŭng-ho. Same *Sŭng* as you and your cousins on our side of the family; and the 'existence' *Jae* and the 'bright' *Ho.* They're your brothers, so you ought to at least remember their names."

Grandmother, sitting beside Uncle, wept the whole time. And then it was her turn to speak.

"Your mom has a lot of regrets. But what can we do? He was born at the wrong time. It was fashionable for the schoolkids to be Red then. Red, White, what difference does it make now— he's sitting in jail. I've tried to talk him into renouncing the Reds, but it's like talking to the wall of his cell. He's a dad, after all, and he's probably afraid his boys up north would come to harm. What can I say? He's thinking of his young ones. Your mom can understand that. And as for us, things could be a lot worse—we haven't come to much harm on his account. I think he told your mom to go on living as if he didn't exist. That's what did it—she didn't go to see him anymore. She was fine all those times they called her into court, but after three visits in prison, she stopped cold. She's done all right for herself, but no matter how disappointed she is, I can't understand why she's been so heartless. The poor guy. You shouldn't treat a husband that way. *Aigo,* the poor cuss."

The sight of Grandmother continually dabbing her eyes choked me with indignation. Father's remarriage, the two boys, Mother joining the Communist party—I had never known these things. What in heaven's name was Mother waiting for? What was she holding out her love for? The burning in my throat was too much for me, and I burst into foolish tears.

That evening I badgered Mother to divorce Father on the spot. Even now I can't fathom Mother, so you can imagine how obtuse I must have seemed to her as a college sophomore. I was taking a course on women and the law then, and I'd learned something about laws relating to divorce and inheritance. I remembered the phrase "The courts recognize certain important grounds for discontinuing a marriage," and my mind was swimming with seven of those reasons. I'd learned, for example, that if the couple hadn't lived together for a certain amount of time, or if a spouse's whereabouts were unknown, then a unilateral request for divorce was permissible.

To my surprise, Mother dismissed my suggestion: "Divorce him? For what? To help that fine father of yours rest content in his jail cell till the day he dies, remaining faithful so his wife and children up north will be safe? Well, I'm no less deserving than her. . . . No, I'm not going to divorce him."

From then on I campaigned to have my name removed from Father's family register, but I learned that the law wouldn't allow that until I married. Not even marriage offered me a complete escape, however.

I arrive at the gray gate of Uncle's house in Hwagok-dong. In my right hand is a bundle in a pink wrapping cloth, in my left the plastic bucket of soybean soup. In the wrapper is a neatly folded traditional ramie outfit. Mother thrust it into my hands as I went out the door. It's one he used to wear, and last night she took it out and pressed it. As long as we're not buying him a new outfit, I should make sure he wears it so he'll at least be comfortable today, she told me. Another light slap in my face.

Standing before the gate, I wonder for the first time what Father will look like. I've seen the pages of yellowed photographs in the album at home, but photos are photos. The very last photo in the album shows him in front of the school where he taught. He's wearing black wool trousers and a white, short-sleeved dress shirt. The thing I notice in that photo is how young he looks—he was twenty-three then. He wears a faint, awkward grin, as if he's camera-shy. And now he's reached sixty-one. What will his face look like? Is he still a committed communist, this man who was involved in anti-government activities, who went north of his own free will, a clumsy spy who volunteered to come south so he could see his mother, only to be arrested two days later, a man still pigheaded after twenty years behind prison walls? Or is he, as Grandmother and Elder Uncle would have it, a pathetic old man who has pawned his life for the safety of his wife and children in the North? Though his fatherly love doesn't extend to me.

Sŭng-o, Uncle's eldest son, opens the gate. He has driven Father up from Taejŏn. I don't see the guard who's come along. They've probably arranged a room for him at a nearby inn. Sŭng-o doesn't make an issue of my late arrival. He relieves me of the bucket and whispers in my ear, "Don't forget to greet him with a full bow. And your husband—is he coming later?"

I answer with a vague smile, then enter Grandmother's room on the ground floor.

Elder Uncle greets me: "Is that you?"

I glance at my two uncles and Grandmother. A stranger sits beside Grandmother; that must be Father. Like Elder Uncle, he has a sharp nose and well-defined lips. But he's taller, and he's haggard and pale. Remembering Sŭng-o's advice, I prostrate myself in a full bow. To no one in particular, but in Grandmother's direction.

"Is your husband coming?" she asks.

"He's at work."

But Grandmother refuses to take the hint. "Then he'll come here on his way home? It's quitting time now. . . ."

Elder Uncle reads my mind and changes the subject: "What do you have there?"

"It's something he used to wear." I can't bring myself to call him "Father." "Mother sent it along for the day."

I place the bundle in front of me. Elder Uncle opens it, then nudges Father.

"Go next door and change. You'll feel cooler. Nothing like ramie on a summer day."

Father obediently leaves with the bundle. He's wearing a gray-striped short-sleeved dress shirt and navy blue trousers, which I imagine Sŭng-o bought just for today. I feel guilty not doing that myself, and at the same time grow irritated for feeling this way. It's because of Grandmother and Elder Uncle that I'm here—

that's all. Acting like a daughter is the last thing on my mind.

"*Eigu*. Damned ism's. What a dreadful fate—how's a body supposed to live inside those walls? I want to die before something terrible happens to him. . . ."

Elder Uncle responds to this tearful outburst: "Mom, you wipe those tears away before he comes back. Now you promised."

Younger Uncle has said nothing. Evidently he's decided to keep his mouth shut after that incident last year.

As of last year, Father had served twenty years in prison. Officially, a prisoner can't be furloughed if he won't recant, but because Father is serving a life term and has been recognized for good conduct, the prison authorities, who use furloughs as an enticement to recant, granted him an unofficial twenty-four-hour leave. It was understood that in return for the furlough document the family would show Father how comfortably they live and try to persuade him to recant. I heard from Sŭng-o's wife that the entire family gathered that night. Younger Uncle got drunk and cursed Father up and down, Grandmother broke into tears, and Elder Uncle, in spite of his advancing age, struck Younger Uncle. In cursing Father, Younger Uncle had brought into the open what everybody already knew. Father had damaged the prospects of his two brothers and their families by going north: Sŭng-o, who had finished law school, had to give up taking the judicial exam and instead go to work for a private company; my cousins who had obtained government jobs had to resign within two or three months, snagged by their background check; Younger Uncle's son Sŭng-t'ae, who was about to go abroad on business, was prevented by the government at the last minute; his sister Sŭng-hŭi, who had married a Korean-Japanese, was denied a passport and had to live apart from her husband for two years; and so forth. And now it was too late for my cousins to change their course in life. There was no one to whom I could appeal on account of the disadvantages I'd suffered because of Father. The same was true of all my paternal cousins. Far from protesting those disadvantages, we hushed up our situation out of a greater concern: we feared rejection by those who might happen to find out about Father.

But what had really prompted Elder Uncle to strike his brother that evening was Younger Uncle's act of defiance toward Father in calling him unfilial toward his mother. Those words had brought tears to Father's eyes. Grandmother had fled to her room, and finally Elder Uncle, telling Younger Uncle he was too insolent with his older brother, had slapped him.

Some ten years ago during one of our holiday get-togethers Younger Uncle had gotten drunk and made a request of my cousins and me: "These are dangerous and complicated times we live in, and none of you can predict the results of your actions. Just make sure of one thing: don't break the Anti-Communism Law. From now on, if any of us gets caught, the whole family is ruined. Understand? I can overlook any other crime you commit, as long as you don't break the Anti-Communism Law."

It sounded ridiculous at first, but we all listened with grave expressions. Now as then, I can understand both Younger Uncle's abuse of Father, and Elder Uncle's violent reaction. But as for Father's tears, I could understand only if they had flowed from someone else's eyes.

Father returns to Grandmother's side. He still hasn't made eye contact or said a word to me. Ramie outfits are pleasant to wear because they're roomy, but his is too big, making him look taller and even more haggard.

Grandmother says not a word, merely holds Father's hand and strokes it, as she did mine long ago.

"Sŭng-hye has two children—a boy and a little girl. Ho-jin's ten now, isn't he?"

I nod.

"Where are the children, anyway? I thought you were going to bring them?"

"Ho-jin was at school, and Ho-jŏng went somewhere to play." Though I had no intention of bringing the children, this is how I respond. I'm thankful that Mother hasn't come up in the conversation. It would seem they've decided not to mention her.

"I think I'll peek into the kitchen for a moment." I quickly rise, wishing I didn't have to go to such lengths to avoid their gazes.

In the kitchen, Sŭng-o's wife and Elder Aunt are preparing dinner.

"I should have come earlier to help out," I say.

"Oh, we're not making anything special. Anyway, how did it go with your father? You've never seen him before, have you?" asks Aunt.

Sŭng-o's wife pauses to observe my reaction.

"I can't really say. He looks older than Elder Uncle."

My aunt nods. "You noticed. Poor old man. I know you've got lots of resentment, but it's not much use feeling that way now. If you could just take pity on him. . . . You understand, don't you?"

I nod. Actually, pity is about all I can offer.

"What did he say?" Sŭng-o's wife asks, eyes full of curiosity.

I shake my head. Father has no more to say than I do. In other words, nothing. There's nothing left for us but to pity each other. Mother knows this. Her hopes for him were all for nothing; what a disheartening realization to have to struggle with. I suddenly wonder if my husband will come.

◆◆◆

We're having dinner on the veranda. Grandmother has seated me beside Father. I guess we're better off side by side. Better than sitting across from each other and trying to avoid eye contact.

My two uncles recall a few of the neighbors and friends from the time we lived in the countryside. Father responds with an occasional smile. With her chopsticks Grandmother keeps placing slices of meat and other morsels in front of him. There's also a shot glass at his place, but it seems ceremonial. Afraid of what alcohol might do to him after all this time, Grandmother has let it be known that we are not to pressure him to drink. Only Father is served the soybean soup; the rest of the family will have it tomorrow for lunch, Grandmother announces. True to Mother's words, Father sips the soup. But he barely touches the rest. As if she can't bear to watch, Grandmother turns away after pushing a serving bowl of short ribs toward him. The rest of us keep our eyes on our rice bowls and pretend to be absorbed in the meal. Even Sŭng-o's two children are unusually quiet as they eat.

The doorbell rings. Instantly Grandmother says, "It's your husband!" I feel myself blush. It's impossible. He's as indifferent about meeting Father as he is serious about the subject of Father. And there wasn't a peep out of him about coming here. The fact that I've admitted this must mean, I now realize, that I have a problem with a husband who behaves like this—it's ridiculous. But the worst is yet to come. Sŭng-o's wife answers the door, and returns with my husband *and* the children in tow. I'm probably the most surprised person in the room.

"My apologies for being late. I had to stop by the house after work to pick up the kids. Children, say hello to your great-grandmother and grandfather. I'm afraid we've arrived right in the middle of dinner. Is it all right if we join you?"

He and the children bow and exchange short greetings with

the others. My husband is talking too loudly and making a fuss. It makes me uncomfortable, but regardless, I have to admit that his appearance has livened up the dinner. Using his salesman's intuition, he seems to have anticipated the oppressive mood of this gathering and is playing the role of the brash son-in-law. He's the same with Father—as unaffected with him as Elder Uncle is.

"Father-in-Law, please allow me to offer you a drink. I've been remiss in not visiting you sooner. As you know, we have a fierce Mother-in-Law living with us, and I have to respect her feelings, so that's made it difficult. I hope you'll forgive me."

It's all I can do to keep from laughing. But you can imagine my surprise when Father accepts the drink and gulps it down. Everyone is taken aback, but no one attempts to stop Father. And in any event the dinner party soon turns into a drinking party; drinks are urged upon one another and promptly drained.

Not long afterwards I notice Father stagger as he heads for the bathroom. Before I know it I'm by his side supporting him. His right arm is feather-light and bone-hard. He glances at me. I meet his gaze.

As I wait for Father outside the bathroom, I think of Mother. I wonder how she is doing. When I was young, she would stand outside the outhouse door at night waiting for me, just as I am doing now. Father emerges from the bathroom and sets out ahead of me. I follow, not supporting him this time. He pauses briefly, and without looking back, says in a soft voice, "Thank you."

Back at the table, the drinking party is in full sway, and as our family inevitably does at holiday gatherings, they ask the children to sing. Ho-jin, a fourth grader now, has grown bored with these impromptu talent shows, but I don't pay much attention to him. I'm more interested in Father: finally he has a sparkle in his eye as he listens to the children sing. Sŭng-o's two children perform several songs apiece, and Ho-jŏng offers a song she has learned at kindergarten. When it's his turn, Ho-jin, displeased with me for not exempting him, keeps glancing at me and barely manages to finish one song. Father presents each of the children with a thousand-wŏn note, telling them to buy something for school.

As soon as the money is safe in their pockets, they all go out to play. I wonder where the money came from. Does Father have any idea how much a thousand wŏn is worth? How could he? He must have wanted to give something, anything, to the children. Father's eyes follow the children out. I wonder next how Father spends his day in prison. What does he see? There are too many things we don't know about each other.

Despite our worries, Ho-jin asks no embarrassing questions of this grandfather he's never seen before. Probably because he's been taught to call his two great-uncles Grandfather all this time, and because, more to the point, there's no reason for him to relate this new grandfather to Grandmother back at home. I wonder how my husband has explained these things to the children.

After graduating from college I went to a newspaper company with a reference from my professor and passed the job test. But when it came time for me to supply the company with supporting documents, I finally realized how naive I had been. I was hired on the basis of such easily obtained documents as my citizen registration card, resume, and references, only to be tripped up by my family register and the background questionnaire, which I was also supposed to furnish. Every petty detail of my personal and family background was to be filled in on the questionnaire, and there was a special section requesting identification of any family member who had gone to the North.

Pressed by the newspaper to submit these last two documents, I managed to put off doing so for three months, and finally turned in my resignation instead. I knew that without passing a security check I wouldn't receive a press card, and I felt it was much better to leave the newspaper voluntarily than to record Father's name and doings on the questionnaire. I then found a job composing and translating telexes at a small trading company. The work wasn't very interesting, but you could say I gained something out of it, because that's where I met my future husband. When he proposed to me I told him about Father, and fortunately he took it in stride—probably because there was no one similar to Father in his own family. It wouldn't affect him, he declared, because he wasn't about to become someone important, a high-ranking public official or a judge, say. We were married, and several years later the guilt-by-family-association system was lifted. But when it came time to issue him a passport for his first overseas business trip, he ran up against the same problem I had experienced. The application forms included something—the background questionnaire or some other security document—on which married men were to note information about their in-laws. At home that night, my husband tried to downplay what had happened.

"Well, it wasn't much fun. I just wrote down your parents' names; I wasn't crazy about volunteering information. If they find out about you after the security check—well, what can we do?"

A few days later he returned home with a sour look on his face. He'd been summoned to the Ministry of Foreign Affairs. He arrived, disconcerted, to find he was being asked to sign a document that began, "The undersigned acknowledges a conflict involving the Anti-Communism Law. . . ."

"If I do anything outside the country in violation of the national welfare, I'm supposed to accept any punishment. That's the main point. I had to sign and date it. Makes me feel like dirt. Like someone grabbed me by the scruff of the neck."

A few days later his passport was issued—clear proof, I guess, that guilt by association had ended—but he was upset for quite some time. His case was over and done with, but in no way did I want the children to go through that experience.

Even now, every June, Ho-jin and the other pupils have to write anti-spy slogans and draw anti-Communist posters for homework. These pictures won't be any different from the ones I used to draw. On the map of our rabbit-shaped nation you color the upper part entirely in red and draw the face of a wolf with black lines, and the wolf's long red claws reaching down toward the south. Sometimes you add a yellow wall with red earlobes, and write at the bottom, "Even the Walls Have Ears." Next year when Ho-jŏng begins school she'll draw pretty much the same pictures.

Will those two children remember today's events when they're grown up? What will they think of their grandfather then?

The drinks are taking effect: Father is dozing where he sits. I perch on the edge of the veranda, where the yard is visible. The long summer day has just now come to an end, and the yard is shrouded like a woman's face behind a dark veil. The children are playing hide-and-seek. Someone has bought popsicles for them; I can see the traces around their mouths. "The rose-of-sharon's blooming!" calls the one who's "it." "Ready or not, here I come!" Before I realize it, Grandmother is sitting beside me, stroking my hand. Just like she stroked Father's a little while ago.

"It's high time they unified the country. Why did they have to split a good piece of land in two and drive nails into people's hearts? Damned ism's; why is it against the law if a man wants to go home to see his mom? Is it such an awful crime that he has to live in that place till the day he dies? No one's ever going to know what a poor, pitiful man your dad is. . . ."

The heavy air of this summer night smells oddly sweet. I soon discover the source of the fragrance—a clump of lovely white gardenia blossoms in a dark corner of the garden. There's something about those flowers, though they've just blossomed and are now at their peak, that reminds me of an actress who flourishes for a season before fame passes her by. A tantalizing smell of something dissolute and overripe. Indifferent to Grandmother's tears, I end up saying something incongruous: "Gardenias are supposed to attract lots of bugs—how did they ever grow so big?"

Father and I stand opposite each other at the front gate. The rest of the family have said their goodbyes and gone back inside. My husband has walked up the alley with the children to turn the car around—and to leave Father and me to ourselves for the moment. Father watches my husband and children at the head of the alley, and I gaze at the gloom that has settled at the base of the wall behind Father. Presently I hear the car start up. I feel I should say something.

"When do you have to leave?"

"They want me ready to go early in the morning."

"I'll see you then," I blurt without thinking.

"That's all right. No need. It's fine like this."

I leave it at that. I had never thought of sending him off in the first place. I gather that Father wants to send *us* off; he doesn't want his back to be the last thing we see of him. All right, I tell myself. Perhaps it's better this way. Yes, it's fine.

I see the car backing around. It's time to go. I bow deeply to Father, then turn and start up the alley.

"Is your mother well?"

I come to a stop. "Yes."

"Well, good. So long, then."

I don't look back. Not far off, the car's taillights are visible.

My husband, so talkative a short time ago, is silent on the way home.

"What happened? Did Mom ask you to go there with the children?"

"No. At work today I got to thinking: Your father deserves to see the children. If I were him, I think that's what I'd want. And the kids should have it different from us. Right now they don't know what's what, but even when they grow up and find out what the real world's like, I don't want them developing irrational fears like we do. Times change, and the children won't be living the same kind of life that we did."

I don't express my gratitude to my husband for coming. Just like I didn't call my father "Father" earlier this evening.

When we arrive at the apartments, the custodian gives me the key. Mother's not at home, he says. He looks bored as he watches his television. My heart drops. Where could Mother have gone this late at night?

"When did she leave?" I ask breathlessly. "Did she say where she was going?"

The custodian's eyes remain glued to the foreign film on the television screen.

"Try the senior citizen hall. I think she's throwing some kind of dinner or something."

My husband is carrying Ho-jŏng on his back, so I give Ho-jin the key and send the three of them upstairs. Then I go around to the back of building 2 where a traditional octagonal pavilion sits in the grass. This structure, so out of place among the apartment buildings, was built for the benefit of the elderly residents of the complex. As I go up the steps I hear music coming through an open window. I poke my head through the doorway and a man playing flower cards near the threshold recognizes me. It's little Hwan's grandfather, who lives on the floor below us.

"Well, look who's here. I understand today is your mom's late husband's sixty-first birthday. Thanks to her, we've filled up on Chinese food. There's a lot of people older than that who never had the big sixty-first celebration; I'd say he's a lucky man, even in death."

Inside, I see a few people singing while they beat out a rhythm with chopsticks on the meal table. About twice their number are dancing in time with the music. Mother is among them. The beautiful light pink traditional outfit she wears is her only colored clothing. She had it made for my wedding, and this is the first time she's worn it since. In the light of the incandescent bulbs its cardinal-red cuffs look like purple butterflies fluttering gently in the air. The thin, aged hands at the ends of those cuffs are doing a dance of their own. Even at this distance I think I can see her fingernails, still youthful with their scarlet color, which she must keep until the winter's first snow.

Dear Distant Love

Sŏ Yŏng-ŭn

Mun-ja looked calmly through the dusty window, and when she saw the wind blowing furiously down the street she put on her wool gloves.

Because the wool shrunk and clumped together when she washed the gloves, she had to press hard with her fingers to get them on. These days nobody around her wore those colorful gloves, which had been out of fashion for several years now. Not only her gloves but everything about her was old-fashioned, redeemed only by the lack of holes: her overcoat with its frayed cuffs, the elastic, slipper-like shoes she wore summer and winter, the short, wide-cut dark gray pants that left her ankles sticking out, the lumpy socks with their layer of lint, the handbag smelling of her lunch whenever she produced it from her desk drawer.

Her appearance made Mun-ja seem all the more pitiable. On the threshold of forty, essentially an old maid, having the highest seniority in the business and editorial departments of this children's book publisher, she had done nothing but proofreading since coming to work here.

Including the director, there were seven in the editorial department. Mun-ja alone had remained over the years; each of the other faces had changed numerous times. Recent college graduates didn't last six months. The complaints started piling up from their first day of work: the chairs wobbled when they sat down, the bathroom was filthy, the stairs were too steep. They grew so irritated, it became almost a ritual to conclude whatever they said with something like, "I've had enough. I'm fed up with this damned place." At that point you could bet they wouldn't last more than a month or two longer.

Mun-ja was excluded from the conversations of these young people. What pride could they take from having as a co-worker an old maid who had always occupied the bottom of the totem pole at this minor publishing house, where they had no future even if they stayed on for the rest of their lives? And what had she to show for the ten years she had worked here, apart from the gray appearing prematurely at the part in her hair?

They liked to think that a frigid wind whirled at Mun-ja's back as she hunched over the proofs on her desk. They imagined coarse gooseflesh sprouting on her chin.

After rushing out at lunchtime for oxtail soup and rice, followed by coffee at a tearoom, they would be welcomed back by Mun-ja, a cup of hot barley tea between her hands. She looked so pitiful it made them sick, and if she happened to speak to them, they snapped back at her.

If Mun-ja was ever upset, she never let it show. The others in the office were embarrassed when the young director occasionally threw the blame for something in her face, but she always accepted the reproaches meekly. And just as she never expressed dissatisfaction, she was stoic and faithful in observing company policies. When the others cursed the company president and reeled off complaints about the facilities and their pay, she listened quietly.

Her young co-workers assumed from Mun-ja's attitude that she was going easy on herself, so afraid was she of being out of a job. And so whenever they saw her, diffident and piteous, they promised themselves they would soon leave the company; they would never become like her.

Mun-ja turned away from the window. Although it was twenty minutes past the end of the workday, the others were still chattering away at their desks. As closing time approached, they had all made telephone calls and appeared to have scheduled the rest of their day.

Mun-ja picked up her bag and approached the director's desk. She waited until he finished a conversation with one of the others, then said goodbye.

She had just started down the stairs when she heard Miss Ch'oe's flippant voice from the office: "It's really too bad. No calls for her even on Saturday."

"And nobody at home to welcome her."

"Oh, no. Even if she's not married, she must have family."

"You ladies are too much," said a man. "Working in the same office and you don't know anything about each other?"

"How? She never tells me anything."

"Well, I've heard a few things third-hand. Seems her parents passed away when she was young, and her only brother emigrated several years ago. She's lived by herself ever since. Apparently she's had all sorts of troubles. And now the only thing she has to her name is the deposit she made on that room she rents in Yongdu-dong, or wherever it is."

"Strange, isn't it? She never shops for new clothes, and she always brings her lunch to work. She's been pinching pennies for over ten years here. Where do you suppose the money goes?"

"Nothing strange about that. Instead of worrying about other people, Miss Ch'oe, you ought to put on a wedding veil yourself—the clock's ticking, you know."

Afraid they would be embarrassed if they discovered she had overheard them, Mun-ja silently descended the stairs.

The wind stung more than she had expected. A car or two was usually parked in the narrow alley, blocking pedestrians, but not that day. Business was slack in the eateries that lined the way, which normally were thronged with lunch-hour customers. The corner of a galvanized-iron roof thumped rhythmically in the wind like a teeter-totter. Had the nails rusted and come loose from the eaves?

Mun-ja raised her coat collar against the chill. As she emerged from the alley she asked herself if her life was as miserable a failure as other people seemed to think. She bit her lip gently, stifling an urge to burst out laughing. What a splendid job she had done in fooling her co-workers and everyone else! What she concealed from the world was not the round seal engraved with horses that Master Yi in *The Tale of Ch'unhyang* hid in his robe. Nor was she the poor heroine of television and movie fame who turned out to be the daughter of the wealthy head of a conglomerate. She could not explain it, but there was, well, something fulfilling and energetic in her mind that others could not sense.

It really mattered little to Mun-ja whether current fashions made her slacks too wide or narrow and her coat too long or short, whether her colleagues called her "Miss" or something more polite, whether her chair wobbled or not, whether the company president nagged her too much.

Sometime ago an older woman who styled herself an expert

proofreader had joined the staff. Not ten days on the job she had a loud argument with the man next to her, because he had called her "Miss" rather than something more respectful, and the following day she threw in a letter of resignation. Why make a big deal over what they call you? Mun-ja had thought as she watched the woman shake her fist and bawl out the man. She had then returned to her proofs, concealing a smile.

When she became aware that others considered her wretched and pitiful, she silently replied: If I look that way to you, fine. Think what you want. One day she had arrived at work to find her desk emptied of office supplies except for a stub of a pencil and some ballpoint pens that had run out of ink. Rather than express her feelings, she had made do with the pencil and had bought new pens. All right, she had thought. If you need something from me, take it.

When a longtime co-worker who had left to become a department head elsewhere kept offering her a higher salary to come work for him, she declined, thinking: It's all right for someone who migrates like a bird to earn a few more wŏn. But I can get by without that measly amount of money.

It was the same when the others in the office dumped their drudge work on her, or their assignment to watch the office on a Sunday or a holiday. Fine, she thought. I can clean the office; that icy water won't make my hands fall off. Go ahead and sneak away.

And of course when she was saddled with work that was even more troublesome and unprofitable than those chores, she never became angry or felt sorry for herself. She never avoided harsh burdens. Her spirit was strong and it always kneeled as if it could bear the heaviest load.

To her co-workers and the others around her, Mun-ja was as

quiet as the dead. But none of them knew that her silence originated from an absolute confidence that she could live under any conditions. Nobody ever dreamed that her confidence had formed while she dealt with a being in a high place, far above the plane of their existence, that it had developed while she walked a solitary road that was longer than they could imagine.

But it was a different matter when she had to ask a favor; she felt entirely humiliated. And by this evening, she simply had to raise two hundred thousand wŏn.

As she walked along, this thought weighing on her mind, Mun-ja noticed a telephone booth. A young man clutched the receiver. Mun-ja, still some distance away, could hear his shrill laughter. When she had called her aunt several days before, the older woman had flatly turned her down. But Mun-ja was desperate now, and there was nothing to do but appeal to her once more.

The young man's conversation seemed endless. It sounded as if someone was pestering him to hurry somewhere, but he was refusing, afraid he would miss the satellite broadcast of a championship boxing match.

Going up behind him and stamping her feet to keep warm, Mun-ja looked fretfully at the dreary clouds scudding above the building across the street. The wind felt as strong as ever. Finally the young man was finished. As if satisfied with having made his point, he remained in the booth until he had lit a cigarette.

Mun-ja picked up the receiver, still warm from his touch.

"Auntie, it's me again."

There was nothing more to say. She heard static, and at last her aunt produced a faint *tsk-tsk* and said, "All right, you might as well come by and say hello."

Tears came to her eyes, blurring her vision, but Mun-ja collected herself. She kept passing her fingernails over the graffiti on the shelf where the telephone rested, as if this were her duty.

Mun-ja never asked why Han-su occasionally demanded a large sum of money in addition to what he took from her every month. As it was, Han-su was uncomfortable putting the money in his pocket. "Damn it! Do you think I do this because I enjoy it? You wait and see; I'll have my chance."

It was always the same story: He needed the money immediately for a meeting with a powerful financier who might invest in his mine. And this time he wouldn't fail. It didn't matter to Mun-ja whether Han-su was telling the truth. As long as he took care of Ok-jo, to help him would be to indirectly help Ok-jo.

It didn't matter if he wasted the entire amount on a night of drinking, like in the old days. That kind of thing didn't hurt Mun-ja anymore. Han-su had carved a thousand invisible scars into her, but Mun-ja could now transcend those scars. For Han-su was already distant from her heart. Whenever Mun-ja overcame one of those wounds her spirit grew stronger, like that of the immortal camel that draws eternal strength as it's burdened with load after load.

But Han-su, like the other people who knew Mun-ja, had no inkling of that. He merely considered her foolishly good. Though once, just once, she had done something that confused and frightened him.

Less than a month after Mun-ja bore Ok-jo, Han-su forced his wife to take the baby. Not that he wanted the child—he and his wife already had a son and daughter. But by taking Ok-jo he felt he could possess Mun-ja forever.

Returning home, Han-su's wife had placed the newborn in front of him. "She must be completely irresponsible. How can she live like that?" she said, her face red with indignation. "I wanted to break something and give her a good scare, but I couldn't find anything to break. Even women who have nothing at least have a vanity. Not her."

Actually, Han-su's wife was relieved to see that Mun-ja had only a single cabinet in the way of furnishings. Her husband had always said that Mun-ja possessed nothing, but she had had her doubts. Back in the days when he had directed a mining operation, businessmen had lined up at his office with money-filled envelopes and expensive gifts, and he could have hoarded these to his heart's content. So whenever he unexpectedly bestowed her with a mink coat, an alligator handbag, or jewelry, she would carefully sound him out, brimming with suspicion that "the bitch" might have received better gifts.

But Han-su had then quit his job and gone into business for himself, buying a tungsten mine. He sold their house and the ancestral graveyard, along with his valuables and real estate, and invested the proceeds in the mine. When his wife had to sell her one remaining gemstone ring in order to sustain them, she began seething all over again, thinking that she was going bankrupt while "that bitch" was swaddled in jewelry, that she was the one who looked the beggar.

Dressed up in a mink coat and an alligator handbag borrowed from Han-su's sister, she had let herself in through the doghole-sized side door of a dwelling next to the Yongdu-dong sewer ditch. One glance and she had sized up Mun-ja's living situation. She realized she had agonized over nothing; she felt ridiculous and drained. Nothing her husband had given her was in evidence there. Mun-ja lacked even a common television, while she herself once had one in every room of her house. Obviously her husband was just trifling with Mun-ja.

When Han-su asked if Mun-ja had resisted giving up the baby, his wife had fixed him with a hawkish glare.

"Does the bitch have any choice? You didn't put her on your family register. It would take a lot of gall for her to put up a stink after she gets herself knocked up. No, she just looked at the baby, not a tear in her eyes, and said, 'If she wakes up and cries in the middle of the night, give her a few spoonfuls of barley tea.' And that's it."

"She's a fool," Han-su had murmured to himself. "Her own baby, and she lets somebody take it away just like that?" But then he clamped his mouth shut; he felt as if he had been speared in the pit of the stomach. Suddenly Mun-ja's utter silence had touched his heart, chilling him to the core.

There had been much more snow than usual that winter ten years before, when Han-su first visited Mun-ja's rented room. Mun-ja was constantly shoveling the roof. If she let the snow pile up, the water melting from it would soak through the concrete ceiling and drip down into her room. Although the ladder wasn't sturdy and she came dangerously close to a high-tension wire, she climbed up and down with her shovel as if she had wings. It didn't matter if the owners, who operated a restaurant, stood on their veranda ridiculing Mun-ja with her flushed cheeks, she scooped up the snow and threw it down as effortlessly as if she were dancing. And if a shovelful of snow landed in a mud puddle and splashed someone passing by, she would fly down, clean the mud from his pants, and apologize until he was satisfied. And back up she would go.

There was no running water in Mun-ja's hutlike kitchen. She had to draw water from the faucet in the owners' yard, which meant going out the back door of the kitchen and descending a long, steep flight of steps. The other tenants, who had moved in earlier, saw those steps as a ladder of humiliation, a necessary means of survival. More than anything else these destitute women hated the thought of the landlady sneering at their backs as they climbed the steps, groaning with the weight of the full bucket they carried in each hand.

Mun-ja lived the same tenant's life as those women, but was altogether different from them. When she appeared at the back door of the kitchen, her cheeks held the glow of someone who enjoyed what she was doing. Occasionally forgetting the buckets she held, she would stand on the steps and gaze up at the sky. That's when the red in her cheeks deepened, as if lit from within. The steps became a musical scale, and the way she came down them spoke of resilience and vitality. It was as if those steps had been made to look crude to others so that Mun-ja alone could enjoy the marvelous, beautiful world above.

The other tenants and the landlord's family often saw Mun-ja at daybreak at the top of the steps vigorously fanning her portable coal-briquette stove. Sometimes they heard her humming, in spite of the acrid smoke she breathed in. She had to use that smaller stove because water was seeping into the fuel hole of her cookstove. The landlord should have fixed the leak by then, and the roof and floor too, but Mun-ja didn't complain. Instead of being thankful, the landlord charged ridiculous amounts for the water and electricity. Mun-ja payed without questioning him, making it seem that she lived comfortably and couldn't be bothered with such trivial matters.

The other tenant women decided that Mun-ja was far better off than she appeared. One day they payed her an unannounced visit so they could inspect her room. What they found was paint peeling from the water-soaked ceiling. They saw no furniture to speak of except the cabinet with its rusty handle. Now they were even more puzzled by the glow that suffused Mun-ja's cheeks and the vitality that seemed to envelop her body in song. And if they were grouped around the faucet and Mun-ja was the first to return to her room, they were left with the feeling that a fragrant flower had briefly touched their hearts. How to explain it? One of them gestured that Mun-ja was crazy, and the rest burst into laughter.

As they had seen for themselves, Mun-ja possessed nothing that others didn't have. For her it was enough to think of the man she loved, no matter what she was doing. Whether she was cleaning bean sprouts, fanning the stove, or shoveling snow from the roof, the far reaches of her heart felt warmed and brightened as if by a hanging lantern, whenever she thought of him. She herself was unaware that this warmth and brightness were what colored her cheeks and infused her flesh with vitality.

Although Han-su came only on Sunday night, she thought of him as a lantern always present on her shelf. If she caught herself haggling at the market she would stop and think, What if he knew . . . ? And if she was about to quarrel with someone, her anger dissolved at the thought of him.

From Monday to Tuesday and on to Saturday she gradually alchemized herself, and on Sunday everything turned golden at her touch.

Before Han-su could knock on her door, Mun-ja recognized the sound of his steps and went out to welcome him. She helped him off with his coat, she removed his socks, she brought a basin of hot water and washed his feet, and each of these objects turned the color of gold.

The meal she prepared for him was like the candle a poor person buys for a shrine with money earned from a week's labor cleaning floors with a rough brush and a wet rag.

When she picked up a piece of lean meat with her chopsticks, Han-su opened his mouth wide and ate. He never thought of reciprocating. Selfish and obtuse, he couldn't see the golden color filling the room; he couldn't hear the melody in their periods of silence. When he stroked her body he was unaware that a smell like that of ripe fruit was settling on his fingers.

Like an impecunious drunk dubiously counting the money in his pocket over and over even when he's found a cheap place to drink, he tried incessantly to read her mind. Could she really be satisfied with what he gave her? Would she devote her life to him? The time he could spend with her was limited to what would escape his wife's notice. And although he had a decent job as secretary to an assemblyman in the ruling party, he earned too little from it to help with Mun-ja's living expenses.

Though Mun-ja never asked him for anything, he was always anxious. What if she requested something he couldn't afford to give her? He knew she wasn't greedy: She didn't use makeup, she didn't dress up, and she gave no indication of buying anything valuable for her room. Still, he kept his guard up.

In the meantime, Han-su's assemblyman became a government minister. Han-su had been a mineral engineering major, and with the minister's help he was appointed to head a semi-public mine. With his new salary he could have established Mun-ja in a home of her own. But he didn't. Instead he provided a splendid new house for his wife and children, along with fine clothes, household help, and more fruit and baked goods than they could ever hope to eat before it spoiled.

He shared nothing with Mun-ja, not one apple, not a single orange. In spite of himself he sometimes picked up a fruit basket for her. But then he would put it back. He was afraid that once he started giving her things she would hold out her hand to him for the rest of her life.

But as always, Mun-ja asked nothing of him. When the landlord raised her rent she managed for a time to find the additional money, but finally she had to move. Prices were soaring, though, and she had to trim her weekly budget even more in order to serve Han-su a dinner as good as before. Instead of paying two bus fares to get somewhere, she would take the first bus as far as it went and walk the rest of the way. For lunch she made do with instant noodles.

In contrast, Han-su's skin looked more glossy each day. And every time he visited Mun-ja, not only his shoes but his shirt, tie, cuffs, buttons, and underwear were different. He built up a collection of suits in various patterns and colors.

One day, as Han-su checked his watch and rose from their bed, Mun-ja clutched at his underwear. "Don't go! Stay with me just for tonight." She buried her face in his back, then immediately released him, just in time to delay a flood of tears. She felt dispirited. The things she had touched and turned golden tore at her heart. As she took his suit jacket from the hanger, she choked up at the sight of a thick wad of money in an inside pocket. Her heart tore some more when she took out his shoes from the quilt on the heated part of the floor, removed the cloth she had wrapped them in, and noticed from the labels on the soles how expensive they must be.

There followed a procession of days that felt to her like the end of the world: she imagined endless tidal waves poised to crash, thunder pealing, violent, swooping winds. The deep sorrow she wanted to pour out in tears at the side of a river or high on a remote mountain washed out the glow in her cheeks little by little.

Again Mun-ja's rent went up. On her way home from a day's search for yet another room she bought two bottles of *soju*. She drank the liquor on an empty stomach and passed out. When she awakened the next morning, bright sunlight and sticky filth were everywhere.

Again she wept, the flood of tears mottling her vision. But then she clenched her teeth, and at that moment, the camel inside her came to life and confronted her pain: "Knife me if you want. Shred me with your cruel blade. You'll never kill me. If I can't stand up, then I'll hold myself erect. My head will never bow. You can hurt me more, but I'll never give up. My love for him is total, and through that love I'll have revenge for the pain he's caused me. I'll stay where I am, I'll live with what's given me, and I'll never run away. Yes, I'll have my revenge, sweet revenge. Not just on him but on the god who gave me this fate and will grant me his mercy the minute I can no longer endure!"

For two days she lay sick in bed, unable to go to work. The day after that was Sunday. She got up as if nothing had happened, took a bath in anticipation of Han-su's arrival, went to the market, and shelled gingko nuts.

That evening she noticed a pearl pin on his tie as she hung it up. But her heart was beyond tearing now. At last she was indifferent toward his possessions. She was no longer concerned with the things he enjoyed.

Mun-ja observed dispassionately as his endless desire reached ever higher, prompting him to scorn the gift boxes and money-filled envelopes from the businessmen who lined up at the door to his house.

And then early one morning the second movement of the Eroica Symphony was broadcast repeatedly over radio and television. Martial law was proclaimed and the National Assembly and Cabinet were dissolved. Not quite two months later Han-su staggered up to Mun-ja's door. His face was haggard and he was badly in need of a shave. He sprawled on the floor of her room, too drunk to control himself, and lay spread-eagled as Mun-ja removed his clothing. Suddenly he clutched the hem of her skirt and said in a husky, tearful voice, "I'm nothing now. Nobody comes to my house anymore. But if you turn your back on me, I'll kill you."

Mun-ja waited in the living room while her aunt finished her bath. The sofa where she sat was like a feather cushion, and the thick Arabian-style carpet beneath her feet was soft and comfortable. Everything at her aunt's was cozy and pleasant.

Beyond the white lace curtains the trees in the yard swayed in the gusty wind. Even cold weather seemed tame and pleasant from inside her aunt's home. The gloomy sky gradually darkened to the color of black ink.

From the bathroom came the refreshing sound of water splashing on the tile floor. Suddenly Mun-ja was struck by a numbing, chilling notion: The weak build their lives on soft sofas and carpets, gilded fireplaces, expensive paintings, and comfortable beds. They grow used to the pleasant touch of such objects, and soon they're enslaved. Their craving is like the mane of a horse that sleeps well after constant stroking. But the mane of my spirit wants to be blown high by strong winds, without knowing satisfaction.

From the kitchen came the scuffing of slippers. Her aunt's middle-aged housekeeper appeared with a glass of juice on a tray.

"It's been a long time," said Mun-ja.

"You should visit us more often. The baby must be getting bigger."

"Yes."

"She looks so much like you it's hard to believe."

"How do you know that?"

"There's a picture of her. Over there." The woman pointed toward the display shelves against the wall.

Mun-ja waited for her to return to the kitchen, then looked at the photo. Mun-ja had asked Han-su to bring the girl on her fifth birthday, and had spent the day with her. The photo had been taken here at the aunt's house.

The photo showed Ok-jo in the arms of Mun-ja's cousins. She was smiling brightly. Her teeth, as even as corn on the cob, were a pure, almost bluish white. Mun-ja took the picture frame and carefully dusted it.

Just before Han-su's wife had taken Ok-jo, Mun-ja had dreamed for several nights that the baby was being stolen from her. Sometimes she dreamed she and the baby were being chased across hills and fields by a figure in black; other times she was a madwoman searching for her stolen child. After she awakened, the screams she had uttered in the dream, screams that sounded so unlike her, continued to whirl and echo about her ears.

She would turn on the light and see that the baby was there, twitching its eyelids in the brightness. And yet she could never be sure she was awake. She would look at the baby, and look again, but the phantom of her nightmare, instead of fading, clung to her more tightly. If only she could run away with the baby, run far, far away. On a sudden urge she knelt and made a tearful plea:

"Why can't I do that? It's been too much for me. I've always made do with as little as possible—that and my bare hands. Hands that have forgotten how to hold. But I don't want to give up my own flesh and blood. Let me be comforted. I can't refuse it this time! I'm hurting too much!"

At that moment the camel within her again came to life: "You can do it. Yes, it hurts to have a high place you want to reach. But the pain is your ladder to that place."

Mun-ja could only shake her head and moan.

But now she was capable of smiling calmly as she looked at the photograph of her daughter.

The splashing stopped, and presently the bathroom door opened. Her aunt's eyes had a fuzzy cast, as if she were enraptured by the feel of the hot water, and there was a pink, milky glow to her skin. As she approached the sofa she brushed her hair, which had been expertly dyed brown. Her undulating bosom, plump and elastic, seemingly ageless, was visible through the deeply cut collar of her silk bathrobe.

Mun-ja carefully returned the photo of Ok-jo to its place and turned to her aunt.

"Are you going to leave Ok-jo with his family forever?"

This bluntness told Mun-ja how little faith her aunt placed in her.

"Yes," Mun-ja replied, clasping her hands squarely in front of her. Her expression was as firm and unyielding as packed earth.

"Why? Did they say they won't give her up?"

"No. In fact, they asked me to take her back."

"Well, thank goodness for that. Then do it, and break up with him. His luck has dried up. The longer you drag things out, the more you'll be hurt—you know that."

"I'll not take Ok-jo back, Aunt."

"No? You're such a strange one. Don't you feel any pity for the child?"

"Yes, I do. And I would love to take her back. But not just for my own satisfaction. When I gave up Ok-jo, in my mind she had already left me. That doesn't mean I don't love her. It's just that my love for her is different from other mothers'. I was reading a biography of Genghis Khan a while ago. Do you know what he did after he conquered China? He left his own son there. He left him with foreign people in a foreign land. He had the strength to abandon his own son, to suppress his love and walk away. And that was what made him such a great historical figure. I think that having a deep attachment to my flesh and blood is like having a deep attachment to possessions—it's something I ought to overcome. I feel like I'm living in a state of tension where I'm constantly having to stand up to someone."

"I don't understand a word you're saying. Why don't you drink your juice?" For herself she requested carrot juice from the house-keeper.

Mun-ja observed her aunt's fleshy, well-preserved hands. They looked so relaxed after the hot bath. The fingertips wrinkled as they dried. The bluish gray nail color had started to come off, and her aunt became absorbed in scraping away what remained of it. And then she spoke up again.

"Actually, I was about to call you, so you came at a good time. Now tell me, isn't it about time you were married? I think I've found a man for you. If you can devote yourself to him half as much as you do with Ok-jo's father, you'll win his affection and have yourself a good life."

Surely she didn't ask me over to tell me this, Mun-ja thought as she stared fretfully out the window. By now the trees in the yard had also turned the color of ink. Perhaps Han-su had left for her room by now.

"Well, what do you think? Would you like to meet him? He's fifty and has two children, but they live with his mother. I understand he has an apartment in Apkujŏng-dong and a hill somewhere this side of Kwach'ŏn that might be good for pasture land. And he's a lawyer. He has a drooping eyelid, and you might think that's a defect, but you have your share of those, too."

Her aunt expected a favorable response, but Mun-ja continued to gaze pensively outside. It was because of the money, her
aunt realized, but she was reluctant to bring up that subject.
She forced herself to yawn, her way of coping with an awkward
moment.

Mun-ja turned back at the sound. The moment she saw her
aunt's eyes, their corners moist from her yawn, she was inexplicably angry. But the next moment she felt the camel within her
tread gently over that anger.

"Aunt, what about the favor I asked?"

"You mean the money?"

"Yes."

"I told you I don't have it. But the housekeeper has some money
I'm looking after. If you want, you can borrow that. But you'll
have to pay interest. Five percent."

"All right."

But Mun-ja's aunt seemed in no hurry to fetch the money. She
scraped at her nail color more aggressively, and continued her
croon-like nagging.

"Am I getting through to you? As long as I can do anything
about it, I'm not going to let my niece spend the rest of her life in
a state where she's not married and not single. Can you imagine
how resentful your mother would be if she knew about this? And
aren't you tired of being strapped for money all the time? If you
marry that lawyer, your luck will change in no time."

Realizing by now that it was useless to respond, Mun-ja merely
said, "Yes, I know."

"The thing is, you've had a monster inside you since you were
a girl. People should turn around if there's mud in their path, but
you're so pigheaded you try to march right through it."

"Yes, I know."

Mun-ja was no longer listening. Her attention had drifted to an essay she had read by a visitor to Libya. Libya's per capita income was ten thousand dollars and its population three million, the writer had explained. One of the government's immediate objectives was to increase the population. Therefore, on one hand government officials advised couples to have large families. And, on the other hand, they tried to lure the people of the desert hinterland with heaps of money. The officials begged these people to move to the cities. They promised them a comfortable life in houses with plush carpets, air conditioning, soft beds, and running water pouring out at the turn of a tap.

But a sizable number refused these enticements. Instead they sank deeper roots into their chosen environment. Most humans will do anything to avoid the constant annoyance of something like thirst. These nomads, however, entrenched themselves more firmly in the desert, where there is nothing but thirst. The thirst of the desert. A land of death where rocks are scorched and broken into sand. When the sun rises, everything between heaven and earth becomes a pink, steaming crucible. And when the sun goes down, the chill can be deadly. To protect themselves from baking or freezing to death these desert people must rely on their own resources. Why, then, do they voluntarily choose a life of thirst?

In Libya there is a legendary map that is said to have come down from the people's ancestors. On that map is drawn a blue waterway flowing deep beneath the desert. The people call it the Path of God. They say that only those who remain in the desert hinterland know the location of this waterway.

Again Mun-ja had to remind her aunt about the money. While the older woman went to her room for it, Mun-ja returned to the display shelves for another look at the photo of Ok-jo.

Poor girl. It's cruel, isn't it, this burden your mother has imposed on you? You'll need your own camel someday, and you'll have it if you can learn to rely on yourself. That camel will help you understand why I've been so obstinate about leaving you beside a swamp of pain instead of a nice, pleasant riverside. You'll understand that I did it out of love.

Her aunt handed her the money. Mun-ja placed it in her bag and turned toward the kitchen to thank the housekeeper. But her aunt, suddenly flustered, stopped her.

"Go. I'll thank her for you."

Perplexed, Mun-ja accepted the shopping bag her aunt had hurriedly stuffed with fruit.

Mun-ja was about to pay the shopkeeper when she noted a look of hesitation on his face.

"Uh, your husband took a dried squid and two bottles of corn liquor a little while ago."

"Oh. All right. How much are they?"

"Let me see . . . eighteen hundred wŏn."

Mun-ja paid and left with her groceries. The yellow glow in the windows of the clustered houses made her feel all the more tired and worn out; she wanted rest. But this was impossible, because Han-su was there. These days he looked burned out and broken down and his drunken outbursts were more frequent.

Midway up the high, steep hill to her room she rested under an old tree. As always, the tree inspired her. Its trunk was gnarled, but the tree was tall and imposing. Each of its many branches resembled a hand longing to caress the sky. For those longing hands to have stretched so high, the roots must have groped their way into the earth several times deeper than the height of the tree. When Mun-ja realized that the roots touching her feet never stopped extending their pure will into the cold, solid ground in search of the water of life, she was comforted, and the chilling pain of her existence lessened.

The landlady was waiting, her face poking outside the front gate. Mun-ja's heart dropped. Not again!

"Ayu, I'm so annoyed I could die. Look there, young lady!" Her landlady indicated the wall that faced the alley. "He pissed there again. Even the dogs don't do that. I can't believe it, leaving a urine stink near our gate. He might as well be doing it in our face. But what I'm really afraid of is if the man next door finds out—he'll go after him."

"I'm very sorry, ma'am. I really am. I'll wash it off right away."

Mun-ja entered her kitchen, set down her bag and groceries, and filled a basin with water. The landlady was still scowling venomously as she emerged.

As this latest humiliation stabbed Mun-ja in all her weariness, a mild skepticism stirred inside her: What if it's useless to climb the ladder of suffering? What if there's no end to this road I'm on? What if it's all a lie? What if my pain and suffering are linked in a cycle of more pain and suffering? But she kept swabbing. Her arms had long since become as tireless as the camel's legs.

Mun-ja had washed the wall clean and was about to go inside when her landlady intercepted her.

"Just a moment, young lady." Her tone had softened. "I have a letter for you."

A moment later the woman reappeared with a blue airmail envelope and handed it to Mun-ja. Her face wore an incongruous, fleeting smile that made Mun-ja's heart drop again. She braced herself.

"I know it wasn't six months ago that you moved here, but I

hope you'll understand. You see, our boy keeps pestering us for his own room. If you can find yourself another place we'll pay the realtor's fee."

Mun-ja responded agreeably: "All right, I understand."

She went inside, picked up Han-su's shabby shoes with the cracked insteps and stood them neatly to one side, then opened the door to her room. He seemed to be sound asleep. The empty liquor bottles lay on their sides next to his head. His disheveled hair had grown below his ears, and the collar of his dress shirt was grimy. Looking at him curled up like a shrimp, Mun-ja wondered momentarily if it was only now that she loved him truly.

She remembered that she was holding a letter. It was from her brother in America. She hadn't expected it, and she skimmed the contents, telling herself that dinner was her first priority.

While she was loading the dinner tray in the kitchen she heard Han-su's voice.

"What's the letter all about?"

"It's from my brother."

"What does it say?"

"He wants me to come to America. His supermarket is doing great and he needs help."

Han-su snorted. "All this time not a peep out of him, and now he asks you to come give him a hand. You write him back and tell him to cut the crap. Wait till I get someone to bankroll me; I'll set up ten of those little supermarkets."

Mun-ja heard the crackle of a match being struck. It probably wasn't the letter that irritated him so much as her failure to tell him if she had brought the money.

Mun-ja left off her dinner preparations and returned to the room. Han-su quickly turned and looked at her out of the corner of his bloodshot eyes. Mun-ja produced the money from her bag and handed it to him. Instantly he crushed out his cigarette on the corner of a newspaper and rose.

"But dinner's ready."

"Dinner, dinner, dinner! Do you have any idea what time it is? What took you so long, anyway?"

Mun-ja silently helped him on with his jacket and overcoat. At moments such as these, when she saw his selfish, heartless character, her lips formed a smile but her heart wept.

While he buttoned his coat, Mun-ja went out to the kitchen and placed his shoes toward the door, slightly apart, so he could slip them on easily. The kitchen was steamy from the rice she'd been scooping for their meal. She tasted the bitterness of grief but smiled without a word.

Leaving Mun-ja at the gate, Han-su stomped down the steps to the street. He descended the hill and soon he was gone from her sight.

He was retreating endlessly from her field of vision. That was her only reaction. Already she considered him not so much a man as the light of a spirit receding to a higher plane in order to present her with a greater ordeal. Her entire being floated like a horse's mane, longing to reach that plane.

IDENTICAL APARTMENTS

Pak Wan-sŏ

Ding. This short, gentle chime is as soft as a timid tap on a xylophone, and yet I'm supposed to hear it in spite of the racket we all make when the after-dinner fun is reaching its peak. It's a difficult business, a business I find dreadful.

To give you an idea of the commotion, it's prime time on the television in my parents' room; my younger brother strums the guitar in his room across the way; and farther down the hall my youngest brother listens to an FM station. My children, who are about the same age as my nephews, cry, laugh, and squabble, then chase each other from room to room playing hide-and-seek. Adults, children, and kitchenmaid, all doing their own thing, produce a chorus of jolly outcries rising to a peak of commotion that reminds me of a huge pot of motley stew cooked to perfection. But that's when I'm supposed to block out the noise and detect that *ding.* I'm used to it. But still it's dreadful. These days my ears are growing tired of detecting, and occasionally I only think I hear the chime. *Yes, that must be the bell.* I go out and open the front gate, but no one is there beneath the light. I close the gate and go back inside, feeling like a fool in the presence of the others, even the teenage kitchenmaid.

The place where I live is not "our house," it's "this house." It's my parents' home, but I've been married off and strictly speaking I'm an outsider now. My parents knew the man I loved was poor, but they were only too happy to give our marriage their blessing. They opposed the idea of our renting a room, though. The least they could do was board us for a few years, they said, and after we had saved up my husband's salary we could buy a house and move out. We pretended we couldn't refuse. Actually, everyone in my family is friendly, and I have nothing to complain about. So we moved into the spacious guest room. My older brother and his wife live here too, but we don't feel we have to be careful in their presence. My father still holds financial power and controls the household, and I'm his precious only daughter. As far as I can tell, Sister-in-Law's situation is similar to my own. She wants to buy a house and live separately, too, and she devotes herself to saving what my brother earns.

We're sisters-in-law, but we're buddies, as close as accomplices in a crime.

To be honest, I've experienced none of the grief or meanness that comes with living with one's parents. Still, it's dreadful waiting for my husband in the evening. Each family member produces a distinct chime, and once we hear it we know which of us it is. When Father rings the bell, the chime is slow and dignified, just like his voice. My older brother tends to press the button forcefully, then kick at the gate. Younger Brother presses the button in a kind of frenzy, the way he strums his guitar, not letting up until someone opens the gate. My youngest brother is hopelessly ignorant of things such as doorbells; he rattles the gate for dear life, exasperating the entire family. "Goodness, Young Master Clown's back!" says Mother. "Hurry and open the gate before he snaps the bolt!" she tells the maid, who drops what she's doing and dashes out. It's been decided that the maid will answer the gate for everybody except my husband. Even my sister-in-law, who knows full well when it's Elder Brother who's arrived, stays plopped in front of the television. It's an accomplishment when she ventures as far as the edge of the veranda to greet him. The maid knows all, and does well by us.

It's my job, though, to recognize when it's my husband ringing the bell, and to open the gate for him. I'm not exactly sure when I inherited this duty. Maybe when we realized he pressed the button so lightly that we wouldn't hear the chime unless I strained to listen for it; it does take exceptional hearing to detect it. Whenever I hear that distinctive, faint *ding,* I feel sorry to the bottom of my heart for my husband as he stands in front of his in-laws' gate, reduced to a coward who can barely touch the bell. Like a girl holding back tears, I leave with a long face to open the gate. And there he stands. But my tears do not gush forth. For the man I see standing there certainly doesn't look like a coward. Instead he is pride itself, as hard and cold as tempered steel. So cold it occurs to me his faint touch on the bell is not timid but deliberate, something he does to play tricks with me.

I fell in love with a warm and tender man whose face looked slightly sad. Because I still think of him that way, I always feel a tinge of bashfulness at the gate. He has no problem with that, and we proceed inside to our room.

Little by little the commotion dies down. Mother has unilaterally decided that her son-in-law doesn't like noise. So the first thing she does is turn down the television. Then she goes from room to room saying, "Shhh, your brother-in-law's home," and that's it for the guitar and radio. My two younger brothers are very understanding in this sense. Even the children pipe down, and finally my children come into the guest room, which is to say our room.

The maid comes in with my husband's meal tray. The dinner served to Father and Elder Brother is a smart, appetizing presentation, and my husband's is no different. But Mother follows it in to make sure none of the side dishes has been left out. And then comes the standard apology: "It's not much, but help yourself." "Please," my husband says, "You make me feel like a guest." To which Mother replies, "My son-in-law will always be an honored guest in our house." And on occasion she brings out from hiding a bottle of Western liquor that has the most beautiful color: "Now I want you to try some of this." My husband accepts Mother's playing up to him as a matter of course, always proud, sometimes indifferent, never overwhelmed or even fazed by her show of favor.

Mother is that good to us. We're not really put out in any way. Mother and the maid know how to take care of us, and except for letting in my husband in the evening, there's nothing for me to do. But that only duty of mine is dreadful. Just how dreadful is something I would like to tell my husband. I sometimes think that the steady growth of our savings is not a reward for my husband's hard work but the outcome of the dreadful duty I put up with. I feel I'm about to suffocate beneath the enormous weight of the million-plus wŏn in that account.

And so I wish I could appeal to my husband to ease my suffering. I wish he could be more sensitive to what I go through living with my family. But somehow I've managed to put up with seven years of this solitary suffering. Though my ears have been abused to the point that I often hear a *ding* that's not there, and my fleshy face has become drawn and nervous. We've saved enough money for a small apartment, assuming we find a good deal, and the children are old enough that they're going to school.

My two kids started school the same year. They're twins, you see. One conception, one bout with morning sickness, one childbirth, and two sons. Talk about killing two birds with one stone. And thanks to living with my family, child rearing is easily managed: no great strain, no big crises.

In my eyes, those dashing boys with their fine features are like a pair of jewels I've gotten for free. I couldn't possibly imagine anyone more handsome, and I couldn't be more satisfied that they're twins.

Mother and Father love those children of mine more than their son's children. My sister-in-law is an optimist and doesn't let this worry her; she thinks elderly people usually love their daughters' children more. But from my perspective, it's not a matter of sons' versus daughters' children. It's just that my sons were born so cute and innocent that everyone loves them.

The time came for those boys to enter school. And with it came my desire to be independent. I've wanted my cute children to come home from school and bang on the gate of *my* house. There is no way I could begin all over again trying to tell who is ringing the bell (though my boys do it more softly and timidly than my nephews). It's dreadful just to imagine.

While my family is sorry we'll be leaving, they also encourage us. I don't for a moment doubt the sincerity of their sadness, which grows from their sweet dispositions.

But I must deal with the opinions of my sister-in-law and mother on whether the first place of my own will be an apartment or a house. My sister-in-law favors an apartment. Because, first of all, we won't have to worry about heating, since we'll be spared the nuisance of coal briquettes; we'll have a kitchen and all the other amenities, so we won't need a maid; we can lock the place up when we're out; we're guaranteed complete independence from our neighbors; and so on. But this independence scares Mother. Cold, uncompromising independence: that's what accounts for the occasional murders and such that take place in apartments, she declares. By her logic, murders in our country never take place anywhere else. On the other hand, consider what a neighborhood has to offer: the aroma of steamed rice cakes prepared together with the neighbors to offer to the spirits, the sizzle of fried cakes, the sharing of food, the huddling over matters great and small, people who are there to help. My sister-in-law and I look at each other and wink.

I agree with my sister-in-law. I don't like this old neighborhood we live in. The people here practice beyond perfection the familiar proverb "A good neighbor is better than a distant brother." God only knows why, but they're too interested in other families' affairs. They're experts at getting as excited as parents whose son has gotten into a first-rate college or high school, or at rushing over with sober faces to commiserate with parents whose children have failed in this respect, or at getting themselves invited to senior citizens' birthday parties, where they eat and have fun; but then they get all the dirt on these families and proceed to mouth it about and speak ill of them.

I know that the moment my husband leaves for work in the morning and the moment he returns in the evening, the neighborhood chatterboxes *tsk-tsk* and sneer at him, asking why a big, strong man like that is living off his in-laws. They consider me a sneaky opportunist and the direct opposite of my sister-in-law, who is the best-natured person they know.

Mother doesn't know how I feel. She assumes we don't have

enough money to buy a house, and this saddens her. She takes to sweet-talking me: Who is going to complain if I live off Father for a few more years? Then she glares at my blameless sister-in-law. But I'm good buddies with Sister-in-Law, and after making the rounds with her, I find a suitable apartment. After we sign the papers, I take Mother there. The first thing she notices is the size. She's surprised at how small it is: only eighteen *pʻyŏng*. We've been deceived, she insists, visibly irritated. "Goodness sakes, we have thirty-seven *pʻyŏng* of floor space at home, a dozen people swarming around inside, and we still have several rooms left over. And you tell me this is eighteen *pʻyŏng?* Goodness sakes, you young folks have been cheated!" By now she is beside herself. I reply that *pʻyŏng* are measured differently now. "Well, that's true," she says. "A *kŭn* of meat doesn't seem to weigh as much as it used to." She looks as if she understands.

As moving day draws near, Mother digs up her old concerns and begins to worry all over again. It seems she can never be pleased with an independent living arrangement where households are separated by thick concrete walls. And she has no confidence that I'm independent enough to run a separate household. In spite of that, she manages not to invite herself to the new apartment to meddle in our affairs, for neither my husband nor I have begged for her help. This is a matter of pride with her.

My apartment building is the "stairway" type: you go up a flight of steps to a landing where the doors to two apartments face each other. At Mother's insistence, we introduce ourselves to the people across the way. Although Mother seems to have expected that the woman of that family will be as old as she, it turns out she is a young housewife like me. But she has a leg up on me, in that she and her husband have been on their own for eight years, ever since their marriage.

"She's just a child." With these words Mother cajoles the woman to help me learn how to do everything. But independent of Mother's request, I immediately form a good impression of the woman. Her apartment is cozy and inviting. It looks like something out of a fairytale. I want to decorate our apartment just like hers. I bashfully ask her help with furniture and interior decoration. She tells me not to worry one bit; the shopping arcade on the ground floor has a furniture shop, a Curtain Center, you name it.

"Well, your sister-in-law is right. This apartment living *is* comfortable." This from my mother, even.

Our apartment is quickly decorated. Father shoulders the expense, rationalizing it as a kind of after-the-fact wedding present. I make up my mind that my apartment will be decorated more tastefully than the woman's, but in the end it is similar in furniture layout and even the color of the curtains. My first reaction to the woman's apartment was to feel overpowered, and so my tastes perhaps mimic hers more than I realized. In any case, my sister-in-law is envious and Mother and Father marvel at how pretty my apartment is.

Finally—freedom from that dreadful business of having to identify the weak *ding* of the bell during the early-evening chaos of our extended family.

In a pretty apron I cook rice and make side dishes for my family. Ch'ŏri's mom—the woman across the way—is my cooking instructor. She samples my side dishes, tasting the seasoning with a smack of her lips, adding a few drops of vinegar here, a sprinkle of hot red pepper there. If she praises the taste of something highly enough, I gladly give her a plate of it. And when she returns the plate it's never empty. We go grocery shopping together. The supermarket downstairs has all sorts of things. That doesn't mean she and I *buy* all sorts of things. But who cares? We simply put on our haughty connoisseur faces and buy bean sprouts, tofu, and mackerel pike. I quickly learn recipes for these things. Mother occasionally visits, and after eating her fill of these dishes she never fails to thank Ch'ŏri's mom.

I get into the routine of housekeeping and people begin to praise my cooking. But from time to time I feel nauseated by the food I prepare, almost as if I have morning sickness. Part of it is a lack of variety in what I cook, but I guess the more important reason is that I'm disgusted with Ch'ŏri's mom's cooking skill. Although I can cook quite well on my own by now, I can't escape her influence. We might as well be eating the same meals as her family. It makes me miserable to think that the same dinner awaits her husband as the one I set before mine. And then my husband gets into the act. At regular intervals he says cruel things about my cooking, pushing my misery to the crisis point. For example, if I serve him a bowl of pickled radish, he might pincer with his chopsticks one of the flower-shaped carrot slices floating in the broth, give me a look of disgust as if he's caught a fly swimming there, and say, "Will you please forget the cute cooking school tricks and give me something with some taste to it?"

And I still dread the evening hours when my husband returns. This is my home, and instead of a doorbell that chimes I have a bean-sized peephole in the door. But it's dreadful having to squint through the lens in that hole and see my husband standing beneath the twenty-watt fluorescent bulb outside our door. Whether it's exhaustion after a day's work or the light from the bulb, his face looks so pale and heartless that it frightens me. It's the face of someone who's hiding a length of cord in his pocket to strangle me with. It's the apartment murderer that Mother worries about! That's always my first reaction, but after I've jumped back from the door, I realize it's my husband. Some of that initial fear and disgust remain, though, while I'm opening the door and helping him off with his clothes.

I want to confess my ridiculous fears to my husband and remove that bean-sized piece of glass from the door, but I'm not sure I can do so without hurting his feelings. I'm not good enough with words to make him understand me. I didn't have to be good with words back in the days when he looked at me with warm and tender eyes. But now I'm forced to realize I need that skill in my relationship with him. And that's when I get to feeling anxious and fretful. "Honey, I feel sort of strange these days—kind of nervous and at loose ends," I'll say. And in the most indifferent tone you can imagine he'll say, "Huh! You're neurotic. That's what we get for being modern." He has a quick mind and is good at snappy answers. But are snappy answers really supposed to solve anything?

I ask Ch'ŏri's mom about neuroses. I thought she'd ask me about my symptoms, but instead she tells me she's neurotic too, just like so-and-so, and such-and-such, and so on down the line until she's named every wife she knows. She knows a lot of the wives in the building, and just as many types of neurosis. I've followed her around to visit a few of these women. They're similar wives with similar households. All around us the apartments are the same, as much so as mine and Ch'ŏri's mom's. Sure, there are differences—one apartment might have a washer, someone else might have a piano—but no one enjoys these advantages long enough to indulge in a sense of superiority. Because someone soon copies her.

Western women go on diets to lose weight, but the women in these apartments diet to imitate others who are on diets or simply to be able to look like them. I shudder in disgust at this behavior. But in order to buy the washer that Ch'ŏri's mom has, I go heavy on the bean sprouts, mackerel pike, and artificial seasonings, using only her recipes. And Ch'ŏri's mom, clearly desperate for an American electric frypan like the one I received as a housewarming gift from my sister-in-law, cuts her grocery shopping to the bone and stops trying new recipes.

And so I waste day after day as I, Ch'ŏri's mom, and women in other apartments try to live better than others. But we only end up resembling one another. And my husband, it seems, has lost seven years of time, tenderness, and warmth for the sake of an eighteen-*p'yŏng* apartment.

There are plenty of cunning wives among the neighbors, women who pray for a miracle to deliver them from such vain, tiresome competition. Ch'ŏri's mom is one of them. She and I lead a mirror-like existence. When I look at her I realize how bored, empty, and dispirited I am. But then one day she appears at my door and I find myself searching her face in vain for the mirror image of myself. Her skin shines and her eyes gleam as if she conceals an ecstatic joy deep inside her. How can this be? I go straight into a funk. How would you feel if one day you looked into the mirror and saw a complete stranger instead of the familiar face you always saw, or if you saw a smiling face when you were sure you were frowning? Well, that's how I feel. What's worse, I can't help feeling humiliated when I see her like that.

I must learn the secret of her transfiguration. Tension quickly enters our relationship. I inspect every clue she gives off—the look in her eyes, her gestures, her speech, her smiles. Sly as the court doctors of old who checked the pulse of females by touching not the subject herself but thread wound about her wrist, I carefully pull my thread tight and focus my nervous energy on the end I hold.

What I eventually learn is that the woman's joy and tension

are cyclical, gradually reaching a climax and then falling off steeply before being reborn. It's a weekly cycle, and Friday evening is the climax.

Friday evening—that's the key to it. Her husband isn't home yet and her son and daughter eat an early dinner and go to building 9 for their piano lesson with a music school student. I quickly catch the scent of a steamy, thrilling affair.

Friday evening, when she looks ready to burst with joy and nervous anticipation; Saturday, when she's limp as a dishrag; and Sunday, when that gleam returns to her eyes, along with the joy that upsets me so—I have no doubt as to the cause.

And so one Friday evening I attack. I'm sure I'll surprise her in the act. What I find, though, is not an adulterer but a lottery ticket.

Lips parched, one hand clutching the ticket, the other beckoning who knows what, she sits on the floor watching a number wheel on the television, and every time the arrow settles on a number she leans forward as if she'll jump right into the television and become the arrow herself, and then her fleshy bottom pounds back onto the floor. All the while she groans in a strange, breathy way.

I realize immediately the reason for this woman's striking transformation, for her glow of fullness. It's the possibility of release from these endless identical apartments.

The next day I go to the booth near the top of the steps leading to the supermarket and buy myself a lottery ticket from a woman whose face is full of dark splotches. But while waiting for Friday, I don't become like Ch'ŏri's mom at all. And she seems as unaffected as I. Now that her secret is out, she's about as joyful as a punctured balloon.

Friday arrives. I worry needlessly, I grow impatient, and of course I feel no joy. I have zero interest in my ticket, but I *am* interested in Ch'ŏri's mom's ticket. Mine has no possibility of being drawn, but hers is sure to be a winner. This thought is maddening. Maybe a group of lifers in prison would feel like I did if one of their number were released without reason.

With the eight million wŏn riding on that ticket, she can go out and buy herself a hillside plot in a beautiful city out in the country where the air is clean, I tell myself. And she can design her own house. She'll build a cozy home with an attic and a pointed roof. That kind of house should be mine. Ch'ŏri and his sister Nani can sit in the den in that attic, listening to the raindrops falling on the roof and reading *A Dog of Flanders*. My boys should be doing that. I *want* them to be doing that. That woman's going to steal it all away from me and give it to *her* children.

She'll plant grass in the yard, grow roses and lilacs, and make Ch'ŏri and Nani their own vegetable patch. She'll plant peas and corn and show the children the miracle of their sprouting. She'll say, "This plant is a dicotyledon and this one's a monocotyledon," and she'll smile the self-indulgent smile of a model mother. That's what *I* want to do, but that woman's going to steal it all away from me and use it up just like it's hers. I pant with vexation.

Ch'ŏri's mom seems to be suffering the same anguish. We look at each other with bloodshot eyes, pretty well played out. One of us, I'm not sure who, comes up with the idea of buying our tickets together. If one of us wins, we'll split the prize half and half. We are only too happy to agree on this.

But the ticket buying soon loses its appeal, and as our interest wanes I suddenly see the light: What am I doing wasting a hundred wŏn every Sunday when the chances of buying a winning ticket are several million to one? Sound thinking on my part.

Ch'ŏri's mom and I finally realize that nothing is happening to us that will offer a release from these identical apartments. And so it's back to our boring lives.

When the days are dull I open the curtains and let my eyes wander across to building 13, then try to calculate the total number of units in the complex. But that only makes my head swim with visions of flickering apartments.

At such times, for some strange reason I find myself disliking my boys. I can no longer stand the fact that they're twins. I get dizzy if I try to tell them apart. I can't tell who is the older and who is the younger.

When I have to ask them, I feel so miserable I want to die. The boys seem to find this hilarious. They giggle and say, "Mom, I'm older" and "Yeah, I'm younger." I'm skeptical about their quick answers and end up asking something stupid, like, "How do you boys know that?"

The boys giggle even louder and say, *"You* told us, Mom." That's right, I did. *I* told them. Otherwise, how could they have told me, all by themselves? But then how did *I* find out? Well, from the doctor. To make sure they didn't get mixed up, didn't he write down the exact times of birth on adhesive and tape it to their chests before releasing us from the hospital?

In the beginning I relied on that tape to distinguish them, but soon I didn't need it. As their mother, I learned to tell them apart before I learned anything else about them. One glance at them playing together or walking toward me, whether up close or at a distance, and I knew. For me this was natural, but others were amazed. Some people pestered me to explain the differences between the boys. But I had risen above explanation; I had a mother's intuition going for me.

But now, time and again I can't tell them apart. As my maternal intuition grows hazy, I begin to suspect the boys themselves. I'm sure the two rascals have hatched a plot: the younger will call himself the older, and vice versa. My suspicions pain me and leave me with a bad taste. If the boys keep fooling me, perhaps the day will come when they'll forget who I am. I'm convinced of it. I panic and call them to me; I won't give them any opportunity to trick me. When they appear, I inspect them from every angle so I won't forget how to distinguish them; I hug them tight, I touch them, I smell them. I try to break down their resemblance but I can't get it in my clutches. It toys with me, and I have to throw up my hands and admit defeat.

The effort wears me out and I decide to go easy on myself. So what if I get them mixed up? Two lives originated at the same time in one stomach, and existed side by side there, but out in the world it's decided that one is older and the other is younger just because the first one came out a few minutes earlier. Is there supposed to be some great significance in this?

But if the boys can be interchanged, does this mean that I, their mother, can be interchanged with another I, just like that? I shudder at this dreadful prospect; I can never let that happen. I'm swallowed up in chaos. What a cursed life if you're the mother of twins!

When I look in the mirror, I'm surprised to discover how weary and used up my face appears. You would think I've lived out my earthly days. I call Ch'ŏri's mom and ask her to help me with a facial of eggs or cucumbers. We take turns doing this. While she pretends to envy my clear, unlined face, she puts on cold cream, pats my face, rubs around and around with her fingertips, covers my face with a steaming washcloth until the skin is cooked, and after all this bustle she mixes up a concoction of eggs, honey, carrot juice, and whatnot and applies it to my face. As it dries it tightens the skin. While she's doing this, I can't laugh or talk. As we all know, if in spite of myself I laugh, I'll end up with wrinkles.

Ch'ŏri's mom is bored with herself and she chatters to me. She picks the most ridiculous stories to tell. Her aim is to make me develop wrinkles first; does she think I don't know this? "You know, girls are more fun than boys. That Nani of ours is such a bright little cutie. Yesterday she asked me, 'Mommy, who was the first diver in the world?' I try to look as if I know, and say, 'Well, I'm not sure, but I think it was an Englishman.' She holds her tummy, giggles, and says, 'Nope, it's Shim Ch'ŏng of Korea. They threw her off the boat for a sacrifice, remember?'" And then Ch'ŏri's mom cackles for the longest time. She hopes I'll laugh too. But I don't. Not because of wrinkles, but because the story isn't funny. Comedians and disk jockeys have used that particular routine a hundred times over. These days there's no fresh material. Professional comics have picked up all the good jokes, East and West, past and present, and put every possible spin on them, and they're all used up. It's like chewing something till the sweetness is gone, then spitting out the remains. All you're left with is stale wordplay. Fat chance of being amused when you feel like gagging. It's like some worthless bum has spit out a piece of gum and popped it into your mouth.

Now it's my turn to help Ch'ŏri's mom. I do unto her face as she does unto mine. A wife lying on her back with an egg facial in bright daylight looks ugly and shabby. Like a cheap, synthetic rag.

I feel bored with myself, too. To get rid of that boredom I'd like to chatter. But I'm in no mood to make her laugh. I dread the thought of the mouth in that ugly, egg-covered face opening up and showing her teeth and tongue and throat. I dread it like I would goblins appearing in daytime. I'd like to hurt that woman. The only way I can do that is to make her jealous. I'll have to tell her about when my husband and I were dating. I know, it'll sound awkward and silly, believe me, but that's what I want to do. Actually, I don't know whether I want to tell the woman or whether I want to hear it myself. And I don't know whether it's the woman or me that I want to hurt. But I ramble on anyway.

Before my husband married me he was a tall, strapping man, but whenever I saw him I felt sorry for him. This feeling came from my heart, and not for a moment did I think I was demeaning him.

We usually arranged to meet on the street. Places like bus stops were good, because no one would look at us funny for waiting there: the end of the Hongnŭng line, the Ewha University bus stop, the Midop'a Department Store bus stop, for example. It's not like we had high-class tastes; we weren't too picky for tearooms, or too poor to buy a hot drink. It's just that we fell into this pattern from the start. I got to know him after he'd finished his military service and returned to school; we ended up in the same graduating class. We preferred to see each other off-campus, and while it was no problem agreeing on the day and time for a date, it wasn't so easy settling on a place. Neither of us had a favorite tearoom, and we couldn't think of a tearoom whose name and location would stick in our memory. Places came to mind, but we weren't exactly sure how to get there. What would happen if we chose for the all-important second date a place we weren't completely sure about, and something went wrong and we didn't connect? The first thing was to make sure we connected. And so we decided to meet at the S Precinct bus stop.

The day arrived, and I went there early. From a far distance I was able to pick him out among a throng of people. He was different from the others. And that differentness was what made me feel sorry for him.

That feeling of pity deepened as I got to know him. I felt sorry for him because he looked nicer and more sincere than others. Other people had the hard, expressionless exterior of shellfish, but he displayed the softest, deepest skin a person could have, warm, gentle skin, and I pitied him for that. While others protected themselves, he was vulnerable, and I felt sorry for him.

And so I enjoyed waiting anxiously as he drew near. I enjoyed feeling sorry for him, grievously sorry.

When we were together we walked around to various places, and when we got tired we took a bus outside the city. We took these buses anywhere, as long as it wasn't a well-known recreational area, and we got off anyplace. Once you get out of Seoul the countryside is pretty much the same. There are places that reek of manure, but if you go toward the foothills, the smell is diluted to something savory. And we enjoyed the sweet scent of green things: the emerald grass, wild edibles, and vegetables that filled the green countryside fields. The green of the low, near mountains turning bluer in the distance, the higher mountains far, far off, spreading out like a blue haze, the poplars along the embankments in the paddies, the ancient trees with the magpie nests at the entrance to a village, the gently winding footpaths— it was so enjoyable to observe these ordinary scenes in his company. But what I enjoyed even more was observing him.

I liked feeling sorry for him as I watched him in a crowd, but I enjoyed observing him even more when we were alone and I didn't have to compare him with anyone else. The fact was, I liked his warmth and gentleness more when I didn't have to feel sorry for him. This was how we grew close.

The first time we kissed, we were on a grassy hill where the paddies ended and the mountains began. We were singing and being playful. My sex education had consisted of my mother and father using wild threats to scare me into believing that all men were robbers. But I was never on guard against him. Quite the opposite. I played games of childlike innocence with him, though at sudden moments I wondered apprehensively if he was one of those robbers.

Anyway, he went and hid somewhere, and a while later I suddenly felt a caterpillar crawling from the nape of my neck toward my cheek. It was disgusting! I jumped and screamed and carried on. But it wasn't a caterpillar. It was a foxtail he'd made into a mustache, and he'd sneaked up behind me to scare me with it. But unlike the face of a child who's pulled off a practical joke, his face was bright red and full of bashfulness and his eyes were sorrowful. I knew then that what he really wanted to do was kiss me, and that he was trying to disguise his desire with the foxtail. I felt compassion and pity for a man who knew no more than that about kissing, and I almost burst into tears.

I drew near to him, removed the ridiculous mustache, and kissed his warm, gentle lips. His kiss, when he was finally able to get rid of his shyness and hesitation, was long and exquisite. I liked him; liked him so much that it saddened me. He said he loved me, wanted to marry me, and I said yes. If he had said he wanted to die with me, I would have said yes.

My story and Ch'ŏri's mom's egg facial finish at about the same time. I clean her face with the hot washcloth, leaving it with a disgusting red glow, as if the cloth has cooked and removed the outer layer of skin. She slaps some strong-smelling toner on her face, shivers in delight, then produces a lascivious smile. "That creep of mine doesn't have an ounce of tenderness. He's rough like an animal. Yuck!" She produces another huge grin that shows her strong white teeth. That grinning mouth gapes at me like an open wound.

Strangely enough, the vividness of her mouth and the blunt way of comparing "that creep of mine" to an animal leaves me with a keen sensation. A hunch runs through me like a surge of electricity, and I shudder violently. The sensation is painful and pleasurable at the same time.

My life continues to be dreadfully tedious. The identical apartments of my neighbors are dreadful, my inability to tell the twins apart is dreadful, but the most dreadful thing of all is squinting through that bean-sized piece of glass to make sure it's my husband, home from work, who stands outside the door. It's dreadful to mistake your husband, inhumanly pale and chilling in the light of the twenty-watt bulb, for the Apartment Murderer.

One thing is not dreadful: my hunch that I will have an affair with Ch'ŏri's mom's "beastly creep." I love that hunch. I love it for colliding violently with my tedious life and for the sparks that collision produces. I love the way that ordinary things change colors in the light of those sparks.

I chafe all over; I simply have to do something. I itch and chafe like a wild animal that is raised on bland premixed feed but gets a taste of fresh wild food. Have you ever craved something to the roots of your teeth?

One day Ch'ŏri's mom tells me she's leaving to visit her family in the countryside. She says she'll buy some run-of-the-mill fabric for clothes for her parents—"Not a bad trade, eh, for the pepper, sesame seeds, garlic, and other stuff I'll bring back"—and she asks me to feed her children while she's gone. She has told her husband she'll be back the same day, but although her parents don't live that far away, it *is* the countryside and it *is* her parents, and if she decides to spend the night there, "the creep" isn't about to kick her out for it.

I play up to her: "Do whatever you want. It's fine by me. Spend the night. Don't worry about the apartment or the meals. I'll take care of it." I even make my eyes smile.

Everything falls into place. I bustle back and forth between the two apartments feeding the two husbands and the children and seeing them to bed.

When it's late enough, I steal over to the woman's apartment. Ch'ŏri's dad is fast asleep, and a blue nightlight burns dimly at the head of the bed. Imagine my surprise when I see him wearing the same pajamas I once went out with Ch'ŏri's mom to buy for *my* husband. I don't know if it's because of those pajamas or because of the blue nightlight, but his face looks paler and more weary than usual, and it kind of resembles my husband's. I feel compassion, but for whom? I'm not sure. I wonder if I should turn off the nightlight. A voice in my mind asks, "What if . . . ," and finally I cut the power to the apartment. Now it's pitch black.

I lie down beside him. I take his head in my arms. His hair stinks of pomade. My husband fancies the very same brand. Grin and bear it, I tell myself. I search for his lips and what I find is the smell of stale tobacco. He and my husband both smoke like chimneys. He stirs and tries to push me away. I cling to him even closer. "When did you get back?" he finally mumbles, half asleep, and reluctantly he embraces me.

His lovemaking is nervous, weak, but sadistic. He makes me feel like a public toilet. His skin gives off an unpleasant metallic odor, the kind that makes you jerk back in disgust. In all of these respects he resembles my husband. I don't even feel like I'm being adulterous. I have a bad habit of fancying myself committing adultery while in my husband's embrace, but now that I'm actually doing it, I don't feel that way. No guilt, no pleasure.

When it's over he sinks into an even deeper sleep. I've begun to doubt that this is really their apartment. I go to the children's bunkbed and reach out for them. I pass my hand along Nani's braids. It's good to have a son and daughter. All we have are sons, and twins at that.

Our children are fast asleep in their bunkbed as well.

I cover them with the quilts they've kicked aside and listen to their even breathing. My mother says that the happiest, most satisfying part of raising us was putting us to sleep, checking our breathing, and trying to imagine how nice and filial we would turn out to be. I try to be that way. But it doesn't work. I have no idea what my boys will end up doing when they grow up, or what kind of relationship they'll have with their mother. I feel emotionally cold and hopeless.

I go in the bathroom and turn on the light. I'm momentarily blinded. I want to see bright and clear what an adulteress looks like. I stand before the mirror. There I am. A woman flush with despairing innocence. A woman who looks like she's spoken with no one, consummated no relationship, in all her life.

It's so odd: my mood is one of pure despair, and yet I feel like a virgin. Here I've played the role of a wife for almost ten years, I have two children, just now I've committed adultery, and I feel like a virgin. A virgin like that is dreadful, but that's how I feel.

The Flowering of Our Lives

Kong Sŏn-ok

I leave the apartment. It's time for my daughter to return from school.

Once I asked her what she does when she comes home and I'm not there.

"Well, first I open the door and go, 'Mom!' And if you don't answer I get my piano stuff and go out."

"What about something to eat?"

"If you're home I eat. If you're not home I don't eat."

"What if you're hungry?"

"If I'm hungry I get mad and forget about it."

She put it very simply. She's eight years old and she knows how to make her case. She says its my fault that she goes hungry, and she knows it worries me, but she'll die before she makes food for herself. That makes *me* mad, and once more as I roam the windy streets I silently denounce her: Wicked girl! Why can't you try to understand your mom!

When she has morning section at school she leaves the

apartment at eight-thirty and returns at one-thirty. Once in a while—yes, once in a while—I feel comfy. And peaceful. There are times when I think I've gotten nicer. At such times, when nothing can rile me, I wait for my daughter to return. The days she goes to school at eight-thirty, I feed her and I dress her well enough so no one will *tsk-tsk* and say, "You look like you're abandoned," or worse. On those days I wait for my daughter. I wash the dishes, clean up, do the laundry, then prepare a meal I'll be proud to serve her when she returns. I'm happy then.

Not so fast, dearie, let's think about that one. In a world where mothers feed their children, is there a mother who would *not* be happy with that? If there were a mom who was unhappy cooking for her children, or a mom who felt miserable cooking for her children, could that person truly be a mom? I think such a woman would have nothing to complain about if she were beaten to death. ("Think." The same old frivolous tone—I don't like it. But I use the word anyway. I dislike that tone, but don't let my dislikes distract you from the truth of what I've written. And maybe we should take a moment to cherish the memory of every frivolous behavior we ever disliked.) In short, if there were such a woman, it shouldn't be enough to simply beat her to death. I have no doubt that such a woman would have nothing to complain about if you gathered all sorts of thugs and had them club her to death.

I'm talking in the grand manner. Shamelessly. But there's a problem, you see. I'm just the sort of woman who deserves to die like that. This horrible reality makes me despair. I can't shake my head and deny it. It's me who deserves to die at the hands of thugs.

Allow me to be more lucid. When I was twelve, when my mother wasn't home and before I had learned from the woman who was my mother that I was also a woman, around the time of my first menstrual period, I once cursed my mother. Out loud. I made a vicious face and said, "Bitch!" as if I were chewing her.

The reason was this: That woman abandoned me. More specifically, she left the house without feeding me. This mom who had no interest in whether the daughter she had given birth to was bleeding from her clamlike genitals couldn't stand the emptiness in her uterus and was often quick to leave the house. On the surface, the reason I had cursed my mother was food. Yes. But food was a simple matter. Simple because at the age of twelve I was capable of preparing rice in my mom's absence, to go with whatever side dishes were available.

Menstruation was different, though. The way my mom pronounced this word when referring to her period, hissing the *s,* was obscene. She was still having her period. My mom was still young enough to conceive. Pronounced in that sibilant way by a woman who had experienced menopause, *menstruation* didn't sound obscene. But from my mom, whose uterus still lived, that hissed word sounded wicked. Of course, I didn't really know what menstruation was. Not even in general terms. I didn't know that once you menstruated, you could carry a baby in your stomach, no matter how young you were, if you had sex with a man. And because I didn't know this, her pronunciation of *menstruation* made it sound disgusting; it made me gag. And I couldn't eat when I felt like gagging.

Why doesn't my daughter eat? Is she mad simply because of her mom's absence? Is that anger only an excuse for not eating? Is there something else she won't talk about that makes her so mad at her mom that she doesn't eat? Is she gagging because of her mom? If so, what's the real reason for that gagging?

It's all right if people want to say bad things about me. I mean, how can a gal who calls herself a mother distrust and reject her own child? Apart from the moral issue, it's just plain cruel, they could say.

The times I have a meal ready when my daughter returns from morning section, the relationship between daughter and mom is as friendly as you please. The daughter is the only object of her mom's love. Mom is a hill against which the daughter can rest, she is the spring sunshine, she is a tree whose leaves shelter a parched road in summer.

But when my daughter started going to morning section, I was already leaving the house, unable to cope with my rebellious feelings.

Mom's running away. From my distant perspective, the little ones in their colorful clothes, those children who are just like my daughter, appear to be crawling as they emerge from the school. I'm running away. I have a strong hunch that she will despair. My heart aches. But still I grow distant in my daughter's field of vision, distant from the school where the children in colorful clothes keep coming out. It's the middle of the day. I'm not ashamed of myself, but I feel like crawling away somewhere.

Sometimes my daughter has afternoon section. When I leave the house on those days, there's a place I can crawl into. A place where the red light of temptation burns in the darkness. There are roads leading far, far into that darkness. Instantly I forget my daughter. Strictly speaking, bothered as I am, I only try to forget her, but it troubles me too much to say that, and so I'm quick to say I forget her. Yes, I forget her. When she has afternoon section, she's home at five. By five o'clock, my heart aches. Because at her age it eventually becomes more difficult to deal with the arrival of what she calls The Black Night than with food. My heart aches twice as much when I run away during afternoon section, and I cry. I run away crying.

Where do I run? Sometimes the best I can do is the vegetable patch visible through the glass door to the balcony of my run-down redevelopment-zone apartment. In the summer, the area between this building and the one next to it becomes a fertile, abundant harmony of beans, potatoes, and corn. I like to sit quietly among these plants, as if building a nest. Absurd behavior for a widow with a girl. Through the thick cover of beanstalks and cornstalks I see the glass door to my balcony. The leaves of the cornstalks rustle against my flesh like the sharp blade of a fruit knife. The keen edges of those leaves show in the darkness. I shudder, quickly gaze up at the sky, and there is the moon shining all by itself.

Later in the night, the girl will drop off to sleep, wake up to the bitter reality of her mom's absence, and turn off the lights. The glass door to the balcony darkens to a black rectangle. And like the moonlight filling that rectangle, the girl's tears fill her hollow bosom and her empty stomach.

Once when I was young, without really intending it, I found myself far from home. I emerged from my house onto a road that was gloomy, hazy, distant. And windy. The shady woods were a good place to hide. As always my heart was bitter and distressed, and I poured throat-burning *soju* into that heart. The studious types used to sneak into these woods from the school library to enjoy brief trysts.

I curled into a ball. It got dark, and I felt cold. Like a stray cat I slunk off to a different place: a place near the fan vent outside the campus cafeteria. A short distance to the right of that vent, steps led up to the activity rooms. I went up those dark, spiraling steps. The door at the top was locked. From inside I heard familiar voices.

Drunk on the *soju,* I had trouble keeping myself steady. I squatted at the bottom of those dark spiral steps and listened to the familiar voices. I curled up as tightly as I could. I was terrified of being seen by unfamiliar eyes, afraid of being seen by familiar eyes. That's when I realized that the difference between terror and fear is the difference between the unfamiliar and the familiar.

Around daybreak I slowly distanced myself from what was familiar and unfamiliar. I decided not to go to that place again. That place of the unfamiliar and familiar. But where would I go instead? There was no place worth going to. I didn't have a boyfriend, and everything I encountered at my young age was unfamiliar and difficult. (I'm not confident enough to declare that I would have been able, even if I had a boyfriend then, to get rid of my perception that everything was unfamiliar. Because I was aware that it's in the nature of youth to make all the circumstances we encounter then seem unfamiliar. But can the characteristics of youth change as the result of a single lover? Ultimately, the fact that I had no boyfriend back then has little relation to the circumstances I found difficult.)

The leaves of a silver magnolia shuddered, sending raindrops pattering onto my chilly forehead and the small bridge of my nose. Dawn had faintly brightened the street before me. The raindrops falling sporadically on that street produced a musty, earthy smell. The video arcade, not yet open, came into view; and then the man who runs the College Market, producing a long, drawn-out yawn after opening his doors; and in front of that store, the studious types, back from their trysts the previous night, also producing gigantic yawns, entering the toilet with the wooden door next to the arcade.

What else was there on that street where the rain pattered down, producing the smell of earth? Broken bricks and the wreckage of tear gas canisters. I carefully hopped over them. What had I been longing for as I shivered through the night, cold and hungry? A long journey. Yes, that's what it was. I wanted to set out on a long journey. And what was at the very back of my mind as I longed for that journey? A mother waiting for a daughter who hadn't returned. That mother's sad despair.

I should have gone home the previous night. I had no reason not to. My mother was getting old, and there was no reason I should act hatefully toward her. If I had gone straight home then, I would have been comfortable enough. Mother, when she was young, felt unfamiliar to me for the sole reason that she was young. But she was older now, and she gave me the feeling of intimacy that comes with aging.

Mother's youth had faded away as I grew up. And now she was reliving that youth through me. She liked to look over my shoulder as I powdered my face in the mirror. Whether it was because her face was unpowdered or was too wrinkled for powder, Mother had a frankness and an unadorned beauty that suited her age. And so she observed me in the mirror. I was aware of her presence, but didn't let on.

"You're old now," I silently told her. "Do you envy me? Are you afraid your daughter will rebel? You know all about it, don't you? About what's squirming inside a young woman who applies lipstick and face powder. Because you went through that stage too."

Mother watched her daughter put on lipstick and pat down her cheeks with powder, took out for her the outfit that she herself had starched, set out her shoes, then watched from outside the front gate as her daughter went far, far into the distance without looking back. In Mother's presence I enjoyed infinite tranquillity and grew complacent. I didn't linger in that sense of complacency with Mother, in that tranquillity she provided me. For I didn't return home. Though there was no reason I shouldn't have.

The tranquillity was shattered. Mother would despair. The despair I had felt waiting for my young mom to return home from her outings—despair that had darkened to anger—would now oppress her. In truth, my heart ached. I cried for her despair, just as my eyes had brimmed with tears of anger when I was little. My sorrowful heart took my footsteps ever farther from Mother.

In our warm home with its warm meals, all would be tranquil with Mother and me when I crawled into her skirt, which had the musty, acrid fragrance of linen and cotton. Mother put her daughter through school by managing a fabric shop in space she rented in the innermost corner of the marketplace, where not a sliver of sunlight shone. To feed her daughter, to earn a living for the two of them, she sold musty, acrid-smelling linen and cotton. To make her daughter's breakfast and get her ready for school, she opened her shop later than other fabric shops, and to be home when her daughter returned and to make her a hot dinner, she closed earlier. Late to open, early to close meant less income. But she accepted this, and took care of her daughter. To the extent that she hadn't prepared meals for her daughter as a young woman, she did so as an older woman. And to the extent that her daughter was hungry and angry as a girl, the mother fed her and despaired when the daughter was grown.

I wished that for one day, anyway, she would come home late or not at all. I couldn't wait to fly away from the daily routine that Mother had woven so tightly about me. How I longed for the mother who was carefree in her younger days! I would have been elated if Mother had said, "Sweetie, I've got a lot of things to do today so I'll be home a little late," or "Sweetie, your mom's going out for a drink, so tonight I'll sleep at the shop" and then had a date with some man who suited her fancy. By going home a bit early I could fill up my absent mother's carefree life.

The daughter didn't join demonstrations, didn't date. The demonstrating types and the dating types led carefree lives. They slept anywhere they could in the school activity rooms and took a shot of energy from instant noodles when hungry. They were the only groups whose spirits could soar with that kind of lifestyle. The daughter wasn't a library type, either.

The mother was well aware that her daughter didn't demonstrate, didn't date, and didn't study. And so her daughter's late arrivals at home gnawed at her more and more. There was no reason for the daughter's rebellion against everything in their daily life. The mother grew anxious. And the daughter, in her anxious mother's presence, rebelled with all her might.

It was right around that time that I met Mi-suk. She was one of those good little girls with fleshy faces and regular features, and she was my classmate in civil ethics, a course I worked hard at because I'd flunked it the previous semester (it was a stupid course, but a required liberal arts course in college at the time), and if you had asked me then what I thought of her, well—she was exactly the sort I looked down my nose at, a typical-looking girl from a wealthy family who grubbed for grades regardless of the course and believed the first priority was to graduate without incident. And I was exactly the sort that Mi-suk, if she didn't openly scorn, would at least laugh at with her eyes for having no clear sense of moral obligation and for showing off and drifting along without good reason, like, for example, the group of our classmates who "devoted their youth to the reform line."

She couldn't stand being sidetracked from the daily schedule her sort observed. To give you an idea, for her it was up at six, lunch at noon, dinner at seven, and bed at midnight. Who would have imagined that I would meet this girl Mi-suk when I finished my overnight rebellion and was returning home at dawn like a prodigal daughter, smelling of earth and asking myself if I shouldn't have returned to my mother, who would remember this incident even in her dreams? Mi-suk and her sort were the library types only during exam time, when they left no seats for the truly studious; they always enjoyed the sunshine. We were having midterms then, and Mi-suk, in bed at midnight and up at six, and evidently bound for the library to find a seat when I saw her approaching me on my way home from my one-night rebellion, shot me a meaningful smile. The moment I saw her, our morning rebellion began. We went to the woods, where the sun was rising.

"On your way to the library?" I asked.

She uncapped a bottle of *soju* with her teeth and laughed. "No. It's just that I can't stand not drinking."

"You *what?*"

I regretted the question and produced a quick little smirk to conceal that regret.

"It's a complete mess."

I let those words sink in. I was about to ask *what* was a complete mess, but decided a direct question would be one more source of regret.

"Why not embrace that mess?" I said instead. And silently I asked her: Wouldn't that be much more like your real self? I can understand your truthfulness this morning. Maybe that's the only kind of truthfulness we have in our lives. Whether there's a reason for it or not. Maybe this truthfulness is the flowering of our lives. Lonely flowers with difficult names, blooming from the wasteland of our messy lives. Sometimes fragrant, sometimes bland, poking out their heads from the core of our lives at a time like this, just when the sun is rising, or in the evening when it's setting. People all around are intoxicated by the fragrance, and collapse exhausted from the banality.

I left. The sun penetrated the shade where Mi-suk had uncapped the *soju* bottle. Drinking in the shade of the woods while the sun came up—was this how Mi-suk rebelled? Probably. I smiled. I wanted to applaud her rebellion, but the morning sunshine was cruelly bright and shrunk me. The part of me that wanted to applaud her grew dispirited. Such desolate beauty and dazzling cruelty in all the rebellion of our lives.

I set out for home and Mother. My mind was no longer agitated; I could go to her now. The sun was directly above, and the familiar alley stretched out ahead with its promise of a familiar and tedious daily existence.

On that lazy morning when the sun was directly above, if my mother hadn't come into sight, I might have gone inside and felt repentant. Mother appeared, though, and instinctively I hid. There was nothing about her to be afraid of. Mother was exhausted waiting for me. Well, it wasn't surprising, considering she'd been standing at the front gate and craning her neck as she peered through teary eyes for the daughter who hadn't returned the previous night.

But the instant that image of her came into sight, I was overcome with a feeling of contrariness. Shuddering, and still hiding, I moved away from her. And I cried. As I cried, I realized that I longed for warmth but was also capable of walking a long, cold road.

That night, during an interval when Mother was not out in the alley waiting, I went inside. Again I grew cold in the presence of my weeping mother. From the moment I returned home, I fanatically plunged myself back into my daily life. And as I stood before my weeping mother I had an uneasy feeling about the spell that my brief breakaway had cast over me, a spell whose lustrous rays penetrated deep to the core of my daily existence.

These are my recollections.

They were nasty times.

Would Mi-suk agree?

Recalling one of those nasty times, a time I can remember only as nasty, I leave the apartment. Why do I recall that period? Much time has passed since that nastiness. It's far off, far, far in the past, so why should it rise to the surface of my consciousness, or rather, why should I raise it? I'm not going to say yet. What I *will* say is that it can be a sort of vindication. Toward the end of this story I can tell you that the truth of this uninteresting account can offer a feeble vindication of my unexplainable rebellion.

Allow me, at this point, to reveal my true identity. You're probably wondering: What kind of woman is this? Why does she confuse us by saying things like "rebellious thoughts" when the simple fact of the matter is that she leaves her daughter alone at home?

Well, I'm a widow. The widow of a public official who died in the line of duty. As the widow of a bottom-level public official, I get by entirely on the measly pension he left me. It's a perilous existence.

My livelihood is tenuous. It's a struggle to buy even the basic necessities. Get a job, I tell myself, get a job. But I procrastinate. When my daughter was a baby, I told myself I'd look for a job when she was in preschool; and then—it's true—around the time she was going to preschool, I told myself I'd look for a job when she was in grade school. This is the fifth year I've been telling myself to get a job.

An uncertain everyday existence easily gives birth to an uncertain awareness of things. The one is cruel to the other. My recollections consist of old, wornout notions that have accumulated in my uncertain awareness. But my day-to-day existence is forever contradicting those notions. I sense a contrariness in those notions I've come to call recollections. And now, when I escape from home at the time my daughter returns from school, the notions are embodied in reality. Free of my daughter, I slowly follow a long, indistinct road, bewitched by a light burning in the darkness.

As always, the lights in the Emperor Cabaret are red, and Nam Chin-i, who appeared there from the eighth to the tenth, is still smiling today, the twelfth, in the ten posters at the entrance. Smiling in multivision.

My first stop is this cabaret. Here I am, falling from grace again. Su-ja in her black scarf, sitting off in a corner, beckons me. I feel like I'm swimming as I approach her.

I'm going to have to offer a partial explanation. My present situation is due purely to her.

I really know little about this woman. I haven't known her that long. One night—yes, a night when the moon was bright— I was sitting quietly, making my nest in the vegetable patch, and someone came up to me. Or maybe I should say she found herself beside me. She was driven by a need.

I could tell she'd been drinking. Her apartment was right in front of her, but her bladder must have been overflowing and she couldn't wait, and she ran to where I was making my nest. She apparently didn't see me among the lush growth of corn. Wanting to observe the greatest courtesy toward her, I didn't make known my presence as she relieved herself.

I had seen her once before, at the neighborhood bathhouse. And there I was overwhelmed by the sight of her huge breasts. She wasn't so much washing those breasts, which were massive compared with her build, as giving them a bath. I conjured an image of the husband of a large-breasted woman, and his abundant happiness. And the flat breasts of a husbandless woman. My breasts.

We took turns scrubbing each other's back. As she scrubbed mine, her voluminous breasts touched me. Long afterward I remembered more vividly the intermittent touch of those swaying breasts than the sensation of the hands that rubbed me. Later I fell in the habit of seeking out that big-breasted woman when I went to the baths. Like a little girl, I wanted through the vivid sensation of those breasts to bury myself in her.

It was strange. Because it's not easy for a flat-chested woman to feel kindly disposed toward a larger woman. It's similar to the way a woman who's not pretty feels about a woman who is pretty. But my feelings toward Su-ja were something I hadn't anticipated. Perhaps it was her frail build, which appeared to have concentrated all of her strong desire toward life in those breasts. I knew that instinctively.

"Your breasts are so pretty," I ventured, head down, as I entrusted my back to her.

"Pretty? Big and stupid-looking, I'd say."

"Better than my little ones, though."

"True. I make my living off of these big boobs."

I smiled. Instantly I could understand her. My flat breasts could understand another woman's full breasts. Flat breasts and full breasts could accommodate each other. It was right that her breasts should be large in order for her to eat. This women and I, one large-breasted and the other flat, lived in the same apartment building.

I separated the cornstalks and revealed myself. She had just finished.

Recognizing me, she flashed a big grin. "You saw me?"

I nodded

"I thought only the moon was watching," she said.

We both giggled.

"I never dreamed you might catch me here," I said.

"And just what have you been up to?"

"Pooping. How about that?"

"Well, I can't let you alone now."

"And what if I don't let *you* alone?"

She produced a bottle of *soju* from her bag.

"Anyway, here's to us and our perfect crime—cheers!"

It was a satisfying ending to my day-long rebellion. My tipsiness could help prevent me from despairing too hastily in the presence of my daughter's despair. I could finally look at my daughter as once again she despaired cruelly in the presence of her brazen, undespairing mom, despaired precisely because of that lack of despair. Would I grow flustered in her presence? Or would I be indifferent? Was I running away from not having a reason, and toward having a reason? Is that what drinking does to me?

I dare to christen that lack of a reason "the flowering of our lives." First my daughter showers me with arrows of criticism. And she opposes me by not eating. Perhaps one of these days when Mom is intoxicated by the scent of those flowers, my daughter will suffocate and the next moment be dead and gone. That is something quite possible to imagine.

I had a call from Su-ja. She'd been to a restaurant on the South Han River that specializes in spicy fish soup. First she'd set up a fishing pole. The riverside breeze was refreshing. She'd ordered *soju,* not bothering with soup. The woman who ran the restaurant acted like a big sister to her. It was all part of a scheme cooked up by the woman. The men who then made advances to Su-ja were old-timers, most of them. Su-ja didn't mind. Generally they were content when she accepted and sipped drinks and ate to her heart's content. For the old guys at this riverside soup house with the balmy breeze, one whiff of a young woman's cosmetics set their manhood throbbing.

Days when business was good for Su-ja were not so frequent. And it seems that manhood is seasonal. When the willows droop over the South Han riverside in front of the fish soup place, when a hot, sticky breeze blows among those willows, that's when a whiff of a young woman's cosmetics seeps into a man's nostrils with a balsam scent.

Su-ja grew persistent in her phone calls: "This opportunity's too good to miss."

Hardly had that opportunity, that balmy breeze, passed me by than she called yet again: "Have to take advantage of this weather. It's a perfect day for perfume," she whispered. At other times she talked as if she were singing a song. "The breeze is up. Put on your dress and make an appearance. Something cotton with polka dots—they'll love it. And a span bra underneath. Don't put up your hair. Just let it fly in the wind."

I turned her down every time. I didn't know her very well. But that's not why I turned her down. I guess I just couldn't get rid of the impression that for her, rebellion and daily existence were practically one and the same.

She benefited from her large breasts, made a living from them, and that's as much as I knew about her. I could also guess that the life of a woman whose large breasts were a help to her had its ups and downs. With such reasons, I couldn't be jealous of her full breasts, at least not because my own were flat. Her breasts were her life's sole support.

What I regarded as rebellion was for her a daily existence. When a day of rebellion became a day like any other, when it became one's life, there was no longer any reason to criticize it. I was disgusted by my rebellion, which had not become my daily existence. It wasn't my only means of sustenance, needless to say, and when it became a weapon that shattered my daily existence, when it shook me out of the lethargy of that existence, when it became a sharp knife that pierced the deepest recesses of my consciousness, I felt despair.

"Listen, there's no need to mope. Look, I'm here beside the terminal, at the Emperor Cabaret. Look once or twice down that alley with the bright lights, and it'll catch your eye right off. Go on in. Smell that aroma of alcohol. And what's better than the smell of a man?"

You bitch, I said to myself over and over as I listened to Su-ja's voice. My daughter wasn't home yet. But while I was calling myself a bitch, I was restless. Mom, the playgirl. I hooted in laughter. Had I caught the playgirl syndrome? Was this the cause of all these problems? I had to scoff at these questions. To be honest, I had never considered whether I was moral or immoral, and the thought of those two words in conjunction with the playgirl syndrome seemed incongruous. As did the question of whether I could state out of hand that the contrariness within me is either moral or immoral.

As a matter of fact, while I'm on the subject of morality and immorality, I was once cursed by a man. I say *cursed* because I strongly felt he was contemptuous of me.

It must have been about a month after my husband died. This man was my husband's protegé and my friend from college. He had worked in one of the political movements, but in spite of his activism he had a broad tolerance for the way people live. For example, he knew how to maintain warm, accepting relationships with former comrades such as my husband who had immersed themselves in new lives. At that time, about a month after my husband's death, he was a fugitive. I told him I was grateful that he, treated like a family member during my husband's lifetime, had come to visit a desolate, bereaved family. Weren't we both equally desperate? I thought. But before I could finish telling him how grateful I was, this protegé of my husband, a man my husband had always considered part of the family, told me I was immoral, or at least amoral.

Was this talk of morality and immorality intended? Perhaps so, but he was also my friend, and had never failed to address me with formal respect.

I didn't know what to make of his crude reference to immorality and morality. As I tried to collect myself, he continued:

"I've seen it in you. Often you didn't go back home, did you? No one knew why. But now the truth behind your behavior is clear. It's been going on for a long time, but I saw it back then. You did it in college, didn't you? We were friends then, and I saw you come out of the woods that time and huddle up at the bottom of the spiral stairs to the activity rooms. We couldn't bring you into our ranks. It was a matter of basic qualifications. There had to be some reason for a person's behavior. Back then, it wasn't clear in your case what that reason was. But now it's come to light: You're immoral, or at least amoral. To put it bluntly. . . ."

I was well aware of my behavior, for which there was no apparent reason. That behavior had caused my mother to despair, and then my husband, and now my daughter. But I couldn't accept those pointed words from my husband's protegé, my friend, and apply them to my unexplainable behavior. Things visible are not all there is to the world. There also exist things unseen. And things unexplainable. So how can we say that only things with a reason can exist in this world? They're rising up, those unexplainable things, and when they rebel all together, the things with reasons grow feeble in their presence. How can I explain this to a man who speaks of such things as morality and immorality?

No, it's not the playgirl syndrome. It's not something that vulgar. It's what I've called flowers. Fragrant flowers. Flowers that occasionally poke their heads through the chaos of our lives.

I enter the Emperor Cabaret muttering about my never-changing fall from grace. Correction: I've plainly said the playgirl syndrome is vulgar, I believe that myself, and I've concluded that my visits to the Emperor Cabaret are part of that fall from grace; and yet there clearly exists in that conclusion an element of realization, an element that *is* changing. And if so, how is that element of change to be explained?

And what exactly do we mean by a fall from grace? If it means immorality, then what exactly are morality and immorality? Where is the boundary between them?

In any event, there's no way my visit to the cabaret today is a fall from grace. Because I believe that the unexplainable contrariness inside me is a quality that cannot be judged against standards of morality and immorality. Yes, I entered the cabaret muttering about my never-changing fall from grace, but as I walk toward the fluid chaos inside, I'm in high spirits, and I pointedly remind myself, "This isn't a fall from grace; it's that damned contrariness inside me."

I swim right over to the corner where Su-ja sits, beckoning me.

Su-ja looks terrific. Looks so marvelous I want to burst out laughing. Su-ja is heartbreakingly beautiful in the Emperor Cabaret tonight. From a distance, it's just a black scarf she's wearing, but on closer inspection, the scarf is terrific too, the black fabric glittering with zigzag gold thread.

"Su-ja, you look terrific."

I greet her with a friendly slap on the palm. Su-ja laughs. At the mention of the word *terrific,* she seems as unaffected as a little girl. Su-ja, terrific and perky. Tonight I've decided to let her cast a spell over me. That spell is enough to handle my soaring contrariness.

"It's the pits if you're alone. Especially in a cabaret."

"Do you really care?"

"I wasn't always like this, you know."

"You're more the fish soup house type?"

"No putdowns, please. I'm in a tailspin. Got three kids. I'm desperate. If business is no good, then I'm wasting my time, wasting my money, and the day goes to hell. And whether business is good or bad, being at a place like this is disgusting."

Su-ja, disgusted whatever the circumstances. Sad Su-ja. Yes, she's in a tailspin, and tonight she has rotten luck. Apart from me, no one gives Su-ja of the Black Scarf a second look.

"I think it's my fault you had rotten luck tonight," I tell her.

"No, it's always like that. The sons of bitches have something wrong with their eyes."

Su-ja is in a rotten mood: no luck that night, or, more precisely, no man to hook who would get her out of that tailspin.

The distance to her house is short enough to walk, but she flags a taxi.

"We're off!" she shouts with a flourish. "Today's not the end of the world. Driver, head for the station!"

"The station? You're going to hop a train somewhere?"

"Nooo. We're going there to have a drink."

I meekly go along with her idea. Because alcohol has always meant the completion of my unexplainable rebellion. Until now, at least. The truth of my feeble rebellions is the belief that they're completed through the temporary effect of alcohol. But isn't it time that I revealed the reality of my rebellions? Did I say they were unexplainable? How irresponsible of me. How sickening. The flowering of our lives—is that how I put it? How childish and hackneyed.

I rebel because I'm distressed. And what is it that distresses me? Let's make sure you heard me, because this is a question that pricks me to the core. What is it that distresses me? As I follow Su-ja I repeat this question, but I have no way to answer it. I follow Su-ja to her cafe. That's what I insist on calling the drinking place she runs. It's in a basement and the interior looks dark. Three of us go down the steps: me, Su-ja, and a man. The man who cursed his life as a taxi driver, saying he'd had rotten luck, that he hadn't made his fare quota for the day. And the weather is gloomy; it puts him in a foul mood. Not meeting his quota, the gloomy weather—nothing's turned out right. So why not accept Su-ja's offer of a drink? He's had a shitty day, and it's clear now that he wants to get away with as much as he can. And all along, he keeps bitching.

"No reason to bitch about your life just because you don't meet your quota."

Su-ja is like a big sister as she serves him drinks. Su-ja, playing the big sister. Telling him not to curse his life, offering him drinks so he'll feel better. I don't miss what happens next. The man is looking at big-sisterly Su-ja's chest. At the cleft of her breasts, revealed as she bends over to pour him a drink. Su-ja's pride and joy. Her lifeline.

I see it today. A full-breasted woman's lonesome existence, which I saw when I first met her at the bathhouse.

I drink in distress, wondering what's distressing me; the man drinks while pretending to be angry at his "bitch of a life" and sneaking looks at Su-ja's breasts; and Su-ja drinks while selling this man drinks and pretending to soothe him by telling him there's no reason to curse his life.

I can't remember falling asleep.

"Sell any drinks?" I ask Su-ja.

"Hell, no. Damn his life and mine! He cleaned me out and took off!"

"You mean we both fell asleep?"

Su-ja titters instead of answering. Her mouth is coated with peanut skins where her face touched the table as she slept.

We both giggle. The giggling soon turns into a mixture of tears and laughter.

"Did our gentleman friend make his quota here?"

"I hope so—thanks to us. We should feel real proud of ourselves."

Off we trudge. It's a long way home. The dawn wind is chilly.

"He really cleaned me out. Didn't even leave a bus token. God only knows what all the bitching was about. Fucking jerk!"

The wind is cold. It digs up the heartburn that comes with too much alcohol and sneaks into its place.

I start to run. I give a reason. I say I'm running because of the wind, because the wind is cold. I embrace the wind and run. I hear Su-ja shouting from behind.

"No big deal. We can go to the South Han. That fish soup place, remember? How about it? We'll make out fine there, I guarantee it."

I give her a nod and keep running. In the presence of a big-chested woman's rebellion, a rebellion that's her daily existence, in the presence of a life that cannot be lived if one doesn't rebel, I watch as my unexplainable rebellion, the days of my feeble rebellion, which I dare to call the flowering of our lives, fall miserably to their knees.

On this cold, windy dawn, Su-ja goes to the fish soup place on the South Han.

I walk slowly, now that it's light. My pace has shrunk. I arrive at the vegetable patch with all of its radish sprouts, beans, and corn. The glass door of my balcony appears up ahead. The sun has just risen, and its rays steal into the thickets within the patch. And up to my balcony door. And over my shadow.

My shadow projects midway between the sun-streaked vegetable patch and my balcony door. I collapse onto my shadow. I struggle to extend my arms, and hug my shadow.

The sun is bright.

WAYFARER

O Chŏng-hŭi

The snow had started that morning. Hye-ja opened the window, sat on the sill, and watched the carefree flakes turn the world giddy. The neighborhood was still, the snow muffling every tiny, squirming noise. There were no calls for the baseballs that came flying into her yard several times a day, no sound of children sneaking over the wall after them. When the young woman who rented the room near the front gate worked the day shift, the neighbor children had taken advantage of the house being left empty and climbed over the wall. Hye-ja would have her hands full putting a stop to it. The day she had returned home, a boy nonchalantly climbed over the wall, glancing at her where she leaned against the door to the veranda watching him. When finally she shouted "Hey!" the boy protested: "We do this all the time, me and the other kids. When nobody's home, what are we supposed to do?" Strangely, the boy's grumbling had reassured her. It had helped her dismiss the notion that the house was haunted, that the cursed, unkempt garden was being kept by some wicked ogre.

Now and then a layer of snow weighing down the bare branches plummeted to the ground and the sparrows searching for food took wing. There were no footprints in the snow between the rented room and the gate; the young woman must not have left for work yet.

Hye-ja went out to the yard and gathered a handful of snow. The white blanket came up to her ankles. If it kept coming down like this, it would easily be knee-deep by nightfall. She ought to sweep it away, she told herself, but she didn't move. The sound of a piano, an unadorned, inelegant melody, had caught her attention. Hye-ja sang along in a soft voice:

> *Hills, fields, trees*
> *Under white, white snow.*
> *We grow up pure of heart, you know.*

She had sung this ditty as a child, and so had her own children. Probably some young mom, alone at home with time on her hands after sending her children off to school, had been watching the snowflakes fall when the melody had come to mind and she had tapped it out on the keyboard.

The music abruptly stopped, leaving Hye-ja standing blankly, mouth open. In the profound silence, her dream of the night before came back to her.

She had first dreamed this dream as a child, but the last time had been long enough ago that she had almost forgotten it. In this dream she was on a street, always the same street, following an endless stone wall, a mossy, crumbling structure that resembled an ancient fortress wall suffering from neglect. "Where am I? I've been here before," she would murmur happily enough, taken with the familiar ambience of the place. She followed that wall seemingly forever, because she had a hunch, which became a conviction, that if she reached into one of the crevices where the wall was worn and crumbling, she would surely find a token of something that had been promised her—a small, pretty button, a secret mark, a tiny, folded piece of paper. But then she would awaken. She couldn't identify the street, not at the beginning of the dream, not at the end; all she did was wander it. Awakening from the dream meant yet again the loss of this street she had constantly followed, and the return of that helpless sensation of being deserted. She felt like a lost child. Where could that street be leading? And why did it all seem so familiar? Her old, wraithlike mother, who was still alive, would have answered right away in her lucid, precise manner: It was the road to the otherworld, or else a road traveled in a former life. That Hye-ja was having this dream again after almost two years offered a hint, no, an assurance, that she was actually back home.

Her hands were growing numb. The snow she clutched was melting. Hye-ja wiped her wet hands on her clothes, stamped the snow from her feet, and returned inside. Her room and the veranda were utter chaos, and it seemed she was always stepping on a water glass, a rag, a transistor radio, her pajamas, and other such things. It was only natural. She had returned home a week earlier and hadn't tended to the house since. Of course she cooked to satisfy her malignant hunger, but the dirty dishes would be shoved aside. She would fill the bathtub and soak for hours, until the hot water cooled, chilling her, and then, without bothering to dress, she would pace the darkened veranda. Two days earlier she had spent much of the day gazing at her daughter's yellow, flower-shaped hairpin, which she had found in a crack in the concrete patio out back. The girl, now in her last year of middle school, was long past the age of using such hairpins.

Her mother-in-law had lived here until the month before, looking after Hye-ja's husband and the two children. But now the house was empty except for Hye-ja's belongings. What to do with Hye-ja when she comes home from the hospital? There must have been a lot of discussion and thought. And finally her husband had made a clean break, removing her name from the family register and turning over the house to her—a rather unusual display of concern on his part. "I'll be moving out before too long," he had told her after the doctor said she was ready for discharge. "One option, if you don't want to go back to the house, is to sell it and get yourself a small apartment. Coming from me, maybe that idea doesn't appeal to you, but an apartment would have its advantages. And you could stay with your family till the house is sold. . . ." Hye-ja hadn't seen him since. In any event, for an ex-husband, he had sounded considerate. Technically she had initiated the divorce, and he tended to agree it was unavoidable. But while she was in the hospital? That seemed to have pained him.

Hye-ja had returned to this house, though, as soon as she was discharged. Humans are forgetful creatures, the doctor had said. She was completely healthy, mentally and physically. She could live a full life, like she had before. And she shouldn't be afraid; that was the most important thing. As if resting after a long journey, she felt extremely lazy. Now and then she was startled into a sense of reality by the sound of the telephone and the voices of people seeking her departed husband and children. "No, they're not here, they moved. . . . I don't know." Curt, blunt responses and the conversation was over, after which she would frantically rummage through the house for some trace of them. It was as if she wanted to obliterate all the time she had been away. The stickers on the wall, the long, black strands of glossy hair in the hairbrush, the handkerchief with the embroidered corner—she discovered these and other traces, but all they did was make her powerfully, vividly aware of the enormous gap that now separated her from them. They wouldn't be coming back, and she could never recover the hours she'd been away from them. Hadn't they been capable of the stronger ties that a deeper love offered? Even if they couldn't conceal from each other the shame and fear that lurked persistently in the depths of their hearts? After scouring the house one last time she had clasped her arms about her upraised knees and silently sobbed. After she had cried herself to exhaustion, she felt a gentle gnawing in her empty stomach. That familiar hunger was like an old friend who had come to comfort her.

The doorbell jarred Hye-ja awake. Her late lunch of cold rice mixed with spicy pepper paste had been followed by a short nap. Who could it be? Confused and startled, she opened the door to the veranda just as the bell rang again. "Registered mail! Your seal, please!" The mailman's cap was visible above the iron gate. Flustered by the mailman's insistence, doubting that anyone could have sent her a registered letter, she opened the vanity drawers in succession from force of habit. Most were empty and sure enough, her seal wasn't there. "I don't have it!" Hye-ja shouted in agitation toward the gate. "For god's sake, then use your thumb!" came the response.

The letter was for Hye-ja's tenant. There was no sign of life from across the yard, and the young woman's kitchen door, which gave access to her room, was padlocked. Hye-ja pushed the kitchen window open, deposited the letter, and went back inside. As she steadied her pounding heart, her hand stopped in the act of closing the yawning drawers of the vanity. There it was, her little appointment book, long forgotten but certainly hers, smudged by her own hands. She fished it out and hastily turned the pages. "29th: Tŏksu Palace"; "dry-clean winter suit"; "16th: 3 p.m., Araya"; "Shinsegye, Bargain Sale, 15th-21st, woolen shirt & vest"—among these notes were items faintly remembered but many she couldn't recall. "3rd: Umi Florist, flower basket, mixed carnations X 60"—a gift for a teacher's sixtieth-birthday celebration? Sometimes smiling, sometimes frowning as she searched her memory, Hye ja read the entries one by one. In the back was a column of telephone numbers, those of her college classmates. They were members of a circle, friends who met once a month, women she felt comparatively close to. Why had she never thought of them? Finally, something to do. She began quickly to dial. First the editorial offices at the women's magazine where Suk-ja worked. But Suk-ja had long since left, she was informed. Then Ae-gyŏng's house. "The number you have dialed is out of service; please check the number and try again." She examined the arabic numerals and redialed. Same result. It was strange. She felt bewitched. Myŏng-hwa's telephone rang incessantly—no answer. Patiently she dialed Ch'un-ja at home. "Not at this number anymore," a voice answered curtly before disconnecting. Hye-ja replaced the receiver and let her mind go blank, oppressed for the first time by the enormous reality of the two years she had lost. She felt bitter and betrayed.

This'll be the last one, she swore to herself, and like a gambler staking her destiny on her last card, she dialed the fifth number with grim determination. She heard ringing and then "Hello," and immediately Chŏng-ok's face rose before her. She forced herself to speak slowly: "Chŏng-ok? It's me, Hye-ja." "Oh, my goodness! My goodness!" This ambiguous exclamation was followed by silence. Hye-ja imagined a terrified look on Chŏng-ok's face, the look of someone who had received a call from the dead. "It's been a long time." "It really has. How is your health?" Chŏng-ok finally added, still flustered. "Where are you?" "I'm home now. How are the others doing? I haven't been able to reach anybody." "Well, that's understandable—a lot of us have moved."

Hye-ja told her friend she would like to see her. There was a brief pause. "Well, as it turns out, we're throwing a farewell party for Pong-sŏn. She's going overseas with her husband. Remember the Sky Lounge on the thirteenth floor of the Kolon Building, in Kwanggyo? We're meeting there at seven o'clock. Everyone'll be happy to see you."

Next, Hye-ja telephoned the puppet show institute. Min, her teacher there, made puppets but he also played an important role in producing the shows. He had produced puppet shows on television—*The Scarlet Hat* and *Master Sun and Mistress Moon*—using puppets Hye-ja had made. Back then Min had praised the originality of her conceptions and the puppets' lifelike expressions. He had piqued her interest by suggesting she hold an exhibition. But now Hye-ja discovered that in Min's case as well, the two years had made a difference. Though she gave her full name when he answered—Kim Hye-ja—Min failed to make the connection. She had to explain she was the creator of the puppets in *The Scarlet Hat* and *Master Sun and Mistress Moon,* and finally Min uttered a faint exclamation. He then slipped immediately into his usual tone: "It's been a while, hasn't it. How have you been?" He must have known all about it, too. Among the people who knew "how she had been," she had no doubt been fodder for dozens of stale conversations. "How is your health?" he asked. "Couldn't be better. Are you still doing puppet shows?" She wished to talk at great length. He'd been kind to her; he'd liked her puppets. "Why don't you come around sometime when you're free," he suggested. She wanted to say she could see him right then, that she had three or four hours till her dinner appointment, but she reluctantly set down the receiver, tempering her regret with the realization that he was perpetually busy. He was so taken with his work that he was still single in his forties, writing books about puppet shows and rushing from little theaters to grade school auditoriums to broadcasting stations. Even so, he wouldn't have forgotten his interest in displaying her puppets. He wouldn't have forgotten his suggestion that she hold an exhibition and do a puppet show in the exhibition hall itself. She had to see him, the following day if possible. She could resume making puppets. With her puppet shows she could tour schools on remote islands and other out-of-the-way places. And if she supplied each of the schools with a set of puppets from the show at a low price, then the children could set up little theaters at home and have their own puppet shows. Wouldn't that be fun. This was exactly the kind of meaningful work she wanted, and she could earn a bit of money doing it. It would be a wonderful thing to do, and it made perfect sense. If she could live on her own earnings, she would for the first time be independent, would have an existence genuinely her own. Determined to begin creating puppets again, she felt a sudden burst of vitality. And then she scolded herself relentlessly for the disgraceful life she had led, a life that had been parasitic pure and simple. That evening she would tell her friends what she was doing now. She would tell them her rosy plans for the future. After all, did any of them know as much about puppets and puppet shows as she did? It wouldn't be stretching the truth to talk about the exhibit she'd do with Min, her teacher, and about the touring performances. True, they hadn't been arranged, but they would be sooner or later, she was sure of it. Hadn't Min always shown an interest in her puppets? Maybe it was all in her mind, that business about herself being the focus of repeated conversations among her friends. And Min's initial failure to recognize her on the phone, the electric shock of recognition, the evasiveness she had read into his vague invitation to visit—wasn't she acting out some sort of victimization complex? Other people don't have as much interest in us as we think they do, her doctor had said. And they don't remember us for as long as we think they should. To Min and her friends, the story about her was merely a single short column buried in the evening newspaper one summer day two years before. Had they spent the last two years making sure they remembered this unfortunate incident involving an acquaintance of theirs? Of course not. While they were raising children, accumulating property, and clutching greedily for some joy in their lives, she had been killing time with endlessly tedious games of cat's-cradle, sitting in the sun from one to three in the afternoon, enduring those stupid question-and-answer sessions with her doctor, and all the while cherishing a desire to put that incident out of her mind. Instead of following her husband's suggestion to change her surroundings she had returned home. And a very good thing it was. If not for the solitude of the empty house, if not for the despair of being alone, would she have thought of resuming her work with puppets? Would she have turned up that little address book?

Hye-ja went up to the attic. Her basement workshop had been filled with odds and ends and locked up, and she had packed her work things in a huge trunk and stored it in the corner of the attic.

Thick dust coated the trunk. The ornamental lock had rusted, but was open. And there, under a single sheet of newspaper, were her things, just as she had left them. Sections of wire mesh of various thicknesses, tubes of hardened adhesive, dyed feathers, a handful of sparkle, the faces of the weaver and the herdsman, and the unfinished winged clothes of the fairy. Strangely, she felt pangs of sorrow as one by one she uncovered these things lying silently like ashes in the trunk she herself had closed and no one had opened. And when she had brought them all into view, the heads, arms, and legs, the remnants of fabric for the various costumes— all of it swept haphazardly into the trunk—another layer of newspaper appeared. She closed her eyes and took a deep breath. She knew all too well what lay hidden there at the bottom, entrenched like a rock in the depths of her bosom. It was her last creation, the lovely princess, sunk deep in a century-long slumber from which she couldn't awaken. Hye-ja had dressed her, was ironing her gorgeous dress one last time—and then it had happened. With trembling hands she removed the newspaper, and there was the face of the princess, lush hair streaming proudly through her coronet. There was her body. And there in her gorgeous costume, like so many severed links of a chain, were the glittering, golden remains of moths.

The snow had dwindled to flurries and the distant skies were clearing in spite of the approaching dusk. It was four o'clock. Plenty of time until Hye-ja's meeting with her friends, but she began to prepare. She couldn't deny the joy and excitement she felt at the prospect of leaving this house where loneliness settled along with the night. She washed her face, then took her time with makeup. At night there was no problem if it was a bit thick. Besides, wasn't this the night she'd finally see her best friends, people to whom her outward appearance didn't matter? She flung open her wardrobe and one by one inspected the clothes on their hangers, but found nothing she cared to go out in. She hadn't tried on those clothes for two years, and she'd gained an enormous amount of weight. She would have been the first to admit that their shapes and colors weren't suitable, but what really depressed her, after she had tried on practically all of them, was not being able to button a single one. Finally she came across something that fit, a sack dress that was fashioniable a decade earlier. It had been made for her, a loose black velvet dress with a great white collar, a dress that fell like a cape from her shoulders. The times she wore it outside the house to meet her husband after work, he had said she looked like quite the little girl—implying that she was too old for it. He was particular about what she wore. And Hye-ja, who followed new fashions closely, had soon stopped wearing it. She realized now how much heavier she was, for the dress confined her as if she actually were inside a sack. She gathered her long hair in a clasp and then looked in the mirror. The person she saw resembled a silent-movie actress.

The glass door to the veranda rattled open and in came the voice of Hye-ja's tenant: "Auntie, I'm going out. Could you please close my coal duct a little later?" Apparently she'd returned while Hye-ja had been rummaging through the trunk. Hye-ja scowled toward the front gate as she heard it open and shut. The young woman had said she worked at a factory where she had day shift one day and night shift the next, but as far as Hye-ja could tell, she'd brought a man home three times in the past week. "That's no good—I should get rid of her," she muttered decisively. "I have better things to do than tend coal for that slut. Ought to tell her I'm selling the house and ask her to vacate, ought to do it right away, tomorrow."

Hye-ja waited until five o'clock, then donned her coat and left. Even with the snow slowing down traffic, she could get to the meeting place in thirty or forty minutes. Still, she left hurriedly, as if being ushered out of her empty house by the gathering darkness.

Deposited by the bus on the broad avenue of Chongno with plenty of time to spare, Hye-ja descended into the pedestrian underpass that crossed to the other side. The poorly ventilated passage stank, and was slushy with tracked-in snow. The subway rumbled underfoot. To the busy stream of people beneath the pale lights Hye-ja gave unguarded looks as she slowly walked along.

The snow had stopped for good, and the darkening streets were windy. At the underpass exit Hye-ja took a deep breath and gained her bearings. She hadn't been downtown in a long while, but her mental map was clear. As she set off, she glimpsed the frozen fountain near the clock tower, which read five-forty, and next to the fountain the giant Christmas tree whose tiny lights were just starting to twinkle. And then, floating hazily in the distance beyond the tree with its coat of pure white were the lights of the Sky Lounge on the thirteenth floor of the Kolon Building. There were no crosswalks, which meant three more underpasses to negotiate. She had more than enough time, though. Should she arrive early and sit there all by herself? No, that wouldn't look good. As she scanned the surroundings for a place to thaw out over coffee, her gaze settled on a brown building across the street and to the left. At that very instant, the Kolon Building, the large tree with its blinking lights, and all the rest, were swept from her field of vision. She saw nothing but that fifteen-story building in which every window was lit. Why hadn't she thought of that? It had never occurred to her, when Chŏng-ok had mentioned the Kolon Building, that her own husband worked across the street. Gently chiding herself, she quickly reentered the underpass. Most likely he was still in his office; he always stayed late. And hadn't he always encouraged her to come to him with any problems? For two people who had been closer to each other than anyone else for such a long period of their lives, what could be so bothersome or complicating about sharing a hot cup of coffee on a cold day? If people begrudged each other such simple contacts, what would that say about their lives, and how could they possibly get along with others? What's more, wasn't she off to a fresh start, full of marvelous plans? If she could resume her work right away, perhaps with her teacher, Min, a man who was unrivaled in the world of puppet shows, it would make even her husband a believer.

Her monologue came to an end when the elevator reached the fifth floor and the Yŏng-u Trading Company, which also occupied the sixth and seventh floors. The custodian intercepted her. "What can I do for you, ma'am?" Hye-ja hesitated at this unanticipated obstacle, but quickly gathered herself. "I'd like to see the manager of the planning office." The custodian picked up the intercom. "Who did you say you were?" he asked while waiting to be connected. "Tell him it's his wife." The young custodian cocked his head skeptically and scrutinized Hye-ja, then handed her the receiver. "Manager, planning office." The resounding voice filled the handset, as if the man were right beside her. "Is that . . . you? It's me, Yŏng-sŏn's mom," Hye-ja stammered, suddenly intimidated by the placid, oddly unfamiliar voice.

"Who's calling? This is the manager of the planning office, but . . . I wonder if it's Manager Yi Ki-dŏk you're looking for." "Yes, could I have Yi Ki-dŏk, please? This is his wife." Hye-ja's flustered response brought a low exclamation from the other end. "This is Yi Kun-ho. One moment, please, and I'll be right out." Presently, from the hallway to the left there appeared a tall, slender man. He'd lost a lot of hair and now wore glasses, but Hye-ja recognized him at once: Yi Kun-ho, who'd joined the company at the same time as her husband and was quite close to him. He'd married late, and until then he could always count on a bed at their house if he was too drunk to go home. Hye-ja was guided to a small reception room where two people were talking. They left at once, and the room fell quiet except for the hiss of the steam heat. Sensing in her counterpart an extreme discomfort that perplexed her, Hye-ja glanced about the stark room, which contained a table and a few chairs. After requesting coffee over the intercom Yi Kun-ho finally said, "You look a lot better. How is your health?" Everyone asked about her health. "Is the gunpowder in a safe place?" was how it sounded to her. Hye-ja smiled but said nothing. "How are you getting along?" "I've started working." "Well, that's good to hear. May I ask what kind of work?" "Sure. It's related to puppet shows. Also, I'm thinking about moving. I remembered what he told me—you know, about how a change of scenery might be a good thing? But I guess he's not at his desk?" Hye-ja ventured a smile. A look of surprise creased Yi's brow. "You didn't know?" A young woman in a short-sleeve sweater arrived with the coffee and set it on the table. Silently Yi added sugar to his cup and began slowly to stir. "Didn't know what?" "He's at the New York office. It's been a month now." Hye-ja found her gaze riveted on the scarlet imprint of her lips on the cup from which she had just drank. The room was so hot! She could feel herself perspiring beneath her undergarments. And her tight-fitting clothes constricted her, made her feel choked. She unbuttoned her coat and her flesh spilled over the collar of the cramped velvet dress. She produced her handkerchief and dabbed at her face and neck, leaving thick smudges of powder, rouge, and eye shadow on the white cloth. She was embarrassed to admit it, but her makeup was too thick. "He took the children, figures to be there about three years. I'm not quite sure, but maybe he didn't tell you out of concern for opening old wounds." "It's all right. I was on my way somewhere and just . . . stopped by. He said I was always welcome to drop in and talk things over. . . . I'd better be on my way," she said in a dull tone, distracted by the suffocating sensation, the perspiration streaming inside her clothes, and the air in the room, which seemed filthy and stuffy. She rose heavily. "Are you all right? You don't look well," Yi said solicitously, noticing her pale, sweaty face. "I feel kind of hot. Thank you for your time—I know you're busy. And I appreciate your kindness." The elevator door closed on Yi's politely bowing form and she began silently to weep.

The electronic display on the clock tower read seven-twenty. Twenty minutes had passed since the appointed hour and not one familiar face had appeared. From her window seat Hye-ja could keep track of the flow of time, second by second, for the clock tower was directly across from her. In the deepening dusk, the Christmas tree lights grew distinct and the lights of the city blossomed in profound splendor. Seven-thirty came and went. The lounge, quiet at first, was now almost full, and with every opening and closing of the door Hye-ja shot an anxious look toward the entrance. Was it possible they didn't recognize her? She really did look different from before. So different she scarcely recognized the face imprinted like a negative on the window with its dark background. Desperate for people and the world to forget what she had done, she had worked hard to change her appearance. She had gained weight with the help of the hunger and the hellish sleep that was regularly induced through a regimen of medication and injections, and she had let her hair grow out. Her hair had turned light gray, something Hye-ja didn't realize until the woman who shared her sickroom accused her of stealing a hairpin, attacked her, and plucked out a handful of it. Hye-ja moved nearer the entrance where she could be seen more easily, and ordered a gin and tonic. An hour had passed. The lounge was well heated and remained warm in its tight glass envelope. Hye-ja removed her coat and placed it over a chair, and discreetly undid the buttons at her throat and chest so she could breathe more easily.

A thin slice of lemon and a scarlet cherry floated in the transparent, ice-filled glass in front of her. The drink tasted like sour water and it made her want to pucker up and spit. The Western saying "Looks good, tastes good" wasn't very apt, she thought as she forlornly watched the floating ice cubes shrink. Presently they melted away and the lemon taste grew suspiciously weak. Her hopes grew fainter that the others would appear. Nine o'clock passed, and as she ordered another gin and tonic she was seized by a doubt that seemed all too real: Had she misunderstood the time and place of the gathering? In her desperation to go out, had she somehow convinced herself that today was the date when in fact it was tomorrow or the day after? It was a lonely business staring at the ice cubes clinking against the glass before disappearing. Staring and waiting. And when ten o'clock arrived and she ordered yet another gin and tonic, the young waiter looked askance at her as if she were a phantom, this obese woman with long, wiry, gray hair tumbling over a broad, white collar that resembled the ribbed semicircle of a folding fan. They weren't coming, she was sure of it. An intense rage came over her. Knowing she would appear at their gathering, they had changed the meeting place—no doubt about it. They were sitting somewhere nearby pointing at her, whispering about her as she sat, all too visible through the window, sick and tired of waiting. "God, she actually

called me. She said she tried the rest of you, too. Consider your-
selves lucky you missed her." "That man died, and she's running
free? But what for? I mean, she's practically an *invalid.*" Hye-ja
covered her ears, as if actually hearing these voices. "Self-defense,
huh? Well, whatever she wants to call it, it happened." "Is it true
he divorced her? Well, I can believe it. How could a person live
with someone like that? I'd be scared." "You suppose she was trying to be faithful to her husband?" "Maybe she lost her head—
I'll bet she was terrified." "That's probably why she ended up in a
mental hospital." When Hye-ja recalled what others had said and
then read between the lines, it was always a *man* that was killed,
not a burglar. Even her husband. He'd kept trying to find out if
the man really was a burglar. Maybe the man didn't have a relationship with her, but wasn't he at least a casual acquaintance?
Her husband had been skillfully circuitous but wouldn't give up.
"I never saw him before," she had said. "Do you want to know
what I was doing? *This* is what I was doing, just like you see here.
Now will you please leave me alone? What do you want, anyway?" These thoughts, thousands of times recalled, she repeated
to herself, and as she did so she clamped her mouth shut and
cried. The fact that she had been wearing only a slip and the man
hadn't been armed had left lingering doubts.

Hye-ja suddenly realized all was quiet. She looked about. The
lounge was deserted except for a couple sitting at a window table,
foreheads touching. The waiter produced a great yawn as he leaned
against the bar watching Hye-ja. The clock on the tower read
eleven.

The subway rumbled beneath Hye-ja's feet before rolling into the
deep of the night. Not much sign of life in the underpasses, just

the slush underfoot, and everywhere the stink. The same three underpasses to negotiate, and when Hye-ja rose to the surface she gazed up at the wind-swept heavens. An uncertain number of stars twinkled dimly in the misty air.

Hye-ja had just climbed the last step when she bumped her knee against something and lost her balance. Coins clinked and scattered at her feet. The fluorescent light was out and the opening to the underpass was dark. Instinctively she stooped over and looked down. She had tripped over someone hunched up in a blanket and had kicked over a tin bowl. "I'm sorry," she hastened to say. "I had something on my mind and just—" Then she realized that the woman beneath the blanket with the sleeping child in her arms was blind. Eyes downcast, chin lifted, the woman extended a hand, groped for the scattered coins, gathered them in. Hye-ja bent over to help and managed in the dim light to pick up the coins that had fallen to the steps. She was about to place them in the bowl when the woman's hand shot out and seized her wrist. The strength and tenacity of her grip startled Hye-ja. The hand didn't release its painful, lurching hold until the woman was sure every last coin had been shaken free from Hye-ja's palm. Hye-ja gazed at the woman as she massaged her stinging wrist. The woman curled back into a ball beneath the blanket, perhaps to sleep, perhaps to doze. You thought I was going to take that money? Well, it's mostly my fault, spaced out and walking right into you. The wind buffeted the opening to the underpass with a chill ferocity. Hye-ja hunkered down beside the woman. The Christmas tree next to the frozen fountain continued its lonely blinking. The clock tower read eleven-thirty. "Aren't you cold? Have you eaten? Look how sound asleep your baby is! Don't you want to go home now? It's supposed to get colder." The woman gave no reply. "Where are you staying? Why don't I help you across the street? You don't want to go to sleep out here and freeze to death. Especially with your baby. . . ." But as Hye-ja gently lifted the quilt her hand was slapped. The woman's eyes glared. "Fucking leech—don't you have anything better to do than bother me! Go home, wash your feet, and go to bed, you hen!" Bloodshot eyes gazing furiously in Hye-ja's direction, the woman clutched her child, took up her bowl, marched a few steps lower, and plumped herself down. Frightened, Hye-ja hurried off.

The wind blew stronger. People raised their collars and scurried along or else chased down taxis. On which side of the street was that taxi stand where she used to catch cabs to her neighborhood? Hye-ja had walked only the distance between two bus stops when she noticed that almost everyone was gone. Vehicles sped past. No taxis waited, headlights off, even at the taxi stands. How to get home? She didn't have a clue. But what troubled Hye-ja most was the hunger tearing at her stomach. Only those three watery gin and tonics since lunch, and it was vexing to think that their sourish, puckery taste was stimulating her appetite. As always when she was hungry, Hye-ja's mouth watered for a heaping bowl of white rice; seafish swabbed in oil and grilled; piping hot fried scallion cakes; and all the rest. It had been the same at the hospital: perpetual hunger. Once her daughter had brought a warmer full of grilled chicken. How the girl in her dazzling white summer hat had cried as she watched Hye-ja devour the food. "Mommy, forgive us. What we did was a crime," she said before offering a short goodbye and leaving. Hye-ja hadn't seen her since. But now, if she could just eat something, it didn't matter what. . . . If she could just put it in her mouth, just a bite. . . . There would be plenty of time later to think about getting home.

Clutching her belly and looking about, Hye-ja finally spied a streetside snack-wagon, its canvas curtains brightly lit from inside.

She entered. A woman was putting away knives, cutting boards, saucepans.

"Could I have something to eat, anything you've got—I'm really hungry."

Startled by Hye-ja's abruptness, the woman observed her before silently serving up two skewers of fish cakes along with soup.

"This is all that's left. I'm out of everything else. I was just about to go home. . . ."

The fish cakes were gone in an instant. The woman ladled out more soup and Hye-ja took it in a gulp, then held out her bowl again while wiping her mouth. The woman apologetically waved her hand no. She obviously pitied Hye-ja. "All that's left is *soju*—really." The woman uncapped a bottle with her teeth, and Hye-ja accepted it, paid, and left.

Hye-ja kept to the old palace's stone wall, which angled away from the street. It was like walking in a dream, quiet except for the slow fall of her feet. The alcohol gently warmed her stomach. Unbelievably, her hunger had vanished. With every gust of wind, the ancient trees inside the mossy stone wall threw back their manes and wailed. Hye-ja stopped every few steps to let more *soju* trickle into her mouth. She had once tried on thick glasses, and now, as then, the ground seemed to fall away under her feet. "You broke your promise," Hye-ja said aloud. These were the heartfelt words she had shouted tearfully in her childhood when she was left all alone by playmates who abandoned her and went home without a word of explanation other than saying that they were tired of playing house; or when they played hide-and-seek and she was "it" and they hid in a place where she couldn't possibly find them and never came out, or else called off the game without telling her.

Again she cursed her liar of a daughter, who had bloomed

more lovely with each new day, even when she cried and said, "I can't believe we put you in this place; I can't believe we have to live like this; I wish I were dead." Yes, her husband and children had left her all alone in an empty house and gone their merry way. Just like those faithless little creatures of her childhood.

Where would this street beside the stone wall lead? Her dream of the previous evening suddenly returned to her. Was *this* the street she walked in her dreams? Although she knew there would be a sign for her in a crevice among the crumbling stones, the memory of waking in distress from those dreams made her anxious. Hye-ja tilted the bottle of *soju* and the liquid gurgled down her throat. She drank it all at once, as if it were a wonder drug in a dream from which she would never awaken. "You all think I'm a murderer, you're watching for me, you're avoiding me. . . ." She said this in a loud voice and with a grand gesture hurled the empty bottle with all her might. "Anyone else would have done the same thing. What was I supposed to do?" On that day, Hye-ja had been making dolls in her basement workshop as she always did after the children left for school. It was a sweltering summer day, she had turned on the hotplate to melt some oxhide glue, and the basement felt like a steamer. The front gate was locked, she expected no visitors, and she was working in her slip. She had finished the complicated process of attaching the sleeping princess's hair and accessories and was intent on adding the finishing touches when she saw the man standing in the doorway. There had been no sound of his entry. What she had seen then was not the man's face but her own nearly naked body. It was pure terror, though, that had caused her to plunge the hot soldering iron into the man's eyes as he approached.

The alcohol made Hye-ja feel as if something was blooming from her body as she swayed down the street. Looking straight ahead, she passed her hand along the stone wall, searching the crevices of the crumbing stones for a token of that pledge of love, that hidden, secret promise of her dream. But then she heard a murmuring in her ear: "They've all forgotten you and there's nothing you can do, is there? And even if you hadn't stuck him with that soldering iron, you wouldn't be any better off than you are now." She vaguely realized that the place where this street ended, this street along the stone wall that she had visited in her dreams, was merely the desolate present of wakefulness. But still Hye-ja moved, one step at a time, deeper into the darkness, her blossoming body telling her the street would never end.

About the Authors

◆◆◆

Ch'oe Yun was born in Seoul in 1953. She studied Korean literature at Sogang University in Seoul, obtained a doctorate in French literature at the University of Aix-en-Provence in France, then returned to Seoul to teach at Sogang. She began her literary career as a critic and made her fictional debut in 1988 with the novella *There a Petal Silently Falls* (Chŏgi sori ŏpshi hanjŏm kkonnip i chigo). She has since published three volumes of fiction and a collection of essays. Her story "The Gray Snowman" (Hoesaek nunsaram) earned her the Tongin Literature Prize in 1992. "The Last of Hanak'o" (Hanak'o nŭn ŏpta), first published in 1994 in *Munhak sasang*, won that year's Yi Sang Literature Prize. In addition to her scholarship and creative writing, Ch'oe has collaborated with her husband, Patrick Maurus, in a series of well-received translations of contemporary Korean fiction into French.

Kim Chi-wŏn was born in 1943 in Kyŏnggi Province and educated at Ehwa University in Seoul. She is the daughter of Ch'oe Chŏng-hŭi and the elder sister of Kim Ch'ae-wŏn, both important writers in their own right. She began publishing fiction in the 1970s after she moved to the New York metropolitan area, where she has lived on and off since then. "Almaden" (Almaden) first appeared in 1979 in *Hanguk munhak*.

Kim Min-suk was born in Pusan in 1948 and studied creative writing at Sŏrabŏl College of Fine Arts in Seoul. She made her literary debut in 1976 with "The Sea and the Butterfly Syndrome" (Pada wa nabibyŏng), which won a new writers' competition sponsored by the *Tonga ilbo*, a Seoul daily. In 1987 Kim received the Nogwŏn Literature Prize for her novella *A Requiem for Time* (Shigan ŭl wihan chinhongok). She has published more than ten volumes of fiction. Among her notable works are the novels *My Name Is Maya* (Nae irŭm ŭn Maya, 1977), *Thursday's Child* (Mogyoil ŭi ai, 1979), and *The Uncharted City* (Chido e ŏmnŭn toshi, 1982). "Scarlet Fingernails" (Pongsunga kkonmul) was first published in *Hyŏndae munhak* in 1987.

Kong Chi-yŏng was born in Seoul in 1963 and was educated at Yonsei University. She made her literary debut in 1985 as a poet, then turned to fiction in

1988 with the publication of her story "The Coming of Dawn" (Tong t'ŭnŭn saebyŏk). She has since published four novels and a story collection. Her most successful novel, *Go Alone Like the Horn of a Rhinoceros* (Muso ŭi ppul ch'ŏrŏm honja sŏ kara, 1993), has sold over half a million copies and was made into a popular movie. "Human Decency" (Ingan e taehan yeŭi) first appeared in 1993 in *Shilch'ŏn munhak.*

Kong Sŏn-ok was born in Koksŏng, South Chŏlla Province, in 1963, and studied Korean literature at South Chŏlla University. She debuted in 1991 in *Ch'angjak kwa pip'yŏng* and has since published a volume of fiction and received the *Women's News (Seoul)* Literature Prize.

O Chŏng-hŭi was born in Seoul in 1947 and studied creative writing at Sŏrabŏl College of the Arts. In January 1968, while still a college student, she captured the annual award for aspiring writers given by the *Chungang ilbo,* a Seoul daily, with her story "The Toyshop Woman" (Wangujŏm yŏin). She has since published seven volumes of fiction. She received the 1979 Yi Sang Literature Prize for "Evening Game" (Chŏnyŏk ŭi keim) and the 1983 Tongin Literature Prize for "The Bronze Mirror" (Tonggyŏng). Her works have been translated into several languages. "Wayfarer" (Sullyeja ŭi norae) was originally published in *Munhak sasang* in 1983.

Pak Wan-sŏ was born in Kyŏnggi Province in 1931 and studied Korean literature at Seoul National University. She debuted in 1970 with the novel *The Naked Tree* (Namok), which draws on her own experiences around the time of the Korean War. In 1981 she received the Yi Sang Literature Prize for "Mother's Post" (Ŏmma ŭi malttuk, 1980). "Identical Apartments" (Talmŭn pang tŭl) first appeared in *Wŏlgan chungang* in 1974.

Sŏ Yŏng-ŭn was born in 1943 in Kangnŭng, Kangwŏn Province, and was graduated from Kŏnguk University in Seoul, where she now lives. She began publishing fiction in the late 1960s. A good introduction to her work is the story collection *How to Cross a Desert* (Samak ŭl kŏnnŏnŭn pŏp, 1978). "Dear Distant Love" (Mŏn kŭdae) first appeared in *Hanguk munhak* in 1983 and was honored with that year's Yi Sang Literature Prize.

Acknowledgments

◆◆◆

We have incurred a number of debts, material and otherwise, while preparing this anthology. Our thanks go first to Patrick Maurus and Ch'oe Yun for bringing this collection to the attention of UNESCO Publishing in Paris, and to Mr. Fernando Ainsa of that organization and Mr. Huh Kwon of the Korean National Commission for UNESCO for accepting the book in the UNESCO Series of Representative Translations. Generous subsidies from UNESCO Publishing and the Korean Culture and Arts Foundation (KCAF) in Seoul made possible the translation and production of the book. We are grateful to Mr. Pak Sang-on of the KCAF for his support with this and other translation projects. We also wish to thank the authors for their cooperation. At the request of Kim Chi-wŏn, author of "Almaden," we made some revisions in our initial English rendering of that story that depart from the original Korean.

Thanks go to Julie Pickering, who read drafts of several of the translations and offered many useful suggestions, and to David McCann, who advised us on the translation of the poem (by Yang Sŏn-gyu) that appears in "Human Decency." We also wish to thank the editors of the following publications, in which earlier versions of three of the stories appeared: *Asian Pacific Quarterly, Korean Culture,* and *Korea Journal.* We are grateful to all the good people at Women in Translation and Seal Press for their assistance and encouragement, especially Barbara Wilson, Katherine Hanson, June Thomas, Rebecca Engrav, Joon-Ho Yu, Ingrid Emerick, and Clare Conrad. Finally, for their patience we bear an eternal debt to our children, Edward and Andy, who are beginning to understand why we rise during the wee hours to work on the computer.

About the Translators

◆◆◆

Bruce and Ju-Chan Fulton are the translators of *Words of Farewell: Stories by Korean Women Writers* (Seattle: Seal Press, 1989), which won the 1993 Korean Literature Translation Prize. With Marshall R. Pihl they translated *Land of Exile: Contemporary Korean Fiction* (Armonk, N.Y.: M. E. Sharpe, 1993). Bruce Fulton is the editor of *Seeing the Invisible,* a 1996 Manoa feature on post-democratization women's fiction in South Korea, to which the Fultons contributed translations. The Fultons are the recipients of a 1995 NEA Translation Fellowship. They live in Seattle.

WELCOME TO THE WORLD OF

INTERNATIONAL WOMEN'S WRITING

◆◆◆

The Cockatoo's Lie by Marion Bloem. $11.95. ISBN: 1-879679-08-6. Family history and a steamy love triangle weave together in this modern novel of Dutch-Indonesian cultural identity.

The Four Winds by Gerd Brantenberg. $12.95. ISBN: 1-879679-05-1. Gerd Brantenberg is one of Norway's cultural treasures, and a lesbian author with a huge international following. This is her hilarious and moving novel of coming out in the sixties at the University of Oslo.

Unnatural Mothers by Renate Dorrestein. $11.95. ISBN: 1-879679-06-X. One of the most original novels to appear from Holland in years, this compelling story of an archeologist and his eleven-year-old daughter's attempts to build a family is by turns satiric and heartbreaking.

An Everyday Story: Norwegian Women's Fiction edited by Katherine Hanson. $14.95. ISBN: 1-879679-07-8. Norway's tradition of storytelling comes alive in this enthralling anthology. The new expanded edition includes stories by contemporary writers.

Unmapped Territories: New Women's Fiction from Japan edited by Yukiko Tanaka. $10.95. ISBN: 1-879679-00-0. These stunning new stories by well-known and emerging writers chart a world of vanishing social and physical landmarks in a Japan both strange and familiar. With an insightful introduction by Tanaka on the literature and culture of the "era of women" in Japan.

Two Women in One by Nawal el-Saadawi. $9.95. ISBN: 1-879679-01-9. One of this Egyptian feminist's most important novels, *Two Women in One* tells the story of Bahiah Shaheen, a well-behaved Cairo medical student—and her other side: rebellious, political and artistic.

Under Observation by Amalie Skram. With an introduction by Elaine Showalter. $15.95. ISBN: 1-879679-03-5. This riveting story of a woman painter confined against her will in a Copenhagen asylum is a classic of nineteenth century Norwegian literature by the author of *Constance Ring* and *Betrayed*.

How Many Miles to Babylon by Doris Gercke. $8.95. ISBN: 1-879679-02-7. Hamburg police detective Bella Block needs a vacation. She thinks she'll find some rest in the countryside, but after only a few hours in the remote village of Roosbach, she realizes she has stumbled onto one of the most troubling cases of her career. The first of this provocative German author's thrillers to be translated into English.

Wild Card by Assumpta Margenat. $8.95. ISBN: 1-879679-04-3. Translated from the Catalan, this lively mystery is set in Andorra, a tiny country in the Pyrenees. Rocio is a supermarket clerk bored with her job and her sexist boss. One day she devises a scheme to get ahead in the world. . . .

Women in Translation is a nonprofit publishing company, dedicated to making women's fiction from around the world available in English translation. The books above may be ordered from us at 523 N. 84th St., Seattle, WA 98103. (Please include $3.00 postage and handling for the first book and 50¢ for each additional book.) Write to us for a free catalog.